MW01139167
Re:ZeRo
-Starting Life in Another World-

“Now cooomes the beginning...of the end!!”

"...Please believe me. I've said a lot of stupid things in my life, but I meant everything I just told you."

じりっ
JIRI
"Felt, just behave and do as you're—"
"Shut up! I am *not* putting on a dress! ...Are you selling me out, Old Man Rom?!"
"Sorry, Felt, but this old man wants to see you in a dress, too..."
"What color would you prefer? I believe bright colors suit you best, Lady Felt..."
"Listen when I'm talking! And die, too! Damn it all!"

(Continued on the cover.)

Re:ZERO -Starting Life in Another World-

The only ability Subaru Natsuki gets when he's summoned to another world is time travel via his own death. But to save her, he'll die as many times as it takes.

CONTENTS

CHAPTER 1

A BEELINE TOWARD SLOTH

1

Subaru Natsuki began the strategy meeting he'd dubbed Witch Cult Hunting Made Simple.

It was before dawn on the Liphas plains. A group of about fifty warriors and mercenaries had gathered together. Standing at the center of attention of so many accomplished people was a little rough on Subaru's nerves.

These people were older, veteran soldiers or rough-and-tumble beast people mercenaries. From Subaru's perspective, they were from a different world. Barring very specific circumstances, Subaru would never have had the opportunity to cross paths with them. And now these residents of a world unconnected to his own were sitting in a circle with Subaru at the center.

That his meandering path had put him in command of such people sent a gale of anxiety and weakness through Subaru's heart. But his passion and will to fight were every bit as intense.

"Figures..."

The scene before Subaru's eyes was what he had yearned for every time he experienced Return by Death, something that had seemed almost impossible to reach. Subaru's piddling readiness and self-respect gave rise to an urge so great that it was almost painful; he didn't want to fail the innumerable people who had guided him so far ever again. He criticized himself for this more harshly than anyone else could have.

"—"

"What is it, Subaru? You went quiet all of a sudden."

When Subaru put his fist to his chest in self-admonishment, someone watching him from the side called out to him. It was the other man who stood out even among their current company, a gorgeous man wearing the uniform of a Knight of the Royal Guard—Julius Juukulius.

"I hardly think you're getting cold feet, but…time is of the essence. You said yourself there's not a moment to spare, no?"

"Yeah, yeah, I know. You don't need to snap at me every time. The first thing you say at times like these is important, so I was just thinking about how to put it best."

"Such concern is unnecessary. Everyone here already knows your conduct before large numbers of people is problematic. Pay it no concern and simply be yourself."

"Gah-ha-ha-ha! Ya sure said it, Julius! Hey, bro, he really got ya there!"

"Grrr…!"

A vein bulged on Subaru's forehead as his darkest moment was dragged out into the open. Ricardo, commander of the beast-man mercenary band called the Iron Fangs, broke into laughter as sympathetic expressions spread among the knights of the expeditionary force. Apparently, news of Subaru's humiliation at the royal palace had traveled further than he'd thought.

"That's so humiliating…!"

"Yes, yes, now that's enough feeling ashamed of yourself! Subawu, it's your duty to work hard to clean the slate so you can live without shame, right? And Julius, I understand your urge to needle him, but think about how you say things!"

"It seems you misunderstand, Ferris. I had no such intention.

Certainly, it would be a happy day if he has become a better speaker for it."

"You really have a roundabout way of doing things..."

Ferris sighed, looking thoroughly annoyed at Julius's sardonic reply. Seeing his reaction, Subaru finally understood the purpose behind Julius's words and deeds. That only gave him the same feelings as Ferris, though.

"A little banter is fine. That said, I believe we should finally address the subject at hand. Our priority should be countermeasures against the Witch Cult."

It was the sharp-looking Wilhelm who dragged the conversation back from the tangent.

Of all his companions, Subaru expected the most out of the Sword Devil, both mentally and in terms of combat. Subaru had cooperated with him in slaying the White Whale, the elderly warrior's mortal foe of many years. In return, he unreservedly lent Subaru his strength.

Joining Subaru and Wilhelm's force were the survivors of the White Whale expeditionary force as well as the Iron Fangs' reinforcements. These fifty-odd individuals formed the Anti-Witch Alliance, which would challenge the Witch Cult.

"Well, since Wilhelm asked and because time's a-wasting, I'll get to the point. The topic of discussion today is Witch Cult Hunting Made Simple... The actual contents are pretty simple. Like with anything, simpler methods give more intense results."

"Logical. What is your plan, then?"

"How about we kick their asses—go in for a preemptive strike to take the enemy commander's head and victory along with it."

"........."

Subaru's conclusion sent a faint whiff of surprise through those present. His words were the very definition of audacity. That "commander's head" belonged to one of the Archbishops of the Seven Deadly Sins commanding the Witch Cult.

"Well, that's definitely simple. Assuming we pull it off, it'd be a huge blow to the Cult."

Amid the group's unease, which was beginning to border on unrest, Ricardo was the first to speak up in admiration. The huge dog-man showed off his fangs as he smiled, touching those sharp canine teeth with a finger as he spoke again.

"That's *if* we can pull it off, though. Anyone can talk big. Can't go countin' our chickens before they hatch."

Ricardo was the first to show he understood Subaru's aim, but he also made sure to call for caution. Subaru thumped his own chest in response and immediately followed up.

"Of course I have a plan. I proved I'm not reckless enough to hunt a whale without a fishhook, didn't I?"

"Man, I already believe you. That's why I wanna hear your reasoning, get it?"

While Subaru was brimming with confidence, Ricardo prompted him to get on with it as he ground his fangs together. Subaru realized his other comrades shared the dog-man's feelings when he saw how they drew closer, eagerly awaiting the details of his proposal.

"Okay, I'll lay this out one part at a time. First, the Witch Cult is targeting the Mathers domain, where Emilia is. This is due to all sorts of background information. We'll leave it at that for now, okay?"

"So those are the starting conditions? Very well. In truth, we anticipated that it was likely an incident related to the Witch Cult would occur in the Mathers domain. The appearance of the White Whale at the same time cannot be dismissed as mere coincidence."

"So what…the Witch Cult used the White Whale to seal the highway with its mist and isolate the Mathers domain, *meow*? Looks like the Cult is getting serious. Well, considering their dogma, that almost goes without saying."

When Subaru began going over the situation, Julius and Ferris both added their thoughts. Apparently, though the Witch Cult was still unfathomable in many respects, the fanatics' obscure activities were underpinned by a pervading hostility toward half-elves. Given that, the current attack on the Mathers lands was no doubt due to the announcement that Emilia was participating in the royal selection.

That indiscriminate cruelty would eventually result in a massacre of the villagers. Subaru genuinely believed the cultists were beyond redemption.

"The Witch Cult is after Emilia's life. But that doesn't mean they'll ignore the humans near her. They don't discriminate—they'll kill women and children without mercy."

"There is no room for doubt on that point, however repugnant it may be."

Seeing Subaru's anger, Julius nodded. His eyes held no surprise in them—only furious indignation. The Witch Cult's capacity for evil was common knowledge in this world, after all.

"I want to save Emilia, the people at the mansion, and of course all the villagers. Now, I thought about getting everyone in the area to the mansion and holing up there, but..."

"Against the Witch Cult, whose members can appear anywhere without the slightest warning, sheltering in place seems a poor plan."

"Yeah, we're gonna pass that one up."

The point of holing up was to maintain one's forces and hold out for some kind of impending victory. Subaru's force couldn't count on reinforcements, so it wasn't much of an option.

Besides, wasting the fighting strength currently in Subaru's hands on a defensive battle would foolishly squander the one clear advantage he possessed. The information he'd gleaned from Return by Death would be worthless the instant events greatly diverged. If an armed group paraded into the mansion, even Petelgeuse would probably revise his plans. He might change the method of attack, or even call off the attack altogether.

Furthermore, if Subaru was to maximize the value of what he'd obtained through Return by Death—

"—We need to go after the Witch Cult lurking in the forest before they figure out what we're up to. While they're prepped to strike first, we've gotta strike even before that, and crush 'em."

"I appreciate the enthusiasm, *meow*, but how do we find the Witch Cult in the forest? No one's managed to grab their tail in four hundred years. We need something to go on."

"Yeah, about that... Long story short, it's like fishing for the White Whale."

"Meow...?"

Subaru's suddenly cryptic explanation made Ferris's big, round eyes bulge even bigger.

"I used my scent to lure the whale in, right? I can do the same thing with the Witch Cult, too."

"..."

"Yeah, this condition I have is scary stuff. It's a real pain in the butt, ha-ha."

"..."

"Ha-ha-ha..."

Subaru's dry laugh was the only sound in the silent atmosphere; when it trailed off, an unsettled air hung over the plains. He looked at the faces of those around him, wondering how they would respond to his long-awaited, long-delayed plan. Subaru himself could not explain it any better; he had no reasoning for why he could lure demon beasts and Witch cultists save his physical makeup. All he could do was recognize the fact and say, *That's how it is.*

Someday the truth behind that would become clear, but even if there was some terrible reason it was so, the best thing he could do right now was rely on it. Hence—

"I figured in advance my story wasn't gonna sound very persuasive."

Subaru surveyed the silent knights and beast people, speaking the truth in the most honest way he could think of.

"I think calling it crazy talk, unbelievable stuff, is the natural reaction to have. But still..."

"Sir Subaru."

"...Please believe me. I've said a lot of stupid things in my life, but I meant everything I just told you. That's how I decided to be, and that's why I want your help."

Up to that point, those around Subaru had reached out to him time after time, only for him to reject them and trample on their feelings. He only realized this now that he was facing his first true challenge.

Subaru was powerless and ignorant before the task that loomed before him. On his own, it would be impossible. He needed help from others—from everyone.

"I only have one head, so it's the only thing I can ask you with. But if this single head won't do, I'll bow it as many times as you like, so please, lend me your strength."

"..."

Subaru pleaded with them, lowering his head for all to see.

Those around Subaru were silent; the only sound was that of the wind crossing the plains. After several moments, the first to speak was a small beast man, a lieutenant of the Iron Fangs called TB.

With an adorable face, he adjusted the position of his monocle and stared straight at Subaru. "I understand what you are trying to say. However, if you ask us to believe you without any basis for...*gah*?!"

"What are you worrying about, TB?"

In the middle of his lecture to Subaru, TB was interrupted by a single blow from his older sister Mimi, who stood nearby. She smacked his back, and as her younger brother groaned, she laughed innocently.

"Mister here worked reaaaally hard to take down that big fish, you know! No one who worked that hard would try to trick us, so it's okay!"

"S-Sis, could you please be quiet?! This is a very important conver—"

"You're always trying to be crofty... Wait, huh? *Cro? Cru? Crufty...?*"

"Crafty?"

"That's the one! You won't grow big if you're doing that all the time!"

Mimi bluntly scolded her teary-eyed younger brother. Then, turning from the wilting TB, she pointed at Subaru.

"You didn't fight that big fish earlier, TB! So if you can't trust Mister here, just trust in your big sis!"

"—"

"Big Sis believes in Mister, so since you believe in Big Sis, you can trust Mister, right, TB? Besides, Mimi will protect TB no matter what happens!"

Mimi puffed her chest out as she spoke, brimming with confidence. Though her words surprised TB, they immediately wore him down. The hostility he'd displayed earlier drained from his face. The sight of the siblings made the others unwittingly break into broad smiles.

Amid the unexpected outpouring of laughter, Mimi tilted her head with a curious look and asked, "What?"

"Nahhh, don't sweat it. That was perfect. You said it great."

His eyes softening, Ricardo patted Mimi's head so hard that his huge palm almost looked like it would pop her head right off.

"There's still things that bug me, but havin' come this far, we're not gonna doubt bro now. We crossed that bridge a long while ago."

"—" Subaru's eyes widened at the unexpected words.

Then, in apparent agreement with Ricardo, Wilhelm stepped forward. "Sir Subaru, a man should not lower his head lightly. Indeed, to avoid meeting a person's eyes when you ask something of them is unacceptable—had you looked, you would surely have noticed it yourself by now."

The Sword Devil's solemn words urged Subaru to lift his chin and look around. As he examined the faces of those surrounding him, Subaru realized that their feelings had not changed. Not a single thing about them was different since the discussion began—

"You know, *meow*, it puts us in a bind if you go quiet all on your own like that. It's not as if anyone thinks your story is a lie, Subawu."

With a subdued look, Ferris passed a finger through his own fur as he spoke. The absence of objections proved that everyone present agreed. Under Subaru's gaze, Julius maintained his usual elegant handsomeness as he stood straight.

"Besides, Subawu, your decoy plan is what decided the fight with the White Whale. It was Lady Crusch who chose to bet on that… which means doubting Subawu is the same as doubting Lady Crusch, and there's no way Ferri could do such a thing."

"That is a very Ferris-like thing to say, but Sir Subaru has simply earned our trust through his actions. That is the plain truth known to all who witnessed that battle."

"H-hey, Old Man Wil?!"

"Of course, I am included in that."

Ferris was visibly nervous, his voice going shrill, but Wilhelm merely nodded strongly in Subaru's direction, paying no heed to the retort.

Such unreserved consideration made Subaru's cheeks run hot as he appreciated the surrounding atmosphere.

"I'm so uncool… Guess I'm as bad at reading the atmosphere as ever."

"I believe an atmosphere is something to be breathed, not read?"

"Oh, shut up! I knew that already! And that the less you can read it the more you obsess about it!"

Julius's comment made Subaru's voice go ragged as he swept away all the excess sentimentality within him.

He'd unnecessarily embarrassed himself *again*. All things considered, though, it wasn't such a bad price to pay.

"Our trust in you is the result of your own accomplishments, Sir Subaru."

Although Subaru could not clarify his reasoning on such an important plan, he'd done enough to earn their trust. Just like Rem had somehow come to believe him, even though the contents of Subaru's words might have given them pause, they did not doubt his motives.

It was the proper way for someone who'd Returned by Death, bearing information from a lost world, to coexist with others—and at that moment, Subaru felt as if it had all come together, right before his eyes.

2

"I—I wasn't crying! I just felt like all the suffering and regret I felt coming all this way had finally paid off, and when I drifted off, some protein-infused alkaline water spilled out of my eyes. That's all! Don't get the wrong idea!!"

Subaru tried his best to hide his tears. At any rate, he glossed over the conflicted emotions inside him, raising his head and diving into the main topic.

"Anyway, if everyone trusts me, that speeds things up a lot. So my selling point is that the Witch Cult and demon beasts react to my scent. I'll use that to lure the Witch Cult."

"So we'll wipe out whatever appears in one fell swoop? If it could become more than an impractical theory, that sounds like a fine plan, but what do you estimate the actual odds of success to be?"

"Odds?"

"The probability that they will detect you and willingly reveal themselves."

Julius, who had not questioned the plan's viability up to that point, voiced his doubts for the first time.

By this point, the members of the expeditionary force who had participated in the battle with the White Whale didn't need an explanation for Subaru's peculiar ability. But Julius and the relief force that had just joined them hadn't seen it for themselves. Naturally they wanted to know Subaru's worth as a decoy—they were betting their lives.

"Given the nature of this strategy, we cannot allow the matter to remain vague. What do you think?"

"The probability of me drawing them out is a hundred percent. They'll come for sure."

"That is a bold statement."

"Those cultists'll come out for sure. It's because they're them, and I'm me."

Julius received an explanation that didn't really explain anything. When it came to confidence in himself, Subaru was second to none. The facts he discovered via Return by Death were absolute. That certainty was his sole advantage.

"You mentioned before…that you have a history with the Witch Cult, didn't you?"

"Yeah. Those are the worst memories I have. I won't let 'em get away with anything like it ever again."

Strictly speaking, that "history" was a future that had yet to come. So long as the actions of Subaru and others did not change it, that horrible future would be realized; he was in this place, at this time, to defy and shatter that destiny.

"...I see. Very well. So we'll be using your presence to lure them out then. Is that right?"

"...You...were easier to convince than I thought."

"I never intended to oppose your plan to begin with. I simply wanted to see if you had the resolve to lead such a dangerous operation. If you lacked the determination, it would have been necessary to find a substitute."

"Say what you want, but it's way too late for me to be getting cold feet now."

Subaru snorted at Julius's mean-spirited prodding as he brushed his meager personal worries aside. If he acted timid now, it would play right into Julius's hands. Subaru made a point to stand up straighter.

"I'm saying this loud and clear. The Witch Cult is gonna show up wherever I am. The Archbishop of the Seven Deadly Sins is no exception. So basically, when they come out, we beat them senseless. As far as that goes, it's a pretty simple plan."

"It really does sound simple when put that way... I have to say, Subawu, between this and the White Whale, you really enjoy using yourself as a decoy."

"Hey, don't say it like I do this every time something comes up. It's only been coincidence up until now. It's not like it's every single..."

Thinking back, his main role during the fight against Elsa in the loot cellar was being a distraction, followed by luring the Urugarum out in the demon beast forest. Then he became the bait for the White Whale. At the present, he was planning an operation against the Witch Cult that centered around his serving as a decoy—

"Huh?! Wait—it really is every time!"

"It would appear you have both ample experience and ample success under your belt. Perhaps we can count on your performance this time as well."

"You can...! You can, but...!"

Though Subaru groaned as he listened to Julius's words, he couldn't find a way to respond.

"So now that we've settled on me acting as a decoy, I wanna focus on everything else. First, the Witch Cult is hiding out in the forest around the manor. There's no better place for it. As for the possibility of other places the cultists could be based...the mist takes care of all that. They wanted to use the mist to cut off the Mathers turf. That means they're hiding out in this region somewhere. Closing off all roads leading out works against them, too."

There was no need to persuade anyone on that point—the White Whale had made it clear. Its obedience of the Witch Cult meant that the demon beast's appearance was necessary for whatever the cultists had planned.

Of course, the White Whale was no help to the Cult this time, having already been slain—

"The White Whale was taken down pretty much right when it appeared. We'll reach the cultists before they figure out what happened."

"Then this will be a battle against time. If we press our blades to the necks of those hiding in the forest, it will come down to a proper contest of strength. With Julius's reinforcements and the Iron Fangs added to the expeditionary force, as well as my modest strength, I do not think we shall lose."

"Well, that's how it is."

Subaru agreed with Wilhelm's assessment.

The fighting ability of the Witch Cult disciples following Petelgeuse couldn't be underestimated. However, many of the troops following Subaru's command were fierce warriors that had survived a battle with the White Whale. Even accounting for Petelgeuse, they were more than a match for a fight with the cultists.

Even Subaru could put up a fight if it was hand-to-hand combat. But considering Wilhelm's skill, it wouldn't be strange to watch heads fly after a single blow. In other words, everything else came down to how much they could tilt the circumstances in their favor, with victory hinging on a single decisive battle.

"Setting up a big ol' ambush means we'll have an overwhelming advantage…!"

In the first place, Petelgeuse had no idea a force was coming for them. The Witch Cult had always been the attacker. Their name was synonymous with irrationality and contradiction. Without a doubt, they'd never even considered that someone might threaten them.

—Subaru would smash that conceit to pieces.

"Maybe everything's been great for you bastards up till now…but we aren't going to let that happen this time."

"—"

Everyone who heard the conviction in Subaru's words wore a tense expression.

They knew. The battle awaiting them was a chance to strike a blow against the vile existence known as the Witch Cult, which had never been possible until that very moment.

"After we enter the Mathers lands, I'll smoke out the Witch Cult lurking in the forest. But the Archbishop of the Seven Deadly Sins is a sly one. He has a bunch of people under him, split into ten or so groups."

"Where did you learn this?"

"From last time Sloth popped his head out. He called his servants fingers, telling them apart with names like right middle finger, left ring finger, and stuff. He didn't seem to go as far as including toes, so we shouldn't have to worry about twenty groups showing up or anything."

Petelgeuse had distinguished between the groups under his command according to fingers. Subaru hadn't had the luxury of confirming that the Cult leader had ten fingers, but he surely ought to have the same ten that any human being did. Moreover, the madman's state made Subaru think that his followers were divided into groups equal to that number of fingers.

For some reason, though, Subaru's reply stirred unrest within the expeditionary force. Subaru raised his eyebrows at their reaction, but Julius's next question helped him realize what was wrong.

"Subaru, does the prior history you mentioned involve the Archbishop of the Seven Deadly Sins? More importantly, is Sloth masterminding the attack?"

"—Sorry. I didn't explain enough. Yeah, the Archbishop of the Seven Deadly Sins we're gonna bump into is that Sloth bastard. He's the one I have a connection with. In this world, he's the owner of the face I hate the most."

"Hmm. Incidentally, I presume your second-most-hated face belongs to me?"

"Don't get carried away. Don't be trying to make yourself a big part of my life, all right?"

It seemed as if Julius joked to hide his admiration, while Subaru could only scowl in response.

When it came to ranking faces he despised, Petelgeuse definitely took the top, with Subaru's own following at the number two spot. Julius was fairly high up on the charts, but it'd take an awful lot to dethrone the leader and runner-up.

"That asshole's put me through hell. But thanks to that, I know for a fact my odor's effective, on top of the knowledge that he splits up his followers into fingers."

"*Meow*, I see. That's why you're so confident… Better not to ask about what happened, hmm?"

"…Yeah, that's right. Please don't. I'll tell you about anything that's important, though."

"Loud and clear. Asking seems like it'll just leave a sour taste anyway."

Somehow, Ferris seemed sympathetic when he saw the unbridled rage Subaru displayed when discussing the Witch Cult. Perhaps Ferris was connecting Subaru's condition with some kind of tragic past of his own. That would have been a misunderstanding, but Subaru made no move to correct him.

"Also, not to put a damper on our plan of attack, but I've arranged for some insurance, too. I asked Anastasia and Russel for that before we set out to take down the White Whale."

"Insurance you asked the lady for? What kind of evil plan is this…?"

"It was just a normal request! Geez, who the hell do you think your employer is?!"

The genuine look of doubt on Ricardo's face drew a yell from Subaru.

"Actually, what I asked both of them to do was touch base with the villages near the highway—I wanted them to hire the dragon carriages from every traveling merchant in the neighborhood. The client is Marquis Mathers, and the condition is that he pays the asking price for everything the carriages are hauling."

"...Ha. That should get 'em fired up."

"There's no question this is going to break the bank, but it's a necessary expense to save people's lives. It's the obvious call to make since Roswaal is off prancing around somewhere again right when we need him."

The lure of gold ought to attract plenty of helpers. The money actually belonged to Roswaal, but it was his own fault for not fulfilling the duty of a landlord that he mentioned so often.

Either way, Subaru had finished laying the groundwork for the evacuation plan—getting Emilia and the villagers out before the Witch Cult attacked—though it had failed before.

"This leaves us with a small problem...namely that we don't want the Witch Cult to get wind of what we're up to, so I wanna hook up with the group of hired merchants along the way."

"Certainly, it would be wise not to put them on guard when we depend on the element of surprise. We should assign people familiar with the circumstances to guide the merchant group. TB."

"I understand. If the lady's involved, I think it's best we send people from our camp. We'll dispatch four messengers. Your instructions, please."

"Oh, that was fast. I appreciate it."

Subaru felt relieved after witnessing Julius and TB's quick decision making.

"Also, I wanna send a messenger from Crusch's to the mansion. If we don't let Emilia know about the alliance treaty and incoming reinforcements, things'll fall into chaos."

"Ahhh, a handwritten letter. *Meow* that I think about it, you wrote one, huh?"

Ferris clapped his hands together. Properly speaking, though, Subaru had merely had a letter written for him. Rem had penned a message with details about the alliance, plus a liberal interpretation of his plans against the Witch Cult. Handling such complex writing was still somewhat beyond Subaru.

If that letter reached the mansion, they'd surely be able to deal with any unforeseen situations on their end. It would give them a chance to prepare beforehand, even if they were forced to rely on the insurance policy Subaru had set up.

"That's...probably all there is to say. It's a plan that leaves a lot to be hashed out along the way, but everyone here ought to already know what this fight means."

"Meanin' it's our best chance to give the Witch Cult a bloody nose!"

As Subaru finished wrapping up the talk, Ricardo burst into ferocious laughter while he stood with his furry arms crossed against his chest. The fierce beast man's conclusion bolstered the morale of every man in the expeditionary force.

"...Throughout the years, there has surely never been a battle against the Witch Cult that has afforded us such an advantageous position."

Wilhelm drew his body straighter, channeling razor-sharp hostility as he spoke. To the Sword Devil, the Witch Cult that the White Whale answered to was as despicable as the beast itself. The only thing that accompanied his overflowing will to fight was a strong sense of reassurance.

"To be granted such an opportunity so soon after finally fulfilling my deepest wish... The greatest problem is keeping my blood from boiling."

"I'm counting on you, Wilhelm."

"As you wish."

The elderly man who had dedicated himself completely to a life of the sword responded very briefly. His demeanor projected a sense of unsurpassed trust. Subaru took this in, surveying the fifty-odd faces of his comrades.

Thanks to them, he could fight. The instant that crossed his mind, words naturally began flowing out.

"The fight with the White Whale was so hard I could've sworn I was a dead man. As a matter of fact, some people did die, while others were erased and will never get to go home."

During the battle, several lives had been snuffed out by the demon beast menace. Its mist had annihilated the memories of their existence; their very names had been scrubbed from the world.

"Right now, I don't think there's much reason or logic behind why we're standing here instead of them. If I had to say it was anything, we were a little luckier. That's all."

There had been many sacrifices, and a great deal had been given up for an opportunity to slay the Demon Beast of Mist. Perhaps, as it was with natural disasters, people set aside their personal differences when pointing their blades at the demon beast. Therefore, Subaru thought both those who had lived and those who had died had given their all.

"—"

Though it wasn't what he'd intended, Subaru's words became something like the speech a commander gives before deployment. For everyone listening closely, the address he gave was like a kind of promise that they braced their hearts with on the eve of their coming battle. It was much like Crusch's address before they set off to fight the White Whale.

Combat knew no mercy and made no distinction between the lives of the highborn and the low-. That was why they should all strive to do everything they could.

But Subaru sympathized so much with those he had come to terms with and accepted that he couldn't read the atmosphere.

"If even the tiniest thing were different, we'd probably all be dead. We're all still here after surviving a fight like that. If that's the case, then let's just get past one more."

"—?!"

"Let's win with such a landslide that not a single one of us dies. Make sure that everyone lives and goes home. We already beat a monster like the White Whale. We ain't gonna lose to the likes of the Witch Cult."

These were the idealistic delusions of a young man who could not grasp the reality of the situation. No matter who had what advantage, casualties were an inevitable part of battle. Subaru knew this, and the warriors, with all their experience, understood far better than he did.

Because they understood that, inside their hearts was something separate from the resolve to march toward death: an acceptance of death. Subaru wanted to challenge their resolve to die specifically because he noticed this lying within them.

"We're gonna make sure no one dies. Dying for the sake of scum like that is just stupid."

Subaru was afraid of death. Dying constantly trashed his life with an unbearable sense of fear and loss. He thought it was like that for everyone; he assumed that was how it had to be. Subaru, who had experienced death more than anyone via Return by Death, didn't want anyone else to know what it was like.

That was why his every action was a rejection of it.

His final words to close out the Witch Cult Hunting Made Simple meeting were explosive.

Before the shocked members of the group, Subaru raised his hand, opening his mouth as he looked out over everyone's face. After all, he'd been told that a man shouldn't make light of bowing his head—and to look people in the eye when making a request.

"On that note, I'm gonna go ahead and ask right out—let me cling to you guys while I rely on you for everything."

3

"Among the Archbishops of the Seven Deadly Sins, the two most famous are probably Sloth and Greed."

Julius spoke to Subaru while riding his land dragon alongside him. Even though they rode together, there was a world of difference in how the two sat astride their dragons. Subaru was desperately clinging to the black dragon he had named Patlash, while Julius rode elegantly.

"And that's why I can't stand you..."

"I shall let that slide and continue what we were discussing. Even among the famous Archbishops of the Seven Deadly Sins, two stand out. In terms of reliable records, information on Sloth is far more prevalent, but in terms of the scale of damage, the unforgivable crimes of Greed are second to none."

"So reliability versus how much damage, huh? Nothin' good from either one by the sound of it..."

"Certainly not."

Julius seemed deflated whenever the Witch Cult was brought up, as if he had also suffered at their hands.

"The individual you know as Sloth is suspected of being responsible for more than half of the Witch Cult's activities. Considering that the Witch Cult operates on a global scale, one can only say he possesses miraculous mobility."

"So the bastard really gets around."

"The name itself rolls off the tongue rather oddly—for a man who dubs himself Sloth, he must be a rather diligent worker. That being said, applying such energy in a direction no one wants suggests a mind that is far beyond help."

The features of the madman—bony cheeks and fiery, gleaming eyes—crossed Subaru's mind. The Archbishop of Sloth, Petelgeuse Romanée-Conti, earnestly strove to be the most diligent, and urged others to be as hardworking as he. Even though he called himself Sloth, he bore a rather substantial hatred toward laziness. His rate of activity, unusual for the Witch Cult, must have been an expression of that hatred.

"It pains me to say this, but the knights have learned little of the Witch Cult. Since they are hidden to begin with, it is difficult to expose them during peacetime. When they cause harm, the first witnesses are always doubted—even then, all that remains in their wake is something akin to a charred plain."

"So the dilemma here is like detectives that don't investigate unless a crime's been committed. I feel you, though..."

Seeing the regret on Julius's face kept even Subaru from poking fun. It would be wrong to criticize the knights' investigative abilities. After all, it didn't change the fact that the Witch Cult was at fault.

"—However, this time, it will be different."

It was Wilhelm, coming up beside them, who interrupted their exchange. Riding his favorite mount, the Sword Devil hemmed Subaru in from the side opposite Julius, staring straight ahead. His eyes were quietly filled with an eagerness to fight as he touched the hilt of the treasured sword hanging from his hip.

"We will take down the leader, allowing none to escape. Just like the White Whale, he will pay for all his wicked deeds. That is the will of every soul in the kingdom, and the earnest desire of the knights."

"Exactly as you say. These cowards have fled from the blade of justice. However, this time, we shall not give them the chance. Our swords will find them."

Wilhelm nodded, and for once Julius's expression hardened as his raw emotion became visible.

Subaru wasn't the only one with a reason to despise the Witch Cult. For some people who'd lived all their lives in this world, cursing the cultists came as naturally as breathing.

"Incidentally, since we got fired up talking about Sloth, who's this Greed guy?"

"Unlike Sloth, Greed is a name associated with few calamities. But the content of those records is more than sufficient. The Empire incident in particular is widely known."

"By that you mean the damage was especially huge?"

When Subaru posed his question with a grimace, Julius indicated yes with a nod.

"The Fortress City of Gackler—located in the Empire of Volakia, found at the south of the world map. It was known as the most solidly defended city of that nation's border regions. It had a standard garrison of thousands of troops, while the settlement itself was enveloped by a complex set of defensive walls. It was a place truly worthy of the name Fortress City, but…Greed conquered it. Single-handedly, no less."

"He took down a whole city?! By himself?!"

This was no mere tale of one knight worth a thousand footmen. Subaru's voice cracked when he heard the shocking account.

"'Soldiers must always be strong'—the common people consider this way of thinking to be 'the Imperial Way.' The Empire is a nation that lives and breathes that ideal, and even its basic infantry are fierce fighters. The Fortress City was manned by such soldiers, but it fell to a single Archbishop of the Seven Deadly Sins who called himself Greed. It is said that even 'Eight Arms' Kulgan, hero of Volakia, was slain in that battle."

It was Wilhelm who explained when Subaru voiced his surprise. Complex emotions appeared in the Sword Devil's eyes when he spoke the name of the hero defeated by Greed. Wilhelm lowered his head when Subaru noticed.

"I once had an opportunity to cross swords with Kulgan. To avoid an international conflict, we represented our two nations in a proxy match. He was a very skilled man. Though I managed to cut down six of his eight arms, he skewered me through the stomach. The match was called off with us both on the brink of death…and thus the match ended without either side declared the winner."

"That was a real casual way to bring up such an intense story…!"

Put plainly, it was difficult for a young man's heart to remain calm after he'd heard a tale about the Sword Devil's prime that was worthy of a novel. He felt a little like digging for more details, but Wilhelm had already mentioned that his worthy rival had landed a blow upon him; even Subaru wasn't insensitive enough to pick at Wilhelm's old scars.

That said, the danger Greed presented weighed heavily on Subaru's mind.

"Sloth and Greed…then on top of that, Pride, Lust, and Wrath, huh? Even without a Gluttony, sounds like a pretty grim future to come, huh?"

"—You seem to be looking quite far ahead."

"I'm not eager to see it. I think the odds of meeting them are pretty high, though."

On the eve of their battle with Sloth, thinking about what was coming made Subaru's chest throb. The unavoidable clash with Petelgeuse no doubt meant earning the permanent ire of the Witch Cult. And if the Witch Cult saw Emilia as an enemy, clashes with the other Archbishops of the Seven Deadly Sins were inevitable.

"Well, the talk about Greed already soured my stomach. Throw me a bone here."

"I have nothing good to say about unsettling the heart with discussions of an uncertain future. You should concentrate on the battle that stands before you, for Lady Emilia's sake."

"Yeah, I get it already. I'm just a little nervous right before the operation's main event."

Clicking his tongue at Julius's attempts to settle him down, Subaru shifted his gaze farther down the highway. Far ahead, in the sky to the east, night had begun to give way to light, with the tip of the morning sun still hidden beyond the dimly lit sky.

The expeditionary force hunting for the Witch Cult had already entered the Mathers domain. Riders and mounts alike went along in exhilaration, morale high as they traversed the plains. From the looks of it, they were not bothered by Subaru's reckless request, for which he quietly breathed with relief.

What Subaru had said earlier was simply his honest feelings. He didn't want to lose a single member of the expeditionary force. There was no reason for there to be casualties against the Witch Cult.

Subaru was determined to do whatever it took to bring about that result.

"That said, being the decoy is about all I can manage…"

"Did you say something?"

"Nothin' at all! I'm just thinking about if that detachment met up with our 'insurance' or not!"

"Ahhh…no reason to worry, I'm sure. They are well aware of their roles. We cannot end this operation in success unless we both meet our respective objectives. They are more determined to fulfill their duty than your thoughts of concern appreciate."

Subaru was just trying to change the subject, but the unexpectedly strong reply left him at a loss. Julius's words showed no hint of concern, making Subaru feel all the smaller.

Before he could smooth any of that over, the scenery in front of them changed.

"—It's coming into view."

"Yeah."

Subaru nodded when Julius murmured, noticing the change of scenery. Down the highway, in the direction of the approaching dawn, they began to see a thin row of green trees. That line marked the end of the plains while showing them the entryway to the great forest that enveloped Roswaal Manor and Earlham Village.

It meant that soon, Subaru would see the combined might of the Witch Cult and that hateful madman once more.

"—"

Just as during the battle with the White Whale, he felt tense, as if something had tightened in his chest. Subaru touched his fist to his abdomen to suppress a pain that he couldn't get used to no matter how often he experienced it.

Then, baring his teeth, he brushed his feelings of weakness aside and spat out a laugh in an apparent attempt to stir his soul.

"Now, then. We've done this before, but…let's do this—Mr. Fate, you're on."

4

"Here—we—go…"

Subaru felt the sensation of trampling fallen leaves as he trod along the difficult-to-navigate path. He stepped over sludge and tree roots as he made his way deeper into the dimly lit forest. If he looked overhead, the sun and the blue sky peeked through gaps in the leaves; the breeze blowing through was rich in moisture. With the lukewarm wind reminding him of the cold sweat on his brow, Subaru wiped it off with the back of his hand, exhaling deeply.

—At that moment Subaru was walking in the forest, isolated and defenseless.

Left to his own devices, Subaru was no longer accompanied by the companions he had traversed the highway with; he was not even riding Patlash. Without even a weapon to rely on, he was the definition of helplessness.

"Had to leave Patlash behind. This is one battle I can't have her stand by my side."

Slightly out of breath, Subaru laughed a little as the words trickled out.

He'd already gone a fair distance along terrain wholly unfit for walking. Squeezing through the gaps between skinny trees, snapping the fallen branches as he passed by, and scrambling up lichen-strewn hills, Subaru forged ahead. Though they were called animal trails by some, the ground was so poor for travel that the barely existing paths barred his way.

It was the third time Subaru had walked through the forest like this.

He'd been carrying someone in his arms both the first and the second time. He'd seemed so much lighter then; he wondered why his current steps felt so heavy by comparison.

"Probably 'cause I'm stunned by my own stupidity that I'm doin' this for the third time. Since it's try number three, I just wanna take it easy and head home… Now, then."

While he was murmuring, right as he leaped over some mushrooms that looked vaguely poisonous, the atmosphere abruptly shifted. It was different from the reflexive sense of tension he'd felt when confronting Elsa or the White Whale. The unpleasantness of the atmosphere clung to him, making Subaru really feel the sweat he hadn't been heeding.

"Here it comes…almost like when you suddenly see a roach in the corner of a quiet room…"

When encountering a black noxious insect, a strange battle of wills would break out—one where it seemed certain that the first one to move would perish. Time seemed to stretch beyond all limits, feeling like infinity.

It was a time much like that, with plain, distasteful trepidation crawling over the entirety of his flesh.

Abruptly, he strained his eyes. To the left and right, the forest scenery seemed uniform. But he felt as if he'd seen this somewhere before—in fact, he actually did recognize this landscape.

"I walk all those paths that ain't worthy of the name and I still get here every time. It's a little funny. I dunno whether to call it a sense of direction or guesswork, but it's too sharp, whatever it is."

Or perhaps he just really had a good nose for evil.

It'd be kind of cool to be known as a hunting dog trained to track down the Witch Cult, but if Subaru was a dog, he was of the beaten variety, having lost every battle to date. He wanted to strip that label off himself this time around.

"—Thanks for the warm welcome."

Subaru squinted, staring into the gloomy darkness ahead of him as he spoke the words of thanks. Of course, there was not even a scintilla of friendliness on his face. But the people to whom he spoke lacked any a smidgen of humanity to care. It was very late to do so, but he wondered who they were.

"I don't suppose you Witch Cultists would tell me even if I asked."

"—"

In an instant, several figures had surrounded Subaru, robed in black outfits that blended with the darkness.

At some point, the sound of the wind and even the chirps of the insects had vanished. It was a rather cliché signal that they had arrived. Now that he understood, suddenly encountering them didn't surprise him anymore.

He felt an out-of-place sense of relief—but that was only because he'd encountered the cultists exactly as planned.

"Sorry, I know you came all this way, but I wanna talk to your leader. That means you guys are in the way."

"—"

"To be honest, it doesn't feel good not to understand any of this, but I probably outrank you, right? Please?"

Subaru waved a hand, seemingly to command them to go away. As he did so, the figures in black robes bowed their heads to Subaru in a show of respect, maintaining the posture as they seemed to glide away, melting into the darkness once more. This, too, was the reaction he had expected.

Though it left him conflicted, the Witch Cultists held no enmity toward Subaru. So long as he did not indicate hostile intent toward them, and Petelgeuse didn't command them otherwise, they would do Subaru no harm.

He didn't really want to know the circumstances that lay behind that judgment.

"Sure would be nice if I could just order them to pack up their things and head back to the family farm..."

Subaru sighed deeply, his shoulders sinking. Things were never so convenient.

Either way, it was clear that he was near his destination. He recognized the scenery around him, and he'd met what he assumed was a Witch Cult patrol. If memory served him correctly, all he needed to do was keep heading deeper into the forest.

His eardrums were filled only by the sounds of his footsteps along the ground and his own breathing. He felt like he was walking through prolonged, never-ending darkness, but that sense soon came to an end.

"—Ohh."

The trees obstructing his path opened before him, and Subaru leaped into a rocky place; a sheer cliff filled his vision.

A sudden break in the forest spread before the tall, precipitous rock face, almost as if the forest had been gouged by a giant claw. Several boulders lay at the bottom of the cliff; the cave within which the Witch Cult was lurking was hidden behind a particularly large one. The malicious group was surely preparing its cruel schemes within.

But it seemed that there would be no need to converse inside the cavern this time around.

After all—

"—I have been waiting for you, DISCIPLE of love."

The man in a priestly habit had come to greet him with arms spread wide, immersed in a world of madness and delight.

His cheeks were gaunt. His eyes seemed ready to fall from their sockets. His hair was a deep green. His skin had an ashen, unhealthy sheen. His limbs, stretching out from under the black habit, were slender and frail, like gnarled branches. He looked like a man in his midthirties, but his deathly overall appearance made fifties seem hardly a stretch.

The only lively part of him was his eyes, but it was with these, and the overwhelming, fiery light of madness within them, that he stared at Subaru.

"I am Petelgeuse Romanée-Conti—Archbishop of the Seven Deadly Sins of the Witch Cult, entruuuusted with Sloth!"

With spittle on the tip of his outstretched tongue, the madman—Petelgeuse—laughed, proudly invoking his name as he extended Subaru his hospitality.

5

When, with a very deep bow and lavish laughter, the madman greeted him, Subaru put a hand to his chest. Standing before Petelgeuse, his mortal enemy, he realized that he was exceedingly calm.

"It's strange…"

This was the enemy he had hated so much, cursed with his desire to kill, the despicable foe that was the cause of all his woes.

He'd raged that he would snap the man's neck with his own hands, had he not? And yet, with the demonic fiend before him that very moment, Subaru was embraced by relief.

"I welcome thee, beloved child, recipient of Her favor! Spleeendid…ahh, splendiiiid! What depths of love entwined about you!

What heights of love wrapped around you! What heat with which love embraces you! I am grateful! I am TRULY, sincerely grateful!!"

In front of Subaru, deep feelings stirring in him, Petelgeuse quickly broke into madness. He plucked at his hair and scratched the back of a hand, drawing blood; the madman was overwhelmed, unable to keep his fierce emotions inside him.

The first time, Subaru had seen his madness in fear; the second, in enmity. Subaru now saw him for the third time. Finally, what he felt was not really disgust; rather, he felt this was just how the madman was.

At the same time, he was certain Petelgeuse's ways would never be compatible with those of normal people.

"—"

Without thinking, Subaru gave his cheek a tug, then took a deep breath. After calming himself, he waved lightly at Petelgeuse, offering the friendliest smile he could manage.

"Yo. Wasn't expecting such a big welcome. I've gotta say, all this doesn't seem real…"

"That iiis to be expected! For many, the beginning comes as a surprise. Anyone can realize one particular day, 'I am loved.' And once realizing it for the fiiirst time, you cannot let that love go—yes, for love is everything!!"

When Subaru sought a place to begin, Petelgeuse eagerly ran with the conversation. Spreading his blood-smeared arms wide, he extolled his particularly insane vision of love—very twisted yet forthright.

"For love! For the love granted to us! I, we cannot fail to reeespond with diligence! Accordingly, we administer the trial, the ordeal! To give meaning to the favor the Witch has granted to this world, to this age, to me! For love, for love forloveforloveforloooove!"

"So you can't be lazy about it. You've gotta be diligent to faithfully repay that love."

"YES—precisely!!"

When Subaru picked up the gist and pretended to understand, Petelgeuse laughed maniacally, deeply impressed.

The understanding and agreement were strictly on the surface. With Subaru keeping pace on the surface, and Petelgeuse unable to peer into his soul, the words were nothing more than sweet, empty nothings. Truly, Subaru wished he could end the conversation there and then.

"Ah, er, so what should I do now? Can I…join you people? What else is needed? A handwritten letter, a formal document with a stamp? I don't have an actual stamp, so will a fingerprint do?"

But Subaru suppressed all the disgust welling in him and turned to face Petelgeuse. The longer he kept the conversation going, the more likely it was that he could drag useful information out of the madman.

"Hmm, hmm…that spirit, that enthusiasm, that forward thinking, is to be treeeeasured… However…"

As the calculating Subaru stepped nearer, Petelgeuse sniffed the air, as if confirming that the scent of the Witch was really present. Then, as an ecstatic smile came over him, the madman extended both hands, showing Subaru his ten perfectly intact fingers. The slender, gnarled digits that resembled branches quivered.

"…The favor that you have been granted is too thick to add you to my fingers at thiiis juncture… I wonder, just how rich is the love of the Witch I see before me? Even Wrath would be envious of this… Could it be that you are Pride?!"

"Pride…?"

"Among the six Archbishops of the Seven Deadly Sins, only the seeeat of Pride is currently vacant! None of this generation worthy of the sin had appeared in this era…but the Witch Factor has suuurely reached the next generation's Pride—you have received your Gospel, of course?"

Taking a step, Petelgeuse closed the distance between them.

Petelgeuse's question, posed with his head tilted ninety degrees, could not fail to throw Subaru off.

He accepted at face value the good news that the seat of Pride among the Archbishops of the Seven Deadly Sins was vacant. But Petelgeuse suspected that Subaru might be the one to fill that vacancy. It was easy for him to claim that he could, but should he do so, and how would Petelgeuse react if he did? It was a hurdle he hadn't anticipated at all.

And he didn't have a clue about the Gospel the guy was asking about. Was it some kind of code word used among members of the Witch Cult, or a trap for the unwary? If the former, it was hazing the rookie Witch Cultist; if the latter, the madman was engaging in psychological warfare.

"Errr, well, you see..."

He didn't want to clumsily say anything rash, but silence would only make him seem more suspicious. Amid that extreme stress, Subaru strongly closed his eyes—once.

Behind his closed eyelids, faces rose up—faces of the people Subaru had to protect.

That was all he needed to harden his resolve.

"Setting aside the Gospel, about this Pride...if it takes a lousy personality to qualify, I just might be who you're looking for. I'm interested, but I'd like to hear a few more details first...about Archbishops of the Seven Deadly Sins, and this trial you mentioned."

With few avenues for follow-up, Subaru kicked the Gospel issue down the road and pursued the madman's statements—about the Archbishops of the Seven Deadly Sins, of which much was unclear, and the trial Petelgeuse had spoken of several times over.

Trial—given the situation, it was probably the current plan of attack. If he could find out details, perhaps even where the fingers were hiding out, it'd be the perfect intel to gather. Naturally, the meddlesome question might send Petelgeuse flying into a rage, but Subaru was already on guard for that.

Behind his lighthearted tone of voice, Subaru was already prepared to commence hostilities when he let the question fly. For his part, the madman slowly stuck his right hand's thumb into his own mouth.

"—My brain—is—shaking."

With a dull sound, he crushed his thumb with his back teeth, sending fresh blood trickling out of the corner of his mouth. There was a slight tremble in his halting murmur, but the mad delight from a moment earlier had completely vanished. His hollow gaze sent a shudder through Subaru, quickening his pulse. His heart beat at such a high tempo it hurt, feeling as if it were slamming against his rib cage from the inside—and right before Subaru's eyes, Petelgeuse withdrew his thumb from his mouth and said:

"The trial… Thaaat is fine. I do not mind at all."

"…"

"It ought to be some time until word reaches all regions that the highway is sealed. Similarly, the trial will not begin yet—for time is something we still pooossess."

In contrast to his disquieting actions, Petelgeuse's words to the eager-to-learn Subaru were, if anything, amiable. A smile came over Subaru at the reaction; he strained not to let his cheek twitch.

"Huh…sealed the highway? What trick did you use to do that?"

"A very simple ONE. The mist. That is eeeenough explanation, I believe?"

"—Yeah, it's plenty."

Subaru nodded at Petelgeuse's brief reply.

The statement, suggesting that the mist and the sealing of the highway were connected, was proof positive that the White Whale and the Witch Cult were linked behind the scenes. Furthermore, from that exchange Subaru learned that word of the White Whale's subjugation had not yet reached Petelgeuse's ears. The cultists hadn't realized Subaru had brought the expeditionary force with him.

"So you sealed the highway so that you could do the trial with no one to interfere. That's a pretty shrewd way to operate, Mr. Petelgeuse."

"Yes, the trial is sacred, inviolable! To fail to overcome at all costs, no maaatter the predicament, would be insincerity toward love! Yes, toward love! The love granted to us! The love poured onto us! We must RESPOND to that love!"

"Yeah!"

Separate from his statements regarding the trial, Petelgeuse got fired up by his personal thoughts on love. The madman bent back, eyes bulging, stretching his tongue as he gazed intently at the heavens, frothing at the mouth as he searched for something intangible.

Ignoring Subaru's double take at the unhinged reaction, Petelgeuse did not stop.

"Aaaaaall must be sacrificed for love! The silver-haired half-demon, whose very existence is insolent, must answer for the deep crime of her very life! Those who bear sins must undergo trials! Yes, they must be TESTED! To find whether they are slothful or diligent! And it is my hand that must be FIRST!"

"So the trials are…to question their sins, to test if they bear sins?"

"For that purpose, the trials! For that purpose, the sins! The Archbishops of the Seven Deadly Sins! Accordingly, I MUST test her! If she is not tested to see if she truly possesses the Witch Factor, then whether she is a suitable vessel cannot be—"

Gripped by madness, Petelgeuse slipped an arm into his habit. Then, after a little rummaging, his fingertips pulled out a small, case-bound book. Subaru thought it about the size of the pocket dictionaries that were common in the world he came from. Deftly opening the book with one hand, Petelgeuse ran his bloodshot eyes along its pages.

"My duty is recorded within the Gospel, and I must fulfill it as proof of my love! If you are indeed Pride, you will understand my loooofty ideals! After all, it has been centuries since the vacancy among US, the forsaken bearing the titles of sins, has been filled!!"

"Hold on a sec! I need to hear more about this Pride and this Witch Factor stuff…"

"—Present your Gospel."

"—!"

Petelgeuse suppressed his madness once more, forcing back a sudden wave of emotion. Subaru, unable to keep up with the shift, unwittingly took a step back when Petelgeuse pressed closer.

At Subaru's reaction, Petelgeuse, the crazed zeal still absent from his eyes, tilted his head ninety degrees.

"Present your Gospel. The proof of your favor—"

Speaking this, the madman extended his blood-smeared right

hand toward Subaru, demanding proof that he was a coconspirator. His undamaged left hand touched the beloved book within it. From his demeanor and actions, Subaru understood.

That book was a Gospel.

And as if to affirm his conviction, Petelgeuse thrust his Gospel text toward Subaru.

"You are not recorded within the text of my Gospel. Therefore, who aaare you, and why have you fortuitously come to appear in this place?"

"Ah! So that book is called a Gospel! I see, I see, I get it, I get it. Well, you should have said so!"

On the brink of a decisive rupture, Subaru made a grand show of patting his chest and putting a hand into his pocket. Of course, he didn't have a single page inside it, let alone a book.

"—"

Petelgeuse's pupils contracted slightly as they watched Subaru's pantomime. His madness-filled eyes caused a countdown to destruction to begin ticking down in the back of Subaru's mind. The numbers were proceeding with unusual speed; failure was surely close at hand.

Therefore—

"Oh, my bad. So, so sorry."

"What IS it?"

"About my Gospel, you see, I…used it as a pot stand and it got dirty, so I threw it out."

—Therefore, this was the watershed moment.

Judging that it was impossible to drag things out any longer, Subaru instantly brought the conversation to a conclusion.

Petelgeuse looked taken aback the instant Subaru's frivolous reply reached his ears. But when the statement immediately transformed to an insult inside the madman's brain, his visage turned fiendish.

"Proof of her favor!! Authority of Sloth!! Unseen HAAAAANDS!!"

The madman screamed with a reptilian look as his shadow exploded—no, the shadow swelled up as if exploding, becoming multiple black arms that stretched toward the heavens.

These were evil hands, imperceptible to normal people, able to destroy a human body with ease.

The hands danced high above like serpentine heads, locking on to Subaru. The black, shadowy, evil hands snapped down like whips, the tips of their fingers aimed at the ground, shooting out at breakneck speed.

And a moment before those black tendrils reached him, Subaru beat a hasty retreat from the spot.

"I told you before—if you can see 'em, they're not *that* hard to dodge!"

"What is this—?!"

Subaru had said it the last time around, so to Petelgeuse it was an assertion ungrounded in fact. However, the madman did not take the time to dismiss Subaru's statement as nonsense.

A total of seven pitch-black hands bore down on Subaru to tear him limb from limb. On bad, rocky footing, he leaped over them with legwork that could not be called pretty, even if one was charitable.

With Petelgeuse to the front, Subaru leaped heavily to the rear, putting as much distance between them as he could. He did this both to escape the range of the attack and to get out of the way of the counterattack.

"Just now, YOU saw my Unseen Hands—"

"Right now, I'm not the one you should worry about."

After his all-powerful move was countered, froth rose to the corners of Petelgeuse's mouth as he seemed ready to raise his voice again. To forestall him, Subaru pointed behind the madman's back. That was the signal for the counterattack.

"Wa—!" "Ha—!"

Overlapping bestial howls formed a destructive shock wave that rumbled through the air and tore up the ground. The rocky ground was stripped bare, kicking up a dusty swirl of wind. The wave caused cracks in the ground, leaving crevices resembling a spiderweb; a hole was gouged into the sheer cliff, precipitating a landslide.

"Wha—?!"

Petelgeuse looked back, raising his voice in shock, eyes bulging as the beast person siblings landed, unleashing their combo attack.

The sleeves of their white robes fluttered as the brother and sister—TB and Mimi—roared on all fours.

The two had landed behind Petelgeuse, opposite Subaru, ignoring the madman as they pounded a roaring wave into the freshly cut cliff. The ferocious shock wave pulverized the rock face, the blasted pieces flowing downward like an avalanche, clamping shut the entrance of the Witch Cult's hideaway.

Rock and earth collapsed into a massive pile, and in an instant the cavern lair had become a tomb.

"Awesome, now they're buried alive—you guys can suffer and regret all that you've done!"

It was Subaru who raised his middle finger, teeth bared as he ferociously pounded the insult home.

As dust danced in the air, and the impact of the landslide was conveyed by the rumbling ground beneath their feet, it went without saying that the fate of the Witch Cultists inside the crushed, buried entrance was sealed. Their plight sent Petelgeuse gazing toward the heavens.

"How...how can THIS be...?"

The madman's throat trembled; he plucked at his head, causing droplets of blood to begin to flow. His violent gesture tore hair away, and as the skin on his head bled, Petelgeuse stamped the ground in fury.

"My fingers...cruelly, without mercy, without order, without warning, without provocation, without meaning, slain, murdered, slaughtered... Ahh, ahh! My brain is shaaaaaaking!"

"Woahoo, that old guy sure has a screw loose!"

"Sis, I think all the Witch Cultists are like that."

Viewing Petelgeuse's passion with childlike disgust, the siblings, Mimi and TB, exchanged sour looks and lighthearted banter. Of course, their intervention at that juncture was no coincidence or miracle. They were Subaru's reinforcements, coordinating with him according to plan.

The two had concealed their presence while accompanying Subaru and had responded to his signal to block the entrance to the Witch Cult hideout. Now the enemy was Petelgeuse alone, putting Subaru and company at an overwhelming advantage.

"...Ah yes, that is right—it is fine."

However, Petelgeuse's tears were just ceasing to flow as he calmly murmured. The madman slowly looked at the faces of Subaru and the others, one by one, and calmly laughed. And laughed—

"IT is fine. It IS fine—it is fine! Ahh, fine! FINE! Yesyesyesyesyes-yesyesyes!!"

"Uhyaa!"

The way the madman's mood rose midway through his words, his voice turning shrill, made Mimi's shoulders jump.

Having exposed his madness, and coated with a thin layer of cold dread, Petelgeuse thrust the fingers of both hands into his mouth at the same time. Then, one by one, he crushed the fingertips with his teeth.

With all ten of his fingertips crushed, a considerable amount of blood flowed as Petelgeuse said, "It is fine. Now I uuunderstand! Now IS the time for struggle! For love, yes, for looooove!!"

Petelgeuse raked the ground with his fingernails, ignoring Mimi and TB as he declared war on Subaru alone. But Subaru shrugged his shoulders toward the madman, his face displaying none of the same militancy.

"...Sorry to disappoint when you're all worked up like this, but..."

"What is this?! I shall attend to this trial with love— This! Very! Moment!"

When Petelgeuse thrust out a bloody finger, proclaiming vehemently, Subaru said to him, "I'm having someone else take you on."

The answer made Petelgeuse's eyes widen. And the instant he tried to raise a skeptical voice—

"Yaaaaaaaa—!!"

Petelgeuse lifted his face in shock as the earsplitting cry crashed down from overhead.

And then the Sword Devil's blade bit into the madman from below the shoulder—slicing him in two.

CHAPTER 2

—FIGHT

1

Let us rewind time to just before the end of the Anti-Witch Alliance conference.

"Oh, right! I forgot the important part!"

When Subaru palmed a fist, it was in the particularly quiet atmosphere immediately following his request to the expeditionary force—on the verge of setting off with great ardor to enter the Mathers domain.

I didn't explain enough, he thought, feeling sheepish as he immediately backed away from his grandiose words, but Subaru could not be negligent about the most critical part. Thus, he addressed one and all:

"I called this plan Witch Cult Hunting Made Simple, but the ultimate target, the Archbishop of the Seven Deadly Sins… I want to pick who goes after him real carefully."

"Carefully?"

"Yeah. After all, whether we take the archbishop down decides whether this plan works or not. I want to pick our best members. What I mean is Wilhelm and some Iron Fangs who're confident about their sneaking abilities. Ah, they have to be okay even if the archbishop's staring straight at them."

Subaru's condition furled the brows of everyone sitting in the circle around him. Their expressions shifted to bewilderment, anxiety, and unease; the men sitting beside one another differed somewhat individually, but their faces surely added up to a sum total of "doubt."

It was a natural reaction. Subaru, knowing he should explain further, scratched his face as he continued.

"Errr, you see. Just like I said, the plan itself is simple—I lure out the Witch Cult so we can hit them. That much is the same as with the White Whale, but…I think it's pretty hard to expect their reaction to be as simple as a demon beast's."

"Ahh, well, that figures. Subawu's scent made the White Whale lose track, but unlike a demon beast, the Witch Cult won't go *grrr* quite that much, huh?"

"Well, that's exactly how the White Whale reacted to me… Anyway, ideally, we hit the Archbishop of the Seven Deadly Sins with a surprise attack and take him down the instant I lure him out. We have to absolutely make sure he dies instantly, so prioritizing that is another requirement."

Subaru affirmed Ferris's explanation and tied the logic together. The surrounding reactions to his plan turned sour, with disgust visible on the faces of many. The sternest face of all was Ricardo's, bared fangs included.

"Wait, wait. We can't do that. Can you leave us out of this one? We can't be sneakily murderin' people after gettin' all fired up about a proper battle like this. No way. I didn't hear about this."

"That's why I'm explaining it now. Besides, I mean just for the Archbishop of the Seven Deadly Sins. The I'm-a-lure plan's other ten parts depend on this. You'll have lots of places to make noise."

Subaru tried all he could to convince Ricardo, the dividing line inside the circle.

"Not that we can underestimate the other Witch Cultists, but the Archbishop of the Seven Deadly Sins is a different story. I want to make extra sure we take him down."

This time Julius interrupted his explanation to the jeering Ricardo.

"So prepare for all possibilities, is it? I commend that line of thinking, but what of your logic for selecting people? Of course, I have no objection to selecting Master Wilhelm."

After glancing sidelong at Wilhelm, who sat with closed eyes, Julius touched his own slender knight's sword as he looked at Subaru.

"I wish to hear the reason why I was not among your initial selections."

"Seems like you're not unhappy about that, but you're not exactly pleased, either..."

The Archbishop of the Seven Deadly Sins was the main event, leaving Julius with some objections to being removed from the decisive battle. Ferris, seeing the two clashing in their opinions, patted Subaru on the shoulder before speaking.

"Hey, Subawu. If this is just you still holding a grudge against Julius..."

"I have no such vulgar suspicions. Such a possibility has never entered my mind...but I would be disappointed to find that you are a human being so obsessed with trivial matters that you lose sight of the greater picture."

Subaru wasn't sure how serious he thought all that, but he felt *Don't give half-hearted orders* was the point that Julius wanted to drive home. Subaru, reflecting on having lost sight of the larger picture through obsession with small things in the past, raised a finger and responded.

"The magic of the Archbishop of Sloth...maybe it's not magic. It's not a spell or a spirit, but anyway, he has a special ability. That's one reason I don't want a big gaggle of people rushing him."

"...Special abiwity? What? First I've heard of it."

"Best I can describe it, it's an ability to extend a bunch of hands invisible to the eye. With one exception, you really can't see 'em, and if they hit you, they can rip your limbs off pretty easily. The range is pretty much as far as he can see."

"Wha...?!"

Subaru's off-the-wall reasoning left Ferris in shock, looking as if someone had poured cold water on him while he slept. Julius's brows furled as well, and a not-insignificant shock took hold of the expeditionary force.

—The Unseen Hands under Petelgeuse's control were literally an invisible menace. Subaru would never forget the sight of that nightmarish power cruelly toying with Rem's body. And in a large-scale melee, the might of that menace could throw everything into utter chaos.

"That's why I don't want to go with numbers. It'll just raise the number of casualties."

"...You're saying that with a completely straight face, huh? I can't check without Lady Crusch here, but..."

"If Crusch were here my answer would be the same. That ability's the biggest obstacle to taking Sloth down."

Deep down, he didn't think that was all there was to it, but even so, he was sure of that part. Taking it in, Julius, the first to have spoken up, lowered his eyes, sinking deep in thought before asking, "Incidentally, you said there was one exception. And that exception is?"

"Me."

"I see. A simple tale."

Faced with Subaru's simple explanation, Julius could only make that curt reply. Julius sank into thought, but in the meantime, someone else clenched a fist.

"I get it!"

It was Mimi who had spoken, vigorously clenching her fist. With an impetuous laugh, she grabbed the shoulders of TB, standing beside her, and shook them hard as she said, "All right, Mimi and TB will go with Mister! And the old man, too! That's best! What, not good? You won't go?"

"Sis, you're being impulsive again..."

TB, accustomed to his older sister's lack of inhibition, made no move to refute her. Subaru was happy for the volunteers, but he wasn't sure they fulfilled his conditions.

"Ya can rest easy. Besides me, Mimi's the best of the bunch at everythin'. She ain't my second in command for nothin'."

"I can really trust you on that? She looks like the type who sneezes at the worst possible time."

"Subawu, you're not really one to talk, are you? …Ha, can't be helped, *meow.* Ferri will go with you, too. That should make you rest a little easier, right?"

"Seriously? That's a big help, but you're all right with this? To be honest, we're crossing a dangerous bridge here."

"To think you would say that…"

When Subaru expressed his surprise at Ferris's declaration, Julius's eyes went wide at Subaru's reply. "Huh?" went Subaru, turning his head at Julius's reaction, but Julius said nothing more.

Julius let the matter of Subaru's intent lie, proceeding to turn Ferris's way.

"I shall leave Master Wilhelm, Mimi, TB, and him in your hands, my friend."

"Yes, yes. Lady Crusch entrusted me with this from the beginning, so don't worry, it'll be fine."

"Even so, I must."

"…Yes, yes. Then I'll stick a little concern for you in a corner of my heart, Julius."

Ferris gave a strained smile; Julius's expression was the very image of seriousness as he drew himself up. The easygoing exchange demonstrated the trust between the two friends. Put bluntly, Subaru was a little jealous.

Either way, the brainstorming seemed to have resulted in Julius agreeing, too.

"Don't feel like arguing anymore?" said Subaru.

"Since you are the only one who can see the archbishop's power, it cannot be helped. If the numbers are increased further, you cannot easily instruct others to evade, I take it?"

"Glad you're quick on the uptake."

As might be expected, people who fought were quick to understand tactics.

Subaru could counter Unseen Hands by dodging the evil hands himself, but beyond that, the asset he brought was seeing the hands' movements and getting other people out of their way. And for purposes of the operation, the fewer people the better. The Unseen Hands power was advantageous against numerous opponents, and that was another reason Subaru wanted to confront Petelgeuse with as few people as possible.

"So that's why I wanted to insist that Wilhelm come with me, but…"

Julius, Ricardo, and others had ceased to object, so Subaru turned the conversation toward Wilhelm, who'd maintained his silence up to that point.

When he cautiously checked on Wilhelm, who had neither approved nor disapproved, the man's eyes opened. The Sword Devil trained his clear blue eyes on Subaru, nodding without a single contrary word.

"—You do not need to ask about my resolve. I am your sword, Sir Subaru. By your will, I shall cut down your foe."

"———"

"Please, employ me however you wish."

Granted such highly refined trust, Subaru could only nod, swallowing his astonishment.

When he looked back, he saw the siblings quarreling, Ferris's shoulders slumping, and behind them Julius, Ricardo, and the rest of the expeditionary force entrusting Subaru & Co. with this crucial matter.

Accepting this, Subaru nodded strongly, this time without worry.

"Yeah, this fight—we're gonna win this!"

2

"Did we get him?!"

Subaru hastily covered his mouth with his hand after he unintentionally exclaimed out loud.

They were at the center of the rock-strewn place in front of the sheer cliff. Wilhelm had just leaped forward, his blade biting into Petelgeuse's slender body at a sharp angle as he sliced it apart.

The madman's body had been slashed from shoulder to hip. His posture swayed wildly from the deep, fatal wound. Even so,

Petelgeuse's eyes remained wide open, glaring at Subaru until the bitter end.

"This cannot b—"

But Subaru would never learn what the madman had intended to say.

A horizontal cut traced an arc, sweeping away blood as it parted the wind. That instant, Petelgeuse's severed head spewed blood like a water fountain as it was sent flying.

The sight of a person being decapitated before his eyes left Subaru speechless. However, adamant denial seemed to drive the headless form forward, causing it to extend its withered, branch-like arms toward Subaru.

"Inelegant to the extreme—fall, like a man."

The Sword Devil's blade mercilessly dismembered the body struggling against its own death. The slice sent both arms flying from their shoulders; the blade returned to directly strike the torso, tearing it from the lower body at the waist, sending the madman-turned-sack-of-flesh tumbling to the ground, innards pouring out.

The gushing blood and muscular twitches soon stopped, leaving only the powerful stench of dead blood.

The spectacular manner of death, utterly lacking in any respect for humanity, made nausea well up into Subaru's throat. But he somehow managed to avoid actually vomiting as he said, "I-it's over…right?"

"If it's not over by now, even Ferri will start believing in this favor-of-the-Witch nonsense," Ferris replied from behind Subaru, who was timidly peering at the corpse. He moved beside the unsettled Subaru, examining the remains without hesitation.

"Though it's not much of a surprise, he's definitely dead," Ferris observed. "You have it on the word of the royal capital's greatest healer."

"Oh…really…?"

The corpse, no longer retaining the shape of a person, seemed more like a prop than anything else. Reassured by Ferris's words, Subaru felt the urge to vomit recede as he looked toward the forest.

As planned, their main target—the Archbishop of the Seven Deadly Sins—had been taken care of. Those remaining were Petelgeuse's fingers in the forest.

"Hope everyone else is doing all right...not taking too many risks."

"Sir Subaru, they are not soldiers who would freelance in violation of your instructions. Even if unavoidable combat does take place, Mr. Ricardo and Mr. Julius are with them. A worst case is unlikely."

Back from checking the severed head for himself, Wilhelm respectfully stood at attention. The Sword Devil's guarantee was reassuring. Yet, it did not wipe away Subaru's worry to any great extent.

The object of his worry was the other detachment—those heading off to deal with the Witch Cultists drawn to Subaru until he could make it to Petelgeuse and lure him out in person.

They had surmised that Petelgeuse's subordinates were scattered around the forest, ten groups in all. Subaru had commanded the two fingers he'd encountered midway to return to base, and their actual retreat had already been confirmed. The idea was to let them go, follow them with the tenacity of a sumo wrestler's leg hold, and use them to work out the locations of the rest—Subaru had strictly ordered his people not to attack, even if they held an advantage in numbers.

But if they were spotted by the opposition, combat was no doubt unavoidable.

"I'm seriously afraid of accidents if that happens. This is the plan I drew up, and it has one crucial hole in it...I don't know what the Witch Cult people are thinking, and this unexpectedly large number of people fighting scares me..."

"Yes, yes, the plan maker must not show worry! Besides, I've heard this talk from Nervous Subawu over and over. It's getting old." Ferris sighed with an exasperated face at Subaru, who was worried about the other side now that his side was taken care of. "I understand you're scared, but with Julius and them, fighting shouldn't be a problem, *meow*. If Julius is fighting seriously, Old Man Wil's probably the only one here who can take him on."

"...That so? He's that strong?"

Ferris had elaborated to address their young leader's inexhaustible worry, but the details still left Subaru conflicted. In terms of his being a reliable ally, Julius's strength was more than welcome—but given his deeply rooted sense of distaste to date, it was difficult for Subaru to accept Julius's worth at face value. Even if the physical wounds from their duel had completely healed, untreatable phantom pains haunted Subaru even then.

"It really does run deep… Setting aside whether it's unconscious or not, I do understand your aversion to him, though…"

"—? What'd you say?"

"Nothing much. In the first place, Julius and them should be much more worried about us! After all, Ferri thought this plan was reckless all this time."

Ferris raised his brows and glared at the acrimonious Subaru, who knit his brow in response.

"…Yeah, I get it. But it worked out, didn't it?" Subaru said as he glanced at the rocky place that had become their battleground.

"Looking at the results only. When the Archbishop of the Seven Deadly Sins suspected you, you were nearly done for, weren't you? It was *definitely* by the skin of your teeth. Ferri hates people in a hurry to die before his eyes."

"I'm not in a hurry to die at all. Well, not that it sounds very convincing right now…"

The sternness of Ferris's gaze told Subaru that apologizing further would be meaningless.

It had actually been Ferris obsessing over the operation's little details right up until the end. Ferris hadn't objected to the broad outline of the operation itself—Subaru "fishing" for Petelgeuse, luring him out as a decoy—but he was abnormally fixated on hammering out the specifics to raise their degree of safety.

In point of fact, Subaru couldn't deny the low reliability of the plan, given that it greatly hinged on Subaru himself. Everything about luring out the Witch Cultists—locating Petelgeuse, the main target; slowing him down; gathering intel—was on Subaru's shoulders alone. If even a single thing happened contrary to Subaru's expectations, he *would* perish. Ferris really, really hated that.

In the end, no useful counterproposal emerged, so he hadn't stopped Subaru from carrying out the plan, but—

"Subawu, you *know* how only going by results leaves a bad taste in my mouth, and still you..."

Ferris's resentful words triggered a memory of other words that had come out of the healer's mouth, spoken close to a half day before at the height of the battle with the White Whale. Ferris had spoken of accepting his role in battle.

Just like Subaru, Ferris was decisively unsuited to the field of battle. On top of that, belonging to the knights meant that, compared to Subaru, he had many more opportunities to feel utterly powerless.

The last words he'd thrown out had an echo of loneliness, as if he'd been betrayed by someone who shared his powerlessness—

"I'm a little surprised, though. I thought you hated me and all."

"Don't be absurd. I don't choose who I heal based on whether I like them or not."

"I wanted you to deny hating me, you know!"

Even if your worth was understood, how you accepted it depended on whether you acknowledged it yourself. When Subaru unwittingly gave a pained smile, Ferris had a sullen face when he touched his only weapon—the dagger on his hip.

"Whether I like or hate someone has no relation to whether it's worth keeping them alive. It's because...that's what Ferri's power is, that others recognize that power."

"Ferris?"

"Besides, a lot of people died in the battle with the White Whale. When someone's squished flat, or erased by the mists, even Ferri... even I can't heal that."

The usual composure in his voice absent, Ferris touched the relief carved into his dagger with a finger. This was the family crest of the Lion Rampant—the same crest on the treasured sword his master, Crusch, had carried.

The touch of Ferris's fingertip seemed to put courage, and more than that, resolve on his face as he glared at Subaru.

"Don't get conceited and think you're the only one who doesn't want people to die in this fight."

"...I'm trying to keep that in mind, too."

He was trying to, but in truth, trying might have been the extent of it. With Ferris's gaze straight on him, Subaru could accept that he wasn't the only one, but he couldn't change his ways. No matter how much Ferris might object, he'd carry out the plan without deviating.

If it was Subaru's own life on the line, he'd probably always bet that chip first.

"We've finished checking the cave. The people inside were completely crushed by falling rock. I feel kind of bad for them."

"Oh yeah, it was perfect! Perfecto-mundo! They all went *booooom*!"

Just when the conversation was at a pause, the beast person siblings returned from checking on the buried cave. Greeting the pair, Subaru walked over to Petelgeuse's remains.

Uncertain elements had been swept away, and the danger had been completely eliminated. Subaru was no longer feeling tense, and his stiff cheeks had finally slackened.

"Wiping 'em all out in an unexpected outside attack—to be honest, it was pretty unsportsmanlike, but don't think badly of me. After all, you're way, waaaaay worse than I am."

With his opponent already a corpse, all he could do was make a hollow declaration of victory. That the victory had been earned with a surprise attack, practically an assassination, made it baser and hollower still.

Even so, Subaru couldn't help but say it, because now it felt real inside him.

Petelgeuse had been struck down—the result Subaru had redone the world several times over to achieve.

"Wilhelm, thank you very much. Also, sorry for making you push yourself."

"Push myself, you say?"

"Cutting him down with a surprise attack from the rear, it's the worst, right?"

Wilhelm's face became slightly clouded. He was complicit in no mere surprise raid, but a sneak attack. A knight would surely have that on his mind.

But Wilhelm's expression immediately broke into a strong smile.

"I abandoned chivalry long ago. It is nothing you need concern yourself with, Sir Subaru."

"But I'm the one who made you tag along and help with a surprise attack, so…"

It was a fact that the opponent was a heretic against whom honest, forthright measures were useless. Even so, asking others to cooperate in a cowardly scheme like this didn't sit well with him at all.

"Well, Ferri didn't mind at all, *meow.* Julius might have hated it… but I think he's shrewd enough to accept it."

"That's why I didn't want to tell him to do it. Well, I could sorta predict how you'd react, though."

"Isn't it better to be a little cowardly and have your friends live than to stick to chivalry and have them die, *meow*? Subawu, whether you or Julius is right is just a matter of your point of view."

Having Ferris intervene was a big help. Wilhelm said nothing, whereas Mimi tilted her head as if she was wondering, *Is there a problem with that…?* She was a mercenary through and through.

And what TB then did deserved mention as even more mercenary than that; having finished looking around the area, the little cat-man walked over to Petelgeuse's remains…and, without a moment's hesitation, began fishing around in his pockets.

Subaru unwittingly gawked at the sight.

"Hmm, seems he wasn't walking around with much on him…"

"H-hey, little guy, you're checking a corpse's pockets like it's no big deal."

"I am not 'little guy,' I am TB. And this is simply checking his belongings."

With a practiced hand, TB searched for the spoils of war deep inside the blood-smeared habit. Mimi did the same. In contrast to their cuddly appearances, the mercenary siblings really did things their own way.

The inside of the habit was surprisingly deep, making TB's hand unexpectedly busy getting everything out. That said, the contents taken out were all mundane articles.

"Field rations, lagmite ore… Ahh, he has a money pouch, too."

"I'm surprised, his inventory's filled with petite bourgeoisie stuff. So what, is pillaging a part of mercenary culture?"

"I believe that it's normally 'to the victor go the spoils'? …What… is this?"

As he made the statement, TB, well-suited to the mercenary trade, had nearly finished his perusal when a black book drew his attention. Seeing this, Subaru went, "Ah!" with a start.

"That's probably the book Petelgeuse called his Gospel."

"Myuu! This is a Gospel?! Uwaa, I touched it!"

When Subaru pointed it out, TB hurled the book away. He looked very much like a kitten as he bounced nervously, drawing a strained smile from Subaru as he picked up the book.

"I know the owner was icky, but you shouldn't mistreat a book. Not even a weird one like this."

"D-don't touch it. I think you should let go right now. Touching it might make you go weird in the head…! It—it might be better to burn it…"

Ignoring TB's concerns, Subaru opened it and glanced at the pages. However, he was unfortunately unable to identify the characters in which the words were written. They were neither I-script nor R-script, nor even H-script, but some other, mysterious language. They kind of looked like hiragana scribbled way too fast, so much so as to be illegible. On top of that, the latter half of the book was comprised of blank pages; a reasonable person might call it a misprint.

"…Well, I can't read it anyway. I know it was careless of me, so both of you calm down, okay?"

"—My apologies."

"Well, it's your fault, Subawu."

Wilhelm and Ferris dropped the combat postures they'd adopted when Subaru unguardedly opened the book before them.

It was for only a brief instant, but the hostility and enmity had been real. With a touch of cold sweat from that, Subaru showed the two the book in his hand, trying to wrap his head around it.

"Does either of you have a clue about this book?"

"Wait a—! Don't just turn it our way like that! Subawu, don't you do something stupid and try to read a Gospel! I genuinely don't know what it'll do to you!"

Ferris averted his eyes, raging like an inferno toward the book raised before him. Surprisingly, Wilhelm turned his back, displaying his aversion to the book as well.

"I know TB reacted like that, too, but what, the book's seriously dangerous?"

The book was about as big and heavy as a pocket dictionary, with binding that was strictly ordinary. As it was from the Witch Cult, he would've expected a cover made out of human skin, but there was no sign of that.

However, the grimaces on the faces of all save Subaru made their sentiments easy to read.

"To the Witch Cult, having one of those books…those Gospels is proof you are a fellow cultist. Yes, I suppose one could say they are like holy scripture to them."

"Scripture…?"

"Rumor has it that the Witch Cult sends them to particular people, *meow*. And when they arrive, that's it…poof, another pious Witch Cultist is born! Or so they say."

"Huh?!"

Subaru's voice went shrill at the unexpected and astounding tale. These Witch Cultists were eerie, creepy people he couldn't understand even the tiniest bit. Yet, they had once been normal human beings, their transformation triggered by the arrival of such a book. A deep reading of Ferris's words suggested that the Gospels were books that brainwashed the human beings reading them.

If that was so, many of the Witch Cultists were brainwashed, ordinary people—

"If that's true, then maybe all the people we buried alive in the cave were just…"

"Sir Subaru, you are mistaken. By the time the Gospel reaches them, they have already passed the point of no return. They are not innocent people brainwashed into obedience that can be saved. Sir

Subaru, did that Archbishop of the Seven Deadly Sins appear sane to you?"

"N-nah. He didn't, but…I thought maybe he was an exception."

Brought back from the brink of thoughts of regret, Subaru passively shut his mouth. So Petelgeuse's madness, far beyond the norm, was just one example of the dangerous mental states within the Witch Cult that didn't involve brainwashing. Put bluntly, a part of him was reluctant to take their current conversation as absolute proof it was so.

"Now, Subawu, I know you did a great job as a decoy against the White Whale and the Witch Cult…but I feel like this is putting you in a lot of danger, *meow*, so don't let the Gospel get you, 'kay?"

"I must ask that as well, Sir Subaru. Please do not make me cut you down."

"I'll try, but is being careful really gonna cut it…?"

It seemed that whether the book "got" someone or not depended on the recipient's mood. If the other side was headhunting, it depended on whether Subaru accepted or declined. The notion left him distinctly uncomfortable.

Sighing at the various things being said, Subaru looked down at the book, which suddenly felt very heavy.

"I guess I'll…keep it with me for now. Even if I can't read it, it might be useful some other way."

It had belonged to an Archbishop of the Seven Deadly Sins. Just maybe deciphering the Gospel might bring him closer to the truth about the Witch Cult.

With that hope in mind, Subaru stuffed the book into his pocket, but no matter how much time passed, the suspicious gazes from the three, looking at him as if he were some crazed daredevil, did not disappear.

"So was there anything else on him that caught your eye? It'd be a super-huge help if he was stupidly walking around with, say, a map with hideouts marked on it…"

"I did not see anything like that among his belongings. Aside from the Gospel text, he was walking around with exactly what one would expect for a man in his attire," TB replied to Subaru's rebound as he checked the confiscated belongings.

Certainly, judging from Petelgeuse's attire, it seemed he traveled light. But even if they wrung his neck, dead men told no tales.

"Hey, hey, can't we just leave? No point fussing over everything here, right? Better to finally head back to everyone?"

At that point, Mimi, having stayed out of the conversation so far, spoke up while tossing dirt over the remains. Her tail sticking out from her hem, she pointed at Petelgeuse, now completely buried, and said:

"We've buried the enemy, so isn't it best to check on how everyone else is doing? Hey, we really should! Really!"

"You say it so innocently, but you're really heartless, wow. With your adorable looks, that contrast's really slapping me in the face."

"Hu-huu, calling me cute's gonna make me blush!"

With convenient hearing, Mimi blushed at the part she liked, drawing a strained smile from Subaru. But it was a fact that she referred to a good opportunity. It really was best to ditch the place and regroup with the main force.

"..."

Looking back, Subaru stared at the place, now completely silent.

The cave was buried in earth and sand, the minions spectacularly crushed, their trump card rendered useless, Petelgeuse slaughtered before he could pull anything—clueless as to what was happening until the bitter end.

Via Return by Death, Subaru had seen what future lay before them if he employed his power to its full extent. They'd scored a complete shutout—and that meant complete victory against the Witch Cult.

It meant that, but—

"Er, no, this is me, right...? There's no way it goes this smoothly. Up till now, no matter how hard I try, there's always a downside. It can't be this good...there's gotta be a catch somewhere..."

"What's with all the suspicion, *meow*? Hurry up, there's still a lot to do, isn't there?"

"A-ah, yeah. That's right... You're right."

Ferris turned a disbelieving eye toward Subaru, who still couldn't believe the fruits of his labors. Nodding at Ferris's words, he tugged on the back of his hair as he departed the rocky place.

Victory. Yes, victory. It wasn't an accident; he'd *won*. What was wrong with that?

"—Maybe he comes back to life as soon as our backs are turned?!"

"What are you going on about? Ferri is really angry already! Sheesh!"

"Ow, ow, ow!"

When Subaru looked back, unable to drop his suspicious mindset, Ferris grabbed hold of his hair and dragged him along. It might have gone without saying, but neither the plugged cave nor Petelgeuse's corpse showed any change.

This time, they would truly take their leave. And then, as the icing on the cake—

"Mister's noisy about it, so just to make sure!"

Saying this, Mimi held her cane in her hand. Magic erupted from it—and Petelgeuse's grave, along with his corpse, exploded.

This time, without exaggeration, Petelgeuse, the Witch Cult's Archbishop of Sloth, was blown to bits.

3

"From the look of things, it would appear you return with fair tidings."

With a modest, composed smile, Julius greeted Subaru and the others, who were rejoining the rest of the group after taking Petelgeuse down.

They were stationed at an expeditionary-force field camp, constructed outside the forest and somewhat far off from the highway. With the Witch Cultists lurking in the forest, they were avoiding prying eyes from there and the highway to not give away their presence.

That said, now that Petelgeuse, their top dog, was dead, it was unlikely the remaining fingers would fail to notice for long. Their future movements required not just caution, but audacious haste.

"What about the fingers' base spotted along the way?"

"One detachment is still keeping it under watch. They will surely contact us if anything occurs. But the other detachment made inopportune contact and engaged the Witch Cultists in combat."

"Serious?! So what happened, then?! Did we lose anyone…?"

Having thought this a routine report, Subaru was stricken with nervousness when he heard it had come to a fight. However, when Subaru pressed closer, Julius gave a strained smile. Hand-combing his slightly disheveled forelocks, he gave his cavalry saber a slight tilt with his hand.

"You may rest easy. Several among the Witch Cultists were formidable, but all were dispatched without difficulty. The base in question was mopped up, so there should be nine fingers left."

"…There's no wounded? Also, none of the enemies got away?"

"Rest easy. We have thoroughly addressed all of your concerns."

Julius was too classy to conceal his own failures. Hearing there had been neither casualties nor failures, Subaru sighed a breath of relief. Julius gave a slightly pained smile at his reaction as he said, "And you were not followed? All went according to plan against the Archbishop of the Seven Deadly Sins?"

"Wilhelm cut off his head, and magic blew his corpse into teeny bits, so that should be it… It should be it, right? Any normal way of thinking, there's no way he'd come back from that, right?"

"You witnessed it for yourself, so I am uncertain why you look so uneasy."

Julius skeptically knit his brows at Subaru's lingering suspicions. Then he continued to grimace when he looked at Ferris, standing at Subaru's side.

"…Besides, though I understand the urge to be certain, destruction of remains lacks elegance. And you were with him, Ferris."

"Sowwy, Ferri desperately tried to stop them, but Subawu just wouldn't…"

"Don't say it like it's some tragedy caused by my violent nature!! What's with all the excess theatrics?! I'll have you know, it was the big sis of those kitty siblings that did it!"

When Julius scolded them for violating the dead, Ferris sold Subaru out with a tear in the corner of his eye. Subaru objected to his statement and pointed to the real culprit—Mimi, who'd returned along with them.

Incidentally, Mimi was sulking from having been scolded for her excess by everyone on the way back. Currently, she was curled over TB's back out of spite, sulking to the point of refusing to walk under her own power.

"I see, Mimi, was it? Then it cannot be helped. She had her reasons, I'm sure."

"Her little brothers do it, too, but don't you and Anastasia spoil her a little *too* much…?"

"That is neither our intent nor fact. Incidentally, it was Master Wilhelm who struck down the archbishop…?"

Evading Subaru's stare, Julius addressed Wilhelm, looking in the latter's direction. Wilhelm reciprocated, pulling back his shoulders as he said, "I cut off his head, and without doubt severed the thread of his life. I know of no living creature able to live through that."

"I am relieved. If Master Wilhelm speaks such a thing, there can be no mistake—so this time we have greatly impeded the future activities of the Witch Cult led by Sloth."

"What, you didn't believe it when I said it?! I'm not playing around here, so I checked the corpse with my own eyes! Two or three times at that!"

"I would like you to take my not checking with Ferris as a sign of my sincerity toward you."

"Sincerity is based on the word *sincere*. You knew that, right?"

A vein bulged on Subaru's forehead as he rebuffed the unapologetic Julius. But Julius did not reply to Subaru as he raised an expectant hand toward the other knights and mercenaries. At his signal, conversing voices died out, and with all eyes on Julius, he motioned to Subaru.

"They, too, await your report. It should come from your own mouth. Am I wrong?"

"You're not wrong, but it annoys me to have *you* set the stage."

"Petty stubbornness, *meow*…"

Ferris sent an exasperated expression toward Subaru and Julius, arguing regardless of the situation.

"Boys really can be so stupid. And Subawu, especially stupid."

"Seen from the outside, a man's pride might often be seen as trivial. Does this ring any bells with you, Ferris?"

"...Who knows? There might have been someone stubborn like that once upon a time..."

Somehow, Ferris's reply to Wilhelm's words sounded awkward. Turning his face away, seemingly to avoid the aged swordsman's gaze, Ferris made a heavy sigh.

With that exchange taking place off behind Subaru, he reported the good news to everyone focused on him.

"So things went pretty much as expected. We took down the Archbishop of the Seven Deadly Sins!"

"Ohhh—"

Narrating with poses and gestures, Subaru made his explanation as vivid as possible, conveying the high points of the success of their operation against the archbishop, bringing joy to the faces of those stewing at having to wait.

"W-wait, wait! No loud voices! They'll hear you!"

"—!"

And they came to the brink of breaking into shouts of joy, which would have made their having camped outside the forest meaningless. No doubt was left that the result was optimal for them all.

"With that done, that leaves moppin' up the stragglers, pretty simple stuff. If we don't hurry, the lady'll be the granny by the time we're done... Ah, that's just a stock joke o' mine."

"Somehow, I don't feel like laughing at that one... Well, that's fine, though."

Setting aside Ricardo's sense of humor, the fact remained that it was best to move nimbly from that point forward. Unfortunately, it was also a fact that the remaining job wasn't as simple as Ricardo made it out to be.

"Just 'cause we beat Petelgeuse doesn't mean everything's wrapped up with a bow, after all."

"Won't do any good to be drunk on victory and trip over our own feet, *meow.* And if they know the Archbishop of the Seven Deadly Sins died, the rest of the Witch Cultists won't be lured out so easily, huh...?"

"Hey, these are Witch Cultists. Best to stop expecting 'em to have sane, rational thoughts."

Ferris and Ricardo picked up where Subaru left off, apparently sharing his concerns. The faces of the others seemed to indicate agreement; not a single one seemed slacker at the news of their first victory.

"First off, smashing the fingers under his command is our top priority. Besides that, there's no one here extreme enough to slaughter all the Witch Cultists, right? I'd like us to capture any of them we can..."

"I have a feeling they'll just kill themselves, though... That's what they've always done to date, after all."

With Subaru plotting to capture some alive, Ferris's lips thinned in dismay. This was not a rebuttal of the idea, but rather an expression of his disgust toward Witch Cultists who would kill themselves to seal their own lips.

To a healer such as him, such craftiness from the Witch Cult was probably a hard thing to take.

"I understand your skepticism, Ferris. But if we can refrain from taking their lives, it is incumbent upon us to do so. I agree that we should prioritize capture when we confront the remaining Witch Cultists. Having said that, we must not lose sight of the fact that our own well-being comes first, to avoid any sudden reversal of fortune."

With Ferris sullen, Julius was considerate toward him while agreeing with Subaru's opinion.

"—And while locating the fingers does come first, we should not neglect that the dragon carriages you arranged should reach us soon enough."

"That so? There's that, too, yeah."

At Julius's declaration, Subaru clapped his hands together, recalling the detachment heading to rendezvous with the expeditionary force.

The dragon carriages, which they'd recruited by gathering traveling merchants together from neighboring parts, were for evacuating Emilia and the rest. That said, with Petelgeuse struck down and nothing left of the Witch Cult but remnants, it seemed highly likely that there would be no need for a wholesale evacuation, making all that extra effort for nothing.

"Though that is as planned, it would surely be difficult for the expeditionary force to act in concert with the merchants concerned. We should order them either to remain at the camp, or to go into the village to proceed with the evacuation as agreed. In that case, we should take care not to cause a panic from the arrival of a large force. What do you think?"

"Think? ...About what?"

"If there is someone familiar to both the village and the mansion, I believe unnecessary panic can be avoided."

"..."

Having blithely followed Julius's lead, Subaru now bit his lips, holding his emotions back. The implicit message was exceedingly simple: now Subaru could return to the mansion in the name of a just cause.

Considering that someone had to explain everything, sending Subaru to the mansion as an envoy made even more sense.

But—

"Don't make me mix public and private business. I still have things to do out here."

"Surely you too are in high spirits. None here would call it mixing the public and private."

"I volunteered to be bait against the Witch Cult, and I'm still the best guy for the job... Besides, I don't deserve to go back to the mansion yet."

Shaking his head at Julius's suggestion, Subaru looked toward the forest—and the mansion that lay beyond.

The proposal was Julius being considerate in his own way. Even Subaru wasn't suspicious enough to view it as an act of malice. But neither was Subaru dishonest about believing he couldn't show his face there yet.

"You still think so, after all this?"

Subaru's moment of reflection made Ferris's eyes go round as he spoke with a look of disbelief. Ferris spoke the words because he knew all that Subaru had done to that point.

He'd formed an alliance with Crusch and her people and cooperated in subjugating the White Whale and crushing the Archbishop of Sloth. Lined up in a row, these successes were more than enough to earn words of admiration.

But inside Subaru, their combined weight was not sufficient to wipe away his own stupidity.

"No matter what you do, you can't change the past—when you make a mistake, you have to clean it up."

"..."

"That's what Anastasia said to me before. It's harsh, but...I think that way, too. Over in the mountain of things I've piled up to date is a big blob of stupidity. That's why I can't let myself stop halfway."

In reality, those words had been spoken to him the last time around. Accordingly, Anastasia had never scolded him so sternly in this world. But it was not so inside Subaru.

Even if no one else remembered, Subaru would not forget, nor was it something he ought to.

"So I finally can go back when the problem—taking care of all of the Witch Cult in the forest—is done."

"If that is what you say, it shall be so. To begin with, it is a fact that having you is an advantage."

When Subaru declined to return to the mansion, Julius honored his choice. Almost all those around Subaru displayed an understanding for his assertion.

Ferris, the only one with a dissatisfied look to the bitter end, said, "I'm a little worried you're that hung up about it... I really can't understand why you'd invent so many reasons not to meet the person you really, really, *really* like. You can just quit if you want to, *meow*..."

"Don't harp on people like that. And it's not that I don't want to. You understand, right?"

"I do not. Ferri's never had a breakup with Lady Crusch like that, *meow*. Don't blame me if you have regrets for not meeting her when you had the chance."

"...Don't harp, geez."

Perhaps Ferris's anger was that of a healer who'd experienced so much human life and death. His words carried great weight indeed.

"Sir Subaru, there is no need to be overly concerned. When people are young, they are emotional, and their feelings lead them astray. However, these things are not irreparable."

"Muuu, Old Man Wil, you spoil Subawu too much."

"If I must say so, you are somewhat excessively strict with Sir Subaru—though I do appreciate the reason why."

"...Don't go talking like you understand it."

Wilhelm's words made Ferris fall silent with a guilty look. The conversation between the longtime acquaintances conveyed sentiments that only they could understand, flying well over Subaru's head.

Though he didn't know the details, Subaru gave Wilhelm a light wave and said, "Thanks for the follow-up. I feel a little better about it now... It's not like it didn't bother me at all."

"At least you seem more at ease. After all, if all it took to solve misunderstandings between men and women were one piece of advice from an old man, far fewer human beings would need worry about such things."

"Wilhelm, you felt bad when you argued with your wife, too, huh?"

The way Wilhelm seemed to speak from personal experience made Subaru inquire with renewed interest. When he did so, Wilhelm closed his eyes, seemingly reminiscing about days long past.

"Of course. In my case, my wife was physically invincible when brought to anger. She pounded me into the floor quite a few times."

"Sword Saints don't do half measures, geez!!"

"Afterward, I forced my arms around her, holding her close until her anger abated."

"That's like an Easter egg for married life?!"

Somehow, Wilhelm's face looked brighter as he related the tale from life with his beloved.

The Sword Devil had plainly come to terms with events in his own past. Subaru, seized by envy, slapped his own cheeks. Awkward as it was, Wilhelm was being considerate to him. He'd be ashamed to call himself a man if he didn't respond to those sentiments.

"I think this is still you thinking too much, Subawu."

"Errr, it's not like I made him just spill stuff out about his wife like that...right?"

"—Now then, it would seem we are prepared to depart."

When Subaru timidly posed the question, Wilhelm pretended not to hear as he looked at the people standing by. Just as the Sword Devil had said, everyone was fully prepared for the next sortie.

That Wilhelm's expression was, in a good sense, without tension was the result of the consideration they all showed for him. In a rather banal sense, the large number of adults had bailed Subaru out.

"Man, I sure come off as young and foolish, don't I…?"

It was doubtless small of him to worry about looking that way in the eyes of adults. Even so, it wasn't in Subaru Natsuki *not* to dwell on it.

"Well, anyway, that's how it is, so…everyone, please and thank you for your cooperation so I can reunite with Emilia-tan on good terms."

"It is mildly deflating to think of that as our objective."

Subaru spoke flippantly to gloss over his blush, and Julius responded in kind. Instantly, the faces of all those lined up broke into broad smiles, and that served as their opportunity to head off.

—To annihilate what was left of the Witch Cult and claim victory with all members safe.

In that moment, Subaru believed without a doubt that they could pull it off.

4

In the immediate aftermath, the Witch Cult hunting proceeded without a hitch.

Naturally, when the expeditionary force redeployed, their first stop was where the fingers had already been located.

Watched by lookouts from the expeditionary force, the fingers they'd encountered just before taking down Petelgeuse were in a field camp within a grove of trees, a frontline base with excellent sight lines in every direction.

But—

"Heya. It's me. Everyone in a good mood?"

"—"

In lackadaisical fashion, Subaru exposed himself, drawing attention from all the Witch Cultists present. They did not regard him with enmity, but rather with indecipherable solidarity that only ran one way.

If Subaru had known nothing of their wicked deeds and acknowledged them as mere enemy combatants, he might have felt pangs of guilt. But Subaru knew the results of the Witch Cultists' vile endeavors, and that their wickedness rendered them unworthy of sympathy.

"Sorry to trick you, but…no, that's a lie. I'm not sorry at all."

Pricked by their upturned eyes, Subaru tossed such words to the Witch Cultists standing in place. They mulled the declaration over, but it was already too late for them to realize that Subaru was hostile.

—A number of silver flashes crossed the battlefield, and the Witch Cultists, reacting too late, tumbled one after another.

"This was more effective than I…"

"Gah-ha-ha-ha! What the heck?! That's the Witch Cult, and look at 'em! Hey, bro, this might turn into one helluva big achievement for ya!"

The conquest of the camp was finished in a matter of seconds. Julius's eyes went wide at the Witch Cultists, cut down with little resistance, while Ricardo, carrying his great hatchet, grinned in high spirits.

By rights, a camp built in a grove like that was to be abandoned at the first sign of an attack. The terrain, open on all sides, made it easy to scatter and escape; worst case, some might slip through and reach other camps, alerting them to the enemy's presence. Such measures had ended before they had a chance to begin.

It was all the result of being taken in by Subaru Natsuki, Cult Killer.

"Having said that, even I didn't think it'd work this well."

The overwhelming results scared Subaru himself more than anyone.

It was a perfect victory: the expeditionary force had suffered no casualties, and none of the enemies had been allowed to escape. If anyone there had doubted Subaru was the driving force behind their success, they doubted no longer.

However, sowing confusion immediately after contact with the enemy was the limit of what Subaru could do. If he had to put what that meant into words—

"—Ah, darn it! This one's done for! And this one! What's with these people?!"

It was Ferris, his tail standing on end, letting up an angry shout as he bound the Witch Cultists. Several black-robed figures rested tumbled at his feet, never to move again.

"They took their own lives?"

Slipping past the indignant Ferris, Wilhelm stripped the hood from one of the fallen figures in black, revealing the face of an ordinary-looking and very dead middle-aged man. Blood had flowed from his eyes, nose, and ears as he expired; if anything stood out, it was his neutral, expressionless look in death.

"The tongue is intact. No sign of using a blade on himself."

"They probably all have magic crystals embedded in their bodies, the sort that kill you by sending poison through your system when activated. Antitoxins won't work if the magical elements aren't deciphered prior to death, so they took the time to plant different rituals for each one...the sophistication disgusts me!"

Ferris, mortified, vented as he checked the abdomen of the man-turned-corpse and found a faintly colored magic crystal. Seven Witch Cultists had killed themselves, but Subaru had no doubt that all ten of the cultists at the camp had such crystals embedded in them.

"Maybe it's not just them, and these things are stuck in all of the other fingers, too...? So they killed themselves with poison even Ferris can't stop."

"Unforgivable. This is...blasphemy against life. What do they think life is...?!"

As Subaru's voice trembled with shock, Ferris used the back of his hand to roughly wipe away the tears brought on by fierce emotion, transferring blood to his pale cheek in the process. However, viewed from the side, his righteous anger at those who would toy with life itself was covered with both ghastliness and exquisite beauty.

It was no doubt because, as a healer, Ferris knew the uncertainties and miracles of life and death more than anyone; he stared at his battlefield, one separate from sword and spell, with a different kind of resolve.

"—"

Standing astride that righteous fury, Subaru couldn't take his eyes off the Witch Cultist corpses lined up in a row. Anyone could see that Subaru lacked the composure to look at them and say, *Here are the fruits of my labors, victory without losing a single drop of blood.*

With the hooded robes stripped from the lined-up Witch Cultist corpses, their faces, hidden in life, were exposed. But the faces that emerged were all those of ordinary men and women. It was hard to believe they'd idolized the Witch Cultist way of life.

"Sir Subaru, it may be best not to pay them so much heed."

Wilhelm stood in the way of Subaru's gaze, shaking his head.

"You are not accustomed to this, and there is no need to force yourself to be. If you feel responsibility or guilt, these too are unnecessary."

"You mean because of the kind of enemy we're facing?"

"That is correct."

The firm, unhesitant reply to Subaru was Wilhelm's idea of consideration. Subaru tried to give a pained smile at the harsh show of concern, but he failed. He could only sigh at himself.

"It's not that I sympathize with them, or that I'm beating myself up with guilt. Even I get why I can't be doing either of those things."

Subaru had no right to lament the Witch Cultists' deaths. He wouldn't even if he did, but it was he who had asked the expeditionary force to annihilate them. Even Subaru wasn't *that* stupid.

But looking at their corpses, Subaru was uncomfortable with the thought that he'd become accustomed to death.

"Not that I'll ever be used to my own death…"

Subaru had already experienced over ten deaths, but he wasn't used to death at all. The sense of loss from his death was always raw, and his fear of it would likely never diminish.

In spite of this, Subaru's heart was becoming numb to the deaths of others, and this fact frightened him.

"Seeing their corpses lined up like that makes 'em look like dolls to me... That scared me."

"Certainly, they might resemble dolls, doing whatever they are told."

However, Subaru had not accurately conveyed his sentiment to Wilhelm. This time, Subaru managed a strained smile at the Sword Devil's agreeing with that part.

As was exceedingly natural, their view of life's worth differed. Subaru, seized by modern Japanese notions of life and death, accepted death differently from Wilhelm, a man who'd seen countless lives ended on the field of battle.

Accordingly, the chasm between their perspectives could not be filled. But Subaru didn't think it needed to be.

"These Witch Cultists..."

When Wilhelm knit his brows at Subaru's strained smile, Subaru continued without switching topics. Aside from matters of death, gazing at their corpses brought a different issue to mind.

"I wonder why they wanted to do all this stuff. The Witch is this weird being hated the world over, so why do they adore her so much...?"

"—"

His murmur deepened the creases of Wilhelm's brow. Stern looks came over the faces of people around them who'd managed to overhear their conversation. But it was a young boy who broke the silence.

"—Perhaps they yearn for destruction?"

It was TB who spoke, his own cane in hand. He did not raise his kitty face, giving his monocle a slight nudge as he said, "The Witch Cult is infamous the world over, but as you can see, there is no shortage of new converts... Though, I believe such thoughts to be a luxury."

"Luxury?"

"I believe it is a choice to make time for such thoughts when we could be taking action to destroy them. It is not as if they deserve such thoughts."

Keeping his head bowed till the last, TB fell into silence. The sight of his adorable kitten face rejected further pursuit of the matter. Perhaps he was reminiscing about painful memories from his past.

"Hmm? What? Mister, something happen?"

Though, the fact that Mimi, who ought to have shared his circumstances, did not react to her younger brother's words meant that even she couldn't guess what he meant.

But TB had a point.

"Despair at everything and yearning for destruction…huh. I can't say there's no part of me that understands, but…"

Surely anyone pressed by despairing circumstances would have a yearning for destruction, a desire to lash out and wreck anything and everything around them. That inclination was especially strong in Subaru, so he could understand that part.

"—You don't need to understand people like *them* one tiny bit. Don't make me say it over and over."

Listening to Subaru's comment, Ferris turned stern eyes toward him. Having finished examining the Witch Cultist corpses, he glared at Subaru with a look full of exhaustion and anger.

"You can't give Witch Cultists the benefit of even a single hair of your fur, or else you'll be sucked into the darkness, too… You're particularly vulnerable, Subawu, so be careful."

"I get it already, you don't need to keep pounding it into me. So enough with the suspicious gazes, please… It just bothered me a little."

Responding to Ferris's sharp glare, Subaru raised both hands, excusing himself as he looked at the corpses once more.

Now that the Witch Cultists' faces were exposed, they seemed to truly be male and female, young and old alike. He couldn't even guess at what had spurred them to join the Witch Cult. Considering the creepiness of that fact, dismissing them as incomprehensible monsters might be the wisest choice.

It was just that Subaru, the trigger for their deaths, felt that dismissing them as incomprehensible monsters was…running from it, somehow.

"Subawu?"

"Nothin'. Did any of the Witch Cultists have useful info on them?"

"Nothing whatsoever. They were walking around with nothing but weapons on them, not even a Gospel, like they never intended to return home alive from the start. So stupid."

They'd reaped neither info nor a sense of success. From the smoldering anger and hostility in Ferris's comment, it'd really gotten under his skin. So Subaru would let him handle raging toward them for the time being.

"Well, I'd better stay calm. Time to get moving and hit a different camp, I guess."

Subaru did a few squats on the spot, switching mental gears to carrying out decoy duty on a larger scale. Unlike dealing with Petelgeuse and the finger at set camps, luring out the Witch Cultists lurking in the forest would be Witch Cult hunting's main event.

Subaru began forging ahead into the forest, searching for a new fishing spot.

"You just watch, you miscalculating bastard. Don't underestimate the power of my posse…!"

"Real roundabout way of talkin'. I can't tell if yer worked up for this or not…"

Hearing the declaration, a fervent appeal to the power of others, left Ricardo beside himself as he grinned.

But despite Subaru's fainthearted statement, their advance continued apace.

5

"—Subaru, the traveling merchants you arranged have rendezvoused with the outer camp."

Julius reported in just after the expeditionary force had annihilated the fourth finger.

After the camp in the grove, they destroyed two more camps—one on a riverbank, one in a marsh—and had determined two things about the Witch Cult: the groups called fingers were organized ten to each camp, and without an Archbishop of the Seven Deadly Sins, the groups were more fragile than they'd ever expected.

This time, Witch Cultists plotting to assault the mansion and the village had very little ability to respond to unforeseen circumstances. With the scent of the Witch wafting around him, they pretty much did whatever Subaru told them from first sight. The effectiveness of Subaru's decoy operation wasn't a one-shot wonder but, rather, a recurring theme.

"Ohh! They really came!"

Secretly elated as he was that things were going so smoothly, Subaru's voice leaped at the report.

He was the one who had arranged for the dragon carriages, but he didn't actually know how many had taken up the offer. Hearing that they had actually assembled eased his feelings of concern.

"Seems like getting 'em all together might prove wasted effort, though. But the fact that they got here safely means that the plains are completely open, then?"

"There seems to be no mistake about that. The enemy has not realized the mist ended in failure. Accordingly, just as we imagined, they have left the highway unguarded, surely thinking it sealed."

"Guess he really didn't have any reason to lie to me. Petelgeuse is the last guy I wanted to take at face value, but that's good news."

The madman had spoken true. Now that this was clear, he wasn't sure what to say.

Either way, Subaru wanted to meet the traveling merchants who had assembled at his behest. He needed to speak to them about the unique situation they'd become involved in, too.

"So we got back to the camp, but..."

Having broken off the decoy operation, Subaru returned outside the forest, scratching his face with a conflicted look. The assembled traveling merchant troupe was the cause of that look. The number of carriages was spectacular beyond his expectations, up to about fifteen. Apparently, the words *Name your price* had quite an impact. Not that he'd taken an accurate count, but the residents of Earlham Village were under a hundred—the carriages were more than enough to evacuate them.

"But they're huddled awfully tight together."

"They are intimidated by the turbulent atmosphere. You can hardly blame them."

The group, clumped together in a corner of the camp, shrank

from the sight of knights keeping strict guard. Seeing this, Subaru concurred with Julius's explanation, twisting his neck as he tried to figure out how to explain everything.

He was grateful that they'd come together. But whether their mercantile souls were in it was another matter.

"If this is how they are about friendlies, won't they head for the hills if they know this involves the Witch Cult?"

"Each individual has his own net amount of courage. But you are likely right to be concerned."

When Julius agreed with Subaru's concerns, the pair's shoulders sank together. By rights, this was where Subaru would clear up the situation, asking them for their cooperation. But looking at them now, he couldn't tell how many had the courage not to flinch from involvement with the Witch Cult.

"Well, having them run off is bad. We'd lose the hauling capacity, but more importantly, I don't want the leftovers to get wind that something's up."

It was callous, but they were already involved in a callous situation. If ignorance helped them get cooperation on happier terms, it was doubtless better for both sides.

"You don't like what I'm thinking, do you?"

"I would not call it elegant. But I am not foolish enough to dwell on that in an emergency. Everything has a time and a place. And in this case, I believe the conditions of time and place have been fulfilled."

"Roundabout, but that's a yes, huh?"

Accepting Julius's roundabout consent, Subaru met the eyes of the other expeditionary force members to see what they thought of the matter. Fortunately, Wilhelm and Ferris did not raise opinions to the contrary; thus, the proposal to explain the circumstances while glossing over the important parts passed by consensus.

"To begin with, it's possible I have to lie to the villagers to get them evacuated, too, so maybe I should just think of this as a rehearsal..."

Concealing the involvement of the Witch Cult was a necessary measure to avoid needless panic. Subaru told himself that for his own benefit as he stepped in the direction of the nervous merchants.

"Er, thank you very much for coming all this way. Since I'm the one who sent for you, I'll explain the circumstances."

"...You did?"

Seeing Subaru step forward as a representative, the traveling merchants looked at one another with surprised faces. Their reaction brought a pained smile over Subaru as he recalled the leading lights in the expeditionary force. With the aged Wilhelm and the chivalrous Julius present, no one had expected Subaru to represent them.

Accepting that as the natural reaction, Subaru switched mental gears. When he did so, he realized that the lineup of traveling merchants contained familiar faces, particularly one smack in the middle of them.

"You're...right, I don't remember your name, but you introduced me to Otto the first time. And a bunch of others were helping out when I ran into the White Whale for the first time."

"First time? White Whale? What are you talking about?"

"Sorry, just talking to myself. So about what's gonna happen from here on out..."

His deeply moved words threw the man off, but Subaru papered it over with a smile. Incidentally, he searched to see if Otto was among the traveling merchants, but apparently, he was not. Apparently, the connection between his fate and that of the young man hauling a large amount of oil had been severed. Subaru felt ever so slightly disappointed.

"Either way, this is an important business discussion for all of you, right? Anyway, the offer was name your price for what you're hauling, so I assume you agreed with those terms?"

"Y-yes, you aren't mistaken. And those terms, your side spoke the truth?"

"Of course. But the terms were to borrow everyone's dragon carriages. I'm sure you've already been told this, but I want your cooperation in evacuating the nearby villagers during the mountain hunt."

"Mountain hunt...?"

Skeptical voices arose, and the traveling merchants all cocked their heads at the discordant ring of the words.

It was true that, at present, they were engaged in a mountain hunt—to wipe out the Witch Cult. But he couldn't just come out and tell them that, fueling the flames of their cowardice. So this was plan B.

"Demon beasts called Urugarum have built a nest in this forest. As you can see, we've put together a pretty large expeditionary force. I want you to help us get the villagers to safety during the mountain hunt."

—A brazen, shameless exaggeration of the situation, some two months out of date.

"You put together a rather lifelike tale. Perhaps you have talent as a fantasist, or a writer?"

"That's not a compliment, is it?"

That was how Julius assessed Subaru, who had eloquently persuaded Team Merchant and secured its cooperation. The details seemed to be resulting in a fight, causing a vein to bulge on Subaru's forehead.

"Cut it out, Subawu. This is just Julius being his normal self. Besides, to be honest, Ferri thinks it was a well-done story, too."

"Geez, both of you… In the first place, I didn't have to make up very much. It's a real story from two months ago."

When Subaru received Ferris's sad assessment, perhaps an attempt to smooth things over (and perhaps not), he let the comment slip with a look of resignation. As he did, the two knights exchanged glances at that particular detail.

"By a real story, were you referring to this forest being colonized by demon beasts?"

"I'm not sure I'd use the word *colonized*, but they were here, yeah. But barriers in the forest split the demon beast habitat away from people. This here's a human being area, no problems at all."

Seeing the wariness in the pair's eyes, Subaru quickly explained why the area around them was safe. The explanation set Julius at ease, but Ferris thinned his lips in Julius's place.

"Subawu, you're not leading Ferri and the others blissfully to their slaughter, are you, *meow*? We can trust you on that?"

"That's putting it way too harshly! Didn't you say that Crusch decided to trust me, so you're not going to doubt me, either?!"

"With all this coming after the fact, it makes me want to start doubting, *meow*… As for the demon beasts, though, I think Marquis Mathers has a screw loose for building his mansion near a demon beast habitat."

Subaru grimaced at the sight of Ferris looking toward the mansion and talking like that. To be blunt, to Subaru, life at Roswaal Manor had felt like this world's idea of common sense. Thus, he'd assumed it was normal to have a residence isolated from a nearby demon beast habitat by barriers, but…

"There's no way that could be true, *meow*."

"Without exception, demon beasts instinctively strive to slaughter living beings. They are simply dangerous creatures, unsuitable for domestication or sustenance. Barriers or not, placing residences next to them is unthinkable."

The pair's instant denials made clear just how nonsensical it had been to place the mansion and village there. Apparently, Roswaal's eccentricity went well past his appearance and personality.

"Along with him not being around this time, I've got way too many things I've gotta say to that bastard…"

Feeling fed up, Subaru shoved the rising sense of weariness to one side. He did so because whether Roswaal was sane or mad, Subaru had experienced firsthand that he always had a convincing excuse. Though Subaru had his doubts about whether such excuses were even necessary, it wasn't the time to think about it.

"Anyway, Team Merchant is happily lending us their resources. That said, we can't bring them on the mountain hunt. So they'll wait at the camp, ready to move any time we need 'em."

"Then, we should demand no evacuation, no reward as part of the d—"

"As if I could do something that vicious! Verbal or not, a deal's a deal. We'll keep our promise… That's right, it's important to keep your promises! Understand?!"

"I—I understand, *meow*, but why are you so worked up about it…?"

Ferris cringed, cowed by Subaru's dramatic overreaction to the issue of the contract.

Standing astride that exchange, Julius touched his own forelocks as he looked toward the traveling merchants. "But it would be careless to leave them here by themselves. Increasing the number of people to protect them all means that we need to divert more people to defending the camp…"

"Yeah, I think we should leave about half back at camp. Right now, the fishing is going super-well, and if we do find a finger camp, I want to have the option to fight or to run… Hmm, but…"

Julius closed his eyes and shook his head at Subaru's lack of confidence. Just when Subaru thought the reaction meant rejection, Julius continued, "That is fine. We shall respect your wishes. I believe devoting half our numbers to defense is an appropriate choice. If the fingers are all groups of ten, double their numbers is more than sufficient to deal with them."

"The way you act makes it super-hard to know whether you're agreeing or not."

"I am often told that it is charming."

"It's mysterious, at least. But with that handsome face… Yeah, I can kinda see it."

Though he was compelled to agree, it rubbed Subaru the wrong way. Accordingly, he stuck his tongue out at Julius.

"The Iron Fangs are cut out for mountain hunting, so we'll have the knights defend the place."

It wasn't exactly a pronouncement from above, but Subaru's declaration reorganized the expeditionary force in short order. As directed, twenty knights remained at the camp to protect the fifteen dragon carriages. The worried expressions on the traveling merchants did not abate, but Subaru gave them an especially cheerful wave, so as not to scare them, before heading for the forest.

If things went sour, their cooperation would be indispensable. But the ideal outcome was for all the advance preparation with them to have been for naught.

And at that moment, Subaru was convinced that this was no mere dream, but a realistic prospect.

6

"That makes—five down!"

"Indeed it does."

Wiping blood from his treasured sword, Wilhelm, having ended his dance of the blade, reacted to Subaru's celebrating shout by drawing himself up.

The place was a depression in the western part of the forest, and they had just destroyed the finger camp located there. Dividing the expeditionary force in half had had no effect on the outcome; they had half destroyed the Witch Cultists in the initial attack. That left the enemy with no time to regroup and recover; they fell quickly to the blades of the Sword Devil and "The Finest."

"Ferris, how about it?"

"...Sorry. Still no good. They got us again."

But as was now usual, success in preventing them from sealing their own lips remained elusive. Subaru and Julius watched Ferris lower his eyes in abhorrence; neither could find words to speak to him. If Ferris could not do it, no one could—but that was no consolation to him.

"Hey, don't get bent outta shape, switch gears. Let's head fer the next one."

"Meow?!"

Ferris was still in the dumps when Ricardo roughly rubbed his head, making his slender body shoot to its feet. For an instant, Ferris was surprised by the pushy attempt to console, but he immediately slapped his own cheeks and began walking anew. Seeing Ferris like that made Ricardo bare his fangs, grinning in satisfaction.

Seeing him behave that way, Subaru could appreciate that Ricardo had long led his organization.

"Mmm, the wins are too easy, I need more exercise... How do you feel, TB?"

"I think it is good when jobs are simple. If I make my darling sister do dangerous things, our brother will raise a fuss, so this is preferable."

"Nnn! You're such weaklings for boys!"

Despite their clash of personalities—the uninhibited older sister versus the intellectual younger brother—the beast person siblings made quite a combo in combat. Mimi left no openings on attack or defense, and TB was surprisingly belligerent in his follow-ups.

Ricardo was leader of the pack in might and command ability, with the powerful sibling lieutenants following in his footsteps. It had been just as hard to get their cooperation as to get Wilhelm's and Ferris's.

As allies, they were incredibly reliable, and so a thought came to Subaru's mind.

"I guess when this is all done we go back to being rivals, huh…?"

"It seems you have the leeway to worry about the future."

As Subaru indulged in sentiment, Julius stood beside him, wiping the blood from his cavalry saber. His crisp handsomeness never seemed ruffled in the midst of combat. He brushed the edge of his white mantle with an elegant gesture.

Subaru hated to admit it, but Julius's point was sound. He averted his gaze while scratching his cheek.

"My bad. Maybe I'm letting my guard down a bit because it's gone insanely smoothly."

"I did not go as far as to call it bad. As a matter of fact, we are functioning so well, none would think we were so hastily assembled. I can understand why you find the relationships between us to be… regrettable."

"…Man, I didn't expect that from you."

Subaru had anticipated barbed sarcasm, but Julius's show of sympathy made him widen his eyes. For his part, Julius's shoulders sank, Subaru's reaction having been an unexpected one.

"The royal selection has begun, and we find ourselves in rival camps. But wherever we stand in the dispute, we can accept the help of others in a common cause. Perhaps we should regard feeling this for ourselves so early after the start of the selection process as our good fortune?"

"...Can't really think of the Witch Cult going after Emilia as 'good fortune.'"

"I suppose not. I am sorry, that was inconsiderate of me."

Julius immediately apologized for his faux pas, touching his own forelocks as he sighed. Subaru felt small for his reflexive indignance in contrast to Julius's forthright remark.

Deep down, Subaru and Julius felt the same way.

Of course, they couldn't ignore the menace closing in on Emilia and the villagers. With that tragic spectacle in mind, Subaru couldn't call it "good fortune" to save his life. But if you set that circumstance aside, the relationships among the people assembled were by no means poor.

Enough to make you think it would be a waste for them to go back to being enemies after driving off the Witch Cult.

"Really is careless of me to worry about it, though. I'm being an idiot."

No matter how smoothly things were going, they were still only halfway to settling the problem. Not that he was putting a wreath of laurel on his own head, but the enemy wasn't even in checkmate; it was far too early to treat victory as assured.

In ancient times or modern, Occident or Orient, one rule held true: the danger was always greatest when you thought everything was in the bag.

"—Sorry for flaking out on you like that. I'll get back to fishing, so I'm counting on all of you."

Pressing a fist into his own cheek, Subaru used the dull pain to get himself going again.

"Fishing" meant casting Subaru as bait for the Witch Cult. In practice, that meant Subaru coming into contact with Witch Cultists without anyone else's intervention. Accordingly, during the time they'd walked around the forest searching, Subaru had acted alone—or at least, with his allies nowhere to be seen around him.

The expeditionary force was tailing Subaru from a medium-to-long distance behind. His allies needed to leave no trace to find, the better to draw the Witch Cultists to Subaru like moths to a flame.

And the next time proved no exception.

"Oh—"

When they finished searching deep in the western part of the forest, he immediately judged that they should switch to the riverside. Subaru was just feeling the cool air around him when he saw shadows gliding in front of him.

"…"

Four Witch Cultists appeared, the largest number he'd bumped into. This development, differing from events at the three camps already crushed since the start of the "fishing," made Subaru's heart strongly leap.

"…!"

Clapping his hands together was the signal that something unforeseen had happened. But if the "fishing" failed once, the other fingers would become suspicious, and straight-up combat with the Witch Cult would become unavoidable. Therefore—

"—Heya. Mind if I take a look around?"

Subaru forced his contracting heart to expand, somehow managing to toss a smile their way. The Witch Cult looked fondly upon his smiling face, which they would have judged harshly in normal times. As was typical, the Witch Cultists were still silent; even in numbers, they displayed no enmity for Subaru.

"Good thinking, moving in bigger groups, but there's no problem over here. There's no problem, you can go back to your place. Mmm, yes, do that, please."

"…"

"I outrank you here, right? Best to grease the wheels and do as you're told, I think?"

"…"

The silence after he gave the directive was bad for his heart. As a matter of fact, stress and unease made its sound and pace skyrocket as cold sweat broke out on the back of his neck.

But the suffocating atmosphere did not continue as long as it felt like to Subaru. Within tens of seconds, or perhaps only ten, the Witch Cultists respectfully bowed and did as Subaru had instructed.

"—Phew."

Relieved of the tension making even his lungs harden, Subaru wiped off his cold sweat. With the cultists on the move, he made the hand signal for success and quickly moved in pursuit.

Normally, the fingers only moved in a limited range from the closest camp. Most likely, these were not out on patrol, but had merely sensed Subaru's presence and been drawn to it. When Subaru told them to return to their lair, they returned to camp without the slightest suspicion.

Thanks to that, it'd take less than five minutes to follow them to the camp. Though the number he encountered had been higher this time, their total would be the same as—

"—?! They split up?"

Subaru gazed in wonderment as the detachment of four people he was following behaved contrary to his expectations—a first. Suddenly, the group of four split into two, with three to one side and one the other. They began walking in different directions without the slightest hesitation in their steps.

"..."

With one acting solo and the others in a group of three, the risk of losing the solo one was far higher. After only a second of thought, Subaru immediately called his allies with a hand signal. Mere seconds later, members of the Iron Fangs lined up beside him.

"They split up. I'll go after the one by himself. The other three..."

"Right on. We got this."

The fox-man—literally a young man with a fox head—accepted Subaru's instructions, heading toward where the group of three had vanished from sight. Before their own backs vanished from Subaru's sight, he cautioned, "Do *not* lay a hand on them. If you spot their camp, regroup with the others."

"You got it."

Giving his slender mustache a flick, the fox-man leaped into the forest to Subaru's right without so much as a sound. Subaru watched him go but had no time to rest on his laurels. He urgently resumed his pursuit of the Witch Cultist heading off solo.

Fortunately, he immediately caught up with the lone Witch

Cultist. Gently and carefully, he followed the figure deeper and deeper into the forest. Keeping his head down, Subaru roughly wiped away the sweat threatening to get into his eyes.

In point of fact, it was pointless for Subaru to keep his breath down and tail the Witch Cultist in secret. Subaru possessed no ability to conceal his presence, and the Witch Cultist walking before him had probably been aware of Subaru's pursuit the whole time.

He said nothing in spite of that because he was obeying the directive of Subaru, who "outranked" him. He'd judged that Subaru's inexplicable actions were for the benefit of the Witch Cult. Not that he could see into their minds, but he could deduce it was probably along those lines.

—But if that was so, Subaru wondered even more why the four-man team would split up.

Not that it was his intention, but Subaru held command authority rivaling that of an Archbishop of the Seven Deadly Sins. He didn't know what would make someone go as far as to defy his orders to head off by himself. Subaru's heart beat a little faster as he wondered if this was connected to some kind of fatal oversight on his part.

"..."

He squinted, focusing on the movements of the cultist ahead of him. The surrounding scenery was bothering him, perhaps because he was abusing his eyesight. The forest all seemed the same to him somehow, as if he'd stumbled into a place giving him déjà vu. He felt as if he was stepping into familiar territory—

—Is that really just a feeling?

As he went down a game trail unworthy of being called a path, stepped over big tree roots, leaped over a gully at his feet, and walked past mushrooms that looked poisonous, the unease inside Subaru changed to certainty.

It can't be!

The biggest alarm bell in Subaru's skull went off. He clenched his teeth and ran forward. When it seemed he might stumble, he toughed it out, plunging forward until the forest before him opened wide. Then—

"What the hell are you doin'?!"

When green fell away from his field of vision, he leaped into the ash-gray scene before his eyes.

Some several hours before, the rocky place that had become a battlefield had been a caved-in cavern and an unmarked grave. But the writhing Witch Cultists were defiling the grave, seemingly trying to unearth the remains of the madman buried there.

—For this was the final resting place of Petelgeuse Romanée-Conti.

"—"

When Subaru spontaneously raised his voice, the Witch Cultists' eyes gathered upon him. The Witch Cultists defiling the grave numbered nine; the lone man he'd followed made ten—a finger.

They'd noticed Petelgeuse's death. At the very least, this finger had to be annihilated.

"—"

The finger moved as one at about the same time that Subaru internally came to that conclusion. The Witch Cultists who knew Petelgeuse was dead instantly reached out toward Subaru.

Subaru didn't know if they were trying to kill him or nab a replacement for their Archbishop of the Seven Deadly Sins. He would never know, for the results were permanently erased by the running silver slash that followed.

Blood spatter scattered as the diagonal blow severed a Witch Cultist in half. The black-robed figure spewed dark red as he collapsed. His silent death throes signaled the start of the battle.

"Sir Subaru, get behind me."

Wilhelm, taking the first kill, lightly pushed Subaru behind him. As Subaru tottered, Ricardo's huge frame and Julius's slender physique slipped past his flanks, with their differing forms of enmity flying.

The battle was one-sided.

Because of Subaru's blunder in impulsively leaping forward, the battle began under fairer conditions. But the expeditionary force paid no heed to this, crushing the Witch Cultists with overwhelming martial force. In a few tens of seconds, the battle was decided, and the battlefield soon contained only the fallen corpses of the cultists.

"What were they trying to do here anyway?"

Watching the end of the battle, Subaru raised his voice in the barren place turned battlefield once more.

No one replied to his question. The Witch Cultists were silent, saying nothing; the last one killed himself in Ferris's arms despite the latter's best efforts. They had no time to be elated at crushing a new finger.

"It is as if they were digging in the earth, searching for something..."

"What they were digging up is the Archbishop of the Seven Deadly Sins' grave. Well, I call it a grave, but Mimi just buried him with dirt, and it was Mimi who blew him up, too."

Having been unearthed from the grave, the madman's corpse was on the surface, lined up with the others. In the first place, the remains were nothing but a headless torso; as a result of the explosion, even that had been cruelly changed to fragments. Subaru couldn't even guess what the cultists had been looking for among the fragments, little more than clumps of flesh. But—

"...I've got a bad feeling about this."

The Witch Cultists had disinterred the Archbishop of the Seven Deadly Sins in search of something. They'd had a reason to unyieldingly persist in the work, even so far as to disobey Subaru's command. There were four fingers left—

"Let's regroup with the other ones following the group of three. Gotta hurry."

The disquieting worry stirring deep inside his chest would not subside. Pressing a fist to his chest, Subaru forced himself to ignore the ache as he hurried to rejoin the fox-man's detachment. They returned to the forest, following that detachment to a different site.

He trusted that the unease would pass once they caught up—

7

"—"

The cruel scent of blood hung in the air.

Lukewarm air wafted among the trees, and the stench of scattered internal organs pricked at his nose. White-hooded leather outfits were strewn around the area, each with its "contents" still inside.

None remained in one piece. Some supernatural power had torn them limb from limb.

"...Don't look like...any survived, huh?"

Subaru was in shock, unable to speak. In front of him, Ricardo spoke with a snort.

A dog-man like him, with sensitive smell even among beast people, had sensed something amiss before anyone else, breaking into a run. When Subaru and the others caught up, he looked back and spoke those words. They succinctly summed up the tragic end.

"H-healing... We've gotta...heal the wounded, or..."

"I told ya. No survivors. There ain't no wounded here, man."

When Subaru spoke with a shaking voice, Ricardo shook his head, his usual haughtiness muted. He wasn't trying to rub it in; it was simply obvious at first glance.

Namely, that the comrades supposed to be there had been slaughtered, leaving not even a single survivor.

"—A disturbing situation. The fight was entirely too one-sided."

"Agreed. Considering how well the Iron Fangs are trained, it is difficult to think they could be so overwhelmed."

With Subaru's mind struck by the surreal sight, unable to keep up, the conversation continued without him. When he looked around, he saw Julius and Wilhelm agree that it was disturbing.

"One-sided...?"

"It is precisely that. There are no corpses save those of Rajan and our other allies here. It is unnatural by any measure."

"—"

"Even against the Witch Cult, it is unthinkable they would be killed without putting up resistance. The Iron Fangs are so elite, it is barely imaginable the enemy would strike down even one... A strange situation, is it not?"

When Subaru stayed silent, Julius mulled over the situation, but Subaru had no time to answer.

In the first place, it was something else that bothered him. It wasn't simply the situation disturbing Subaru's thoughts. It was the initial impact, well before that, which he couldn't move on from.

"Why are you acting like this is normal…?"

"Subaru?"

"We came rushing and our buddies are dead, you know?! So why are you acting like this is no big…"

"We cannot change what has happened, just as one cannot change the past."

Subaru was speechless, and Julius pulled his gaze away, walking toward Ferris.

Ferris had said nothing to this point, but unlike Subaru, he hadn't been standing still. He was looking at one beast person corpse after another, examining their wounds.

—When joined together, these clumps of flesh would surely turn into their former comrades.

Subaru wondered if the young fox-man pursuing the Witch Cultists was the one Julius had called Rajan. Subaru recalled his aloof face and witty phrases uttered in Kararagi dialect. He and the other four beast people had been cruelly ripped apart to the point that they were unrecognizable.

"Ferris, have you learned anything?"

"…Let's start with no survivors. Based on the state of the wounds, it seems like they were taken down by the same person, but these aren't blade wounds. Of course, it wasn't magic, either. They were torn apart by force."

"Some guy was sayin' there were demon beasts around, huh? Gimme a break…"

When Ferris calmly gave his report, Ricardo gave an appropriate sound through his canine teeth. Subaru, brought back to reality by the sound, wobbled into the exchange.

"Torn apart… You're not saying this was by demon beasts?"

"These aren't bite wounds, so I don't think we need to worry about that. It feels more like brute strength. But it seems like they died pretty much instantly, so I don't think they suffered much."

"…Why are you mentioning something like that…?"

"Because I thought it might put your mind at ease a little, Subawu."

Unfortunately, Ferris's show of consideration had no such effect on Subaru's mind.

There was nothing to death save death. As a result, whether they'd suffered or not was of little import. It didn't change the fact that Subaru and the others had not saved them, or that they had died without putting up a fight.

"I...I should have been...more on top of things...!"

"Sir Subaru, I understand your feelings of regret. However, this is not the time or place."

"Wilhelm..."

"A Witch Cult site is likely nearby. Since our allies were attacked, we should assume the terrain favors the enemy. We should pull back and regroup."

With Subaru threatening to be engulfed by the scene, Wilhelm shook his head as he grasped the boy's shoulders, making Subaru set his regrets aside.

The Sword Devil's words were heartless, but true. If they persisted in standing still due to the deaths of their allies, they would only put their other allies in danger—a foolish exercise. They were already in combat with this finger. Just as with the finger at the rocky place, Subaru was useless, nothing but dead weight.

"Then let's pull back fer now, come back for revenge later."

With a heave of his jaw, Ricardo announced their departure from the tragic sight. He asked if any objected, but none did, certainly not Julius or Wilhelm, or even Mimi as she consoled a tearful TB.

"...We should at least take something of them."

"That's accounted for already. No more than rings or hair, though."

Ferris quietly replied to the reluctant Subaru. When he gave a pocket a light pat, Subaru realized Ferris had taken care of it while he'd been standing stiff.

Having lost all reasons to remain, Subaru seemed to cling to the tragic sight as he looked back at it one last time.

"..."

The remains, lined up atop bare soil, were comrades he'd traded words with tens of minutes before. As he gazed upon that death, Subaru's mind let out a heavy, painful scream.

Why was Subaru's mind continuing such frenzied shouts that moment? It was because—

"Subawu, we have to go."

"...I know."

Neither time nor his allies gave Subaru any chance to wallow. Ferris called out to Subaru, still unable to find the words to give to the remains, and Subaru followed the others, the last to leave that place.

And then he noticed something.

The presence of jet-black hands slipping through the gaps in the trees, creeping closer without a sound.

"Get *down*—!!"

"—!"

When the evil hands seemed to slip out from the darkness, Subaru was in a daze as he shouted.

The ones able to instantly respond to the sudden directive were Wilhelm and the other heavy hitters. They didn't ask why like a bunch of idiots—they instantly crouched, escaping the hands sailing over the ground.

However, the hands caught those who reacted too slowly, displaying their thoroughly wicked might.

"Gya—!"

Those who remained standing screamed—no, they were not screams; they were death cries.

The black-dyed arms stretched the necks of the slow-to-react knights, fatally gouging out their throats. The fingers seemed to move without resistance, rending human flesh with the ease of passing through water.

Blood spurted forth, and multiple lives were snuffed out right before Subaru's eyes. Subaru was in shock from this, but immediately after, others unfroze and raised their own voices.

"—What is it? What happened?!"

"I don't know! Blood spurted from their throats all of a sudden…"

They, aghast at the slaughter of their allies, could not see what had created this death. In other words, this was greater proof than anything that they were the black, evil hands known to Subaru.

Thus, Subaru thrust aside his feelings of disbelief.

"—It's Unseen Hands!!" he shouted.

The black hands that had brought death to their allies—these were none other than Petelgeuse's Unseen Hands.

But that was impossible. The madman controlling them had died for certain. His torso had been cut in half, and the only things they'd found left of his corpse were fragments. Ferris had firmly stated that recovery was impossible.

"So who the hell is using Unseen Hands then?!"

Subaru's voice was raw with surprise. The pitch-black hands dancing in the sky reacted. Multiple hands moved like the heads of snakes, their fingers turning menacingly toward him.

Their numbers were probably thirty—an invisible menace in numbers somewhat above what Petelgeuse had controlled.

"Sir Subaru! Indicate the arms' locations!"

Wilhelm shouted, sword poised, with Ferris tumbled at his feet. The Sword Devil's request caused those who had initially taken flight to look at Subaru. Their morale was hardly broken, but they had no countermeasure beyond Subaru.

Understanding his duty, Subaru squinted at the evil hands. He would *not* let them add to the corpses of his allies. However, as if to mock his determination, the evil hands…

"They vanished…?!"

The hands made of black mist gently dissolved into dust from the fingertips down. In an instant, the thirty hands dissipated. Subaru, unable to discern his opponent's intent, watched with a stiff face.

"Bro, what happened to the attack?! Where's it comin' from?!"

"They vanished! They were pulled back! I don't know why!"

Replying to Ricardo's angry shout with an angry shout of his own, Subaru desperately swept his gaze across the area.

Subaru was the only one who could detect Unseen Hands, which attacked with neither sound nor aura. The life or death of his allies depended on his actions. That fact made Subaru earnest in his efforts.

Accordingly, he neglected to care for himself.

"Ugh—?!"

The bad feeling suddenly arising at the back of Subaru's neck made him raise a cry of pain. The next moment, his neck bones seemed to creak from the powerful grip raising him, pulling his feet off the ground. Floating in the air, he could neither kick at the ground nor stand firm. His limbs writhed and flailed, but Subaru's body was pulled into the darkness in a single swoop.

"No! Subaru—!"

"Julius, don't! The enemy's here!"

Julius immediately reached out, but he was interrupted by Ferris's bloodcurdling cry.

The instant before they were separated, Subaru's eyes spotted a group of black figures bursting out of the forest—Witch Cultists attacking his wary allies from the flank.

"Shit! Let me go, damn it…!"

As sword began to ring against sword, Subaru alone was being pulled away from the battlefield. As he swung his limbs, they struck tree branches, picking up painful scrapes in the process, but he had no time to care about that.

The hand restraining him possessed tremendous physical strength, carrying Subaru with movements impossible for any man-made device. That, and the fact that he couldn't break free, made it easy for him to guess what was pulling him. That very moment, Subaru was being whisked away by Unseen Hands. Therefore, his enemy was—

"Gu—aaah—!"

The impact forced an interruption in his thought process.

The forced floating in midair came to an end when his back was slammed against a large tree. After that, Subaru was pressed against the trunk, legs still off the ground, suspended in midair as he came face-to-face with his foe.

"*Geheh!* Shit! Who the hell is…?"

"Ahh—my brain—is—shaking."

"—"

When Subaru coughed, turning his eyes toward his surroundings, that phrase froze his heart.

The nonsensical line seemed to flow into his ears as if it were teasing him, but it was far too evil to ignore.

Slowly, the darkness seemed to dissolve as a slender figure walked out of it.

So far as Subaru knew, the Witch Cultists all wore the same hooded black robes, and this figure was no exception. But this individual left the hood down, leaving a face exposed.

"—"

For an instant, Subaru hallucinated that this figure was Petelgeuse's body double. But an instant later, he rejected the idea. The figure resembled the madman yet was different somehow. After all, the person appearing before Subaru was a young, redheaded woman with conspicuous freckles.

"So why…? What are you…? What the—what the hell…?!"

With strong pressure over his entire body, Subaru writhed, moaning in pain as he looked down at the woman.

The previous finger exterminations had already established that the Witch Cultists were male and female, young and old alike. Having a woman as his enemy was nothing to be shocked over, but Subaru's fright would not abate.

The problem was not his opponent's gender—it was that the woman and that madman were two of a kind.

The woman made Subaru feel disgust and terror rivaling those caused by Petelgeuse Romanée-Conti himself. They absolutely had nothing to do with the fact that the shadows wriggling at her feet were keeping Subaru bound.

"You're…Petelgeuse's…what…?! Get these hands off me…!"

"—A finger, you SEE."

"Ah?"

Forcing his shudder back down, Subaru wrung out a raspy voice with which to speak to her. The instant after that voice raised Subaru's doubts, the woman forcefully shook her head like a spring-operated doll.

Then she raised her right hand and put a finger into her mouth; this, she violently bit and crushed. The dull sound, the droplets of fresh blood, they were that madman's blasphemous self-harm through and through—

"I am a finger! One rewarded with Her favor! A diligent diiisciple carrying out the trial, faithfully obeying the guidance of Her love! Ahh! Ahh, are you *lazy*?!"

"Uu…!"

The woman waved her bloody finger, scattering droplets of blood around as she instinctively unveiled her madness. The sight of the angrily raging woman who called herself a finger made Subaru squirm, forgetting all about how hard it was to breathe.

That madness, that insanity, that irritable behavior, repeating that same stupid phrase to vilify his opponent—it wasn't just her ability to use the authority. Even setting aside the eccentric mannerisms, the woman had far too much in common with the madman to ignore.

Confidant. Successor. A Priest of the Seven Deadly Sins rather than an archbishop. Various possibilities raced inside his head.

But she didn't fit any of them. If he had to put a more proper, more accurate label on what he felt—

"A dead ringer…a copy? With Petelgeuse's exact personality…!"

He couldn't help but think of the woman as Petelgeuse himself rather than someone who merely resembled him. Perhaps that itself was what the term *finger* signified.

Perhaps the fingers had literally been part of Petelgeuse…

"If that's so, worst case doesn't even cover it…!"

"Being able to recover you this early is a great relief! You are troublesome, you are dangerous, you are particularly vile! You can see Unseen Hands, can you not?"

"…No comment…"

"You cannot hold your SILENCE with me! You have been captured by

Her favor, when by riiights you would be discarded as rubbish! Thiiiis cannot be mere happenstaaance! When it is not once, but twice, it is not happenstance, but inevitability! And inevitability INSTILLS diligence!"

Her inability to listen to others was just like the original's.

As she opened her eyes wide enough that her eyeballs threatened to pop out, saliva scattered from the madwoman's long tongue. Ordinarily, that would be bad enough, but the ugliness of her fury ran far deeper than that surface.

"Now, now then, then then then. Although THIS is extremely regrettable, there is something that I SIMPLY must confirm. Who are you, and what is your purpose?"

"What am *I* doing…?"

Subaru grimaced at the question, his disgust with his unsightly opponent plain. When he parroted the words back, the madwoman stretched a hand to the sky.

"Yes! That is precisely what I ask! The favor you wear is far greater thaaan that of an ordinary believer, rivaling the Archbishops of the Seven Deadly Sins themselves! If so, are you indeed this generation's Pride? Pride, come here to carry out the trial in the place of Sloth?!"

"You pull this as soon as you make me think you're gonna take it easy and spare my life…? And if you think I am him, why are you puttin' the screws to me like this…?!"

"Even if you are an archbishop, it is an unwritten rule we do not interfere with one another! Beyond that, if this is to result in conflict, there is only greater diligence! To push forward and persist against any obstacle in THE way of love! After all, illogical clashes are far from rare!"

The madwoman responded to Subaru's question with a loud, derisive, insane laugh.

Sure, fanning the flames of internal competition sounded great in theory, but she'd just proudly exposed her organization as a collection of egotistical maniacs. In other words, as far as she was concerned, if Subaru *was* Pride, that made him her enemy.

"If you are Pride, the empty seat among the sins has beeeeen filled! Once the trial is completed, we must assemble the remaining sins so that the Witch may display her favor to us! And for that, among other things—"

"—"

"I must begin the trial early so that you may sever your lingering attachments. Tomorrow? No, beginning right now! Naturally, I ask that you watch until the very end!"

The madwoman gleefully thrust her demand into Subaru's face from a position of absolute superiority. This was a worst-case scenario. She meant to move up the trial—in other words, to rush the plan of attack. The madwoman continued to loudly extol her misunderstanding, making her murderous urges all too clear to Subaru.

Of course, he couldn't let her go through with it. There was little merit in playing for time, keeping the madwoman tied down in that place. The worst thought to strike him was that it was possible this female Petelgeuse copy was not the only one who could use the authority.

Accordingly, Subaru had to convey this to his comrades without a second to lose—

"Even so…shit! Even if I see 'em, I can't do anything about 'em from my end!"

The largest obstacle to regaining his freedom was the Unseen Hands still keeping him pinned. When he felt his neck grabbed and reached back, Subaru's fingers passed through the haze, unable to affect it.

As Subaru cursed the wholly unnatural phenomenon, the madwoman nodded.

"So you can indeed see my Unseen Hands. I am exceedingly dissatisfied, disturbed, dismayed, discontented at the absurdity of this, but this proves you are iiindeed Pride!"

"Don't make me say it twice… Ahh, it's the first time for you, is it? I'm not your Pride—I haven't even gotten my special admission book yet…!"

"What obstinacy! However, even you shall become more cooperative, and s—"

When Subaru resumed struggling, the woman's visage twisted in wicked delight as she stared at the sight. But the instant her slender arm subconsciously groped in a pocket, the woman's words were cut off, her expression vanishing.

"...That is right."

The woman drew her hand out of her own pocket as she haltingly spoke. It held nothing in it. The fact that it held nothing made the madwoman claw at her own face, gouging the flesh as she shouted, "—Gospel!!"

"—?!"

Subaru's body went rigid at the reverberation of the throat-splitting scream.

It was a sudden explosion of emotion. Her scratch wounds did not fit the rawness of the word, so the woman deepened the lacerations on her cheek as she looked up at Subaru, the object of her rage, flesh under the fingernail she turned toward him.

"Even if this diminutive body offers ten thousand words spent, ten thousand lives taken, ten thousand human laments, it is insufficient! A guide is necessary so that my foolish, immature self MAY properly repay Her favor! And for that purpose, the Gospel! Which is now beyond my grasp!"

"Uu..."

"If it was lost, then where?! Ahh, but I understand. My Gospel, the guide of my love! You, youyouyouuu must have seized it!"

When she directed her unstable hatred toward Subaru, the malice thrust through him, chilling his spine. The madwoman, rightful heir to Petelgeuse's spirit, brought her bloody visage close to Subaru.

"Stay back...!"

Her approach made Subaru feel the presence of death, something he had not tasted in some time.

When death drew near, it had a scent that only Subaru could pick out. It was this death that hovered around the woman's body as she came to seal Subaru Natsuki's fate.

"It is futile to struggle any further. This is as far as youuu..."

Responding to the madwoman's mocking voice, the evil hand's

grip made Subaru's neck bones creak. He was on the verge of losing consciousness, sinking into a lethal abyss.

"—What is this?"

"—Aah—"

The questioning voice led to a slackening of the grip, letting Subaru breathe easier for that single instant. Subaru forced his hazy eyes open to see for himself what had created that time for him.

Then Subaru saw it: a wavering, flickering cluster of red light, right before his eyes.

"What th…?"

"Spirit—!!"

Before Subaru could figure out what the light was, the madwoman raised a vivid, hateful shout. For its part, the light responded with vibrant clarity.

The light surged, as if about to explode, burning Subaru's and the woman's eyes with white light.

8

"—"

When the light exploded without warning, Subaru let out a shriek and bent backward. The pain, like needles stuck in his retinas, brought a flood of tears, making him cover his face with his palms—and the next moment, he was hurled free.

"Whoaaa!"

The instant Subaru, overtaken by the floating feeling, realized he had escaped from the hand, he moved to break his fall. He rolled feetfirst over the root of a large tree, minimizing the damage from the fall. Thanks to the Sword Devil's lessons, he was an expert at breaking falls after being sent flying. He rubbed his eyes with the backs of his hands and lifted his face.

"That was…er, uh-oh!"

When he lifted his head up to check the situation, the pitch-black hand came at high speed to mow him down. Subaru shuddered at the attack, which would have knocked his head clean off had it hit, and glared at the culprit in outrage. When he did so, the madwoman concerned was covering her face with her palms as she blindly flailed at the surrounding area with innumerable evil hands.

"Spirit…! Spiriiiiit!!"

The woman poured hatred onto the spirit, perhaps simply that aggrieved from the blow it had given her. However, the light was nowhere to be seen. The madwoman was merely wrecking the woods in anger, as if trying to inflict even a glancing blow on the offending spirit.

She'd completely taken her attention off Subaru. That moment, he was free to choose whether to attack or flee.

"I'll run, then!"

A greedy choice, like evading the wildly flailing hands and landing a single blow to the madwoman's vitals was beyond Subaru's means. Rather than engage, the better option was to secure combat capability.

"We can't let her be. But I need Wilhelm-level combat strength here! Should be that—"

"—You called, Sir Subaru?"

In his haste to rendezvous with the others, Subaru's eardrums were greeted by the voice he most wanted to hear. When he turned around, his eyes were greeted by the sight of a white-haired, elderly man—the Sword Devil—slipping through a gap in the grove and rushing over.

"Wilhelm!"

"That was most concerning. I am very sorry I could not be here sooner."

Wilhelm, carrying his treasured sword in pursuit, breathed a sigh of relief when he saw that Subaru was safe. Subaru, delighted at the best reinforcements he could hope for, blinked hard when he noticed the red light floating atop Wilhelm's head.

That glow was none other than that of the spirit that had just saved Subaru from peril.

"That's the spirit from earlier… Wilhelm, don't tell me you use spirits?!"

"Unfortunately, I have no talent beyond the sword. It is purely on loan from its proper contractor. However—it would seem you are in need of my specialty."

Wilhelm had stepped in front of Subaru by the time he finished those words. The ghastly aura radiating from the Sword Devil was great enough that the madwoman, eyes seared by the light, noticed and turned toward it.

"Ahh, SO there you are... You, you shall not escape...!"

The bloodstained woman's madness was directed at both Wilhelm and the spirit attending him.

"The enemy's in the same league as an Archbishop of the Seven Deadly Sins! You saw earlier how strong Unseen Hands are. Even you can't just take her on from the fr—"

"No matter. Knowing they are invisible, I have ways to deal with them."

When Subaru warned him of the seething woman's madness, the Sword Devil made that firm reply as he stepped forward. The sudden move startled Subaru, and even amid her villainy, the woman was dubious as well.

"What is this? Your head, your life...do you come to present these to me? If so, that is a WISE and diligent choice! I would like to respond with all due respect. However..."

"Invisible hands, is it? A most interesting parlor trick—I must experience it at least once."

"...Did you call this a parlor trick?"

For a moment, Wilhelm's words made the madwoman's madness vanish. Wilhelm responded to her utterance by lowering his sword, beckoning her with his open hand—*Come on*, he taunted.

"—! This foolish endeavor is to abandon all logic! And to discard logic is *lazy*!!"

"Wi—"

Mad with rage, the woman thrust both hands forward; simultaneously arms spewed from her shadow, assaulting the Sword Devil.

Their ferocity compelled Subaru to instantly shout for him to dodge, but he wasn't in time. The black, evil hands ought to have grasped Wilhelm's limbs, cruelly rending his flesh asunder—

But they did not.

A silver flash ran across the sky, and droplets of blood spurted from the woman's neck.

"If the human launching the attack is in plain sight before you, it can be anticipated, invisible or not. By watching the movement of her eyes, feeling her hostility, reading how she breathes as she aims, it was all too clear."

"—"

The Sword Devil made that frightening declaration having completely anticipated the pitch-black, evil hands, striking them down with his sword. Without exaggeration, his evasive timing was perfect; his talk of reading her breaths was no mere boast. His shocking combat skill had blunted the advantage posed by the invisible hands.

"How, how, how can this…?"

And without doubt, the madwoman's shock was even greater than Subaru's. She pressed a palm to the right side of her neck, taking in the feeling of the blood smearing it from the fresh cut. The very fact that the woman had dodged just prior to Wilhelm's sword strike, the action saving her life, was itself abnormal.

"Damn it, she threw herself with her own power…"

In concert with the sword strike, the woman had leaped backward in an unnatural pose and with unfathomable speed. The shadowy arm had grabbed and tossed the woman's body, narrowly saving her life from the Sword Devil's blade.

However, as a consequence, the evil hand's gripping power had crushed her left shoulder. It was a violent emergency evasive maneuver of sorts with no room for subtlety. However, the woman patted her crushed shoulder, glaring at Wilhelm as she said, "What…what a diligent concept, such diligent skill, aaa diligent way of life!"

Her cheeks flushed, the woman praised Wilhelm with delight in her eyes. Receiving what was, by her standards, unreserved adulation, Wilhelm grimaced in visible displeasure. However, the woman paid this no heed.

"None have ever challenged my love with such a method, such technique, such cunning! What diligence! Ahh, splendid!"

"Even this world is not so barren that I would waste words upon the likes of you."

"Do not say such hurtful things. I want you to show me more! Of you! Your sword! All OF you! Captivate me more!!"

Her body half smeared with blood, the madwoman stretched her hands out to Wilhelm as if seeking his affections. The Sword Devil did not conceal his displeasure at her statement, giving his sword a swing as he charged once more.

"Then then thennnn! HOW about this?!"

Together with her pronouncement, Unseen Hands gushed out from the ground, forming a black wall in front of the woman. It was a wall Wilhelm could not see. If he kept charging in like that, he'd be enmeshed in the evil hands, unable to evade.

"She made a wall of arms in front! Go around!"

"—Understood."

At Subaru's shout, Wilhelm kicked off from the ground, evading just short of the black wall before his eyes. The Sword Devil proceeded to leap sideways, escaping from the arms' range, thrusting his sword into the ground and swinging it upward.

"—!"

The angular sword strike gouged out the earth, sending a shower of dirt pouring onto the madwoman. He had kicked up a completely mundane smoke screen of dust. Naturally, the woman showed no signs of damage from it.

"—? Did that have a point…?"

"I hoped you would not disappoint me! Come! Come, come! Diligent old bones! You, the beloved child that knows love is the greatest thing in this world! Demonstrate your diligence to me!!"

The Sword Devil's behavior drew comments from both Subaru and the madwoman. But Wilhelm said nothing to either set of words. The aged swordsman simply continued his nimble run as dirt showered down upon the woman over and over.

Brushing away the unpleasant downpour, the madwoman turned eyes toward the Sword Devil like a maiden in love. The arms of instant death obstinately pounded down wherever she was looking.

"Are you finished? Is there no more? If so, dismay! Disappointment! Despondency of the soul, despair! Ahh, AHH! Are you *lazy*?!!!"

"N-no way?!"

At the woman's shout, shadow exploded; it was a terrifying volley of power that squarely locked on to Wilhelm. The hitherto sporadic evil hands now numbered above thirty, literally filling the sky in the narrow gaps between the trees. Subaru felt dizzy from the overwhelming number of them.

Fatally, there were thirty-odd of them, and Subaru could only point out one or two at best—

"Anyway, it's bad, Wilhelm!"

At the same time as Subaru's woefully insufficient cry, the evil hands cascaded straight down onto the Sword Devil. This time, malice that mercilessly destroyed all it touched would trample Wilhelm flat.

As he raced across the ground, Wilhelm looked overhead, his blue eyes narrowing as he said, "I told you."

The Sword Devil's tranquil voice rode on the warm forest breeze as he easily evaded the encroaching invisible hands.

"Huh?"

Both Subaru and the woman were taken aback; not even they knew which one had spoken the word.

The evil hands poured down on all sides, twisting around to assail the Sword Devil's limbs. With superhuman agility, Wilhelm dodged, evaded, and overwhelmed them.

When he had finally shaken off all the ferocious attacks, a vicious smile came over the Sword Devil's cheeks as he glared at the woman.

"—So long as I know the arms are invisible, I have ways to deal with them."

Certainly, he had just proven that his earlier proclamation was in no way false. But the results were so majestic that Subaru could scarcely close his wide-open mouth. Even Wilhelm shouldn't have had the super-senses to detect that many arms coming at him.

"Absurd. Absurd, absurd, absurdabsurdabsurdabsurdsurdsurd-surdsurdsurd…!"

Stricken senseless as she was by the foiling of her best move, the woman's eyes lost all focus. Trembling, the woman crushed her remaining fingers in true Petelgeuse fashion, but her emotional outburst did not relent as blood flowed from her nose.

The nosebleed was still dripping when the woman thrust her blood-smeared right hand at Wilhelm.

"Impossibleimpossibleimpossibleimpossible! How could you escape my Unseen Hands?!"

"Of course, I evaded them by sight. Once I knew their nature, foiling them was mere child's play."

Wilhelm tediously made the declaration as he once again made dirt shower with the tip of his treasured sword.

Dirt poured onto the madwoman, incomprehension on her beet-red face. But after seeing it repeated over and over, Subaru finally understood Wilhelm's objective in making that move. At the same time, he was in shock.

—The repeated showers of dirt were his opening moves for making Unseen Hands visible.

The hands themselves were invisible to the naked eye, interacting with whatever they touched by destroying it. In other words, the evil hands left a trail as they tore through the dirt showers.

Of course, even if he could see the ferocious attacks by thirty-plus hands, evading them was no easy task. And yet, Wilhelm's superhuman, godlike combat capabilities made even this seem like child's play.

"Now then, both of our tricks have been sufficiently exposed. I shall obtain vengeance for my comrades."

Thrusting the tip of his treasured sword forward, Wilhelm threatened with suppressed anger. The hostility radiating from the tip of his sword sent a thrill through Subaru, not even the direct target of that blade. Naturally, his fear was nothing compared to that of the madwoman on the receiving end of that sword tip.

In spite of this, the madwoman spread her blood-smeared arms wide, laughing as if granting his bloodlust a warm welcome.

"Ahh, ahh, it is splendid! Your actions are diligence personified! To inflict this situation, this development, this predicament upon meee…! I, always striving to be first among Her adherents, to repay Her favor and love with diligence! And yet, you have…!"

"To repeat *diligence* and *laziness* over and over is foolishness."

Exhaling once in the face of the woman's unsightly cries, the Sword Devil gazed at her with enmity winning out against the bloodlust in his eyes.

"'—If I do this, I will be loved. If I do enough, I will be loved.' The frivolity with which you speak the word rots my ears. It is not love of which you speak. It is merely your own conceit."

"What do you know about love?! Love is eeeverything to me!!"

Wilhelm did not reply to the woman's shriek; rather he slammed his sword down and advanced. The dirt shower recommenced, and the Sword Devil put his foot down, carving a wound in the ground as his body shot out like a bullet.

Even though, like a whip, like a spear, like a maul, like a sword, the madwoman's evil hands raced to mow Wilhelm down, he saw through them all, and was thus allowed to draw near.

And then—

"It is over, heretic."

As he stated this, the treasured sword in Wilhelm's hand plunged to the hilt, deep into the madwoman's belly. The sword ran through her, coming out of her back; when he yanked it out with a twist, a great deal of blood and entrails poured out.

When Wilhelm pulled back, the woman fell to her knees and bent forward as she touched the wound with a hand.

"Ahh, this cannot…"

Her palm was impotent to stop her blood from gushing out, her intestines from pouring out.

Wilhelm silently looked down at the madwoman, unable to stem the spillage of her life. Having cut down so many lives, the Sword Devil knew that she had little time left to live.

"It seems you require a mercy blow?"

"—Mercy is unnecessary. My life drains away, my blooood, disappearing… My diligence, the heartbeat that sustains me, is stopping, vani…sh…ing…"

Refusing the Sword Devil's mercy, the madwoman fell onto her side with a smile on her lips. The light proceeded to fade from the woman's eyes. Subaru stood rooted to the spot as he watched her final moments.

"…!"

"Ahh, my brain is shaaa…"

While Subaru stared, the woman left only those final words before her breathing completely ceased.

It was the death of the second user of Unseen Hands, the second Sloth.

Watching until the end, Subaru let out his breath. The conclusion of the battle had made him practically forget to breathe. His body resumed its life functions, as if remembering that which it had forgotten.

"I-is it…over?"

"—At the very least, this woman has most assuredly ceased to breathe."

Wiping the blood from his sword, Wilhelm replied thus to Subaru, who was nervously peering at the corpse. Subaru bit his lip, feeling as if the meaning behind those words bolstered his earlier deduction.

But Subaru immediately shook his head, switching gears. He knew it was no time to sink into contemplation.

"Setting her aside…anyway, we've gotta head back! I'm worried about everyone else. If we don't link up with them…!"

"—No, Sir Subaru. I have just been informed that they have wrapped up their end."

"Informed…?"

With Subaru agitated, Wilhelm offered a hand toward him. A pale light was floating above his hand. The spirit swayed left and right, emitting a faint red light, asserting its own existence.

"That's the spirit from…er, a minor spirit? Anyway, you're saying that this spirit told you the others are safe on their end?"

Subaru spoke toward the flickering light on Wilhelm's hand in hope of a reply. However, the spirit did not reply with words; it merely floated into the air, entering the forest as if to lead the way.

"That means *Follow me*, doesn't it?"

"—Let us go, Sir Subaru."

Grasping that it wished to guide them, Subaru and Wilhelm chased after the spirit.

They returned to their comrades after repelling a foe rivaling an Archbishop of the Seven Deadly Sins; considering the circumstances, it was good news to return with, but grave emotions were carved onto the pair's faces.

"—Shit."

But that moment, the only thing on Subaru's mind was the state of the allies with whom he would be reunited.

9

"—Who's there?"

"Hold up! It's us! Sorry to startle you!"

Checked by a sharp yell, Subaru came out of the thicket, showing himself with his hands up.

The knights who had sensed them returning from deep in the forest, and thus pointed their swords at them, immediately relaxed their guard, relief on their faces as they lowered their blades. But that relief was marred by sadness and regret.

Subaru had a feeling that the result of the fighting in the forest hadn't been a pure victory, something to take joy in.

"It seems you have both returned."

"Julius…"

As Subaru and Wilhelm surveyed the area, Julius ran over. Seeing that Subaru and Wilhelm were each without injury, he stood at attention without any change in expression.

"At the very least, it is good that you two are safe… Shall I make the damage report?"

"…Yeah, please do."

Having confirmed the other was safe and sound, Subaru granted approval for Julius to shift to the damage report. Accepting, Julius indicated the forest-turned-battlefield with his hand.

…The forest littered with fallen trees and traces of bloodshed, the aftereffects of combat.

"Five died instantly from the initial, invisible attack. Two more died while engaged in combat with the Witch Cult in the attack immediately following—our total casualties for this engagement were seven."

"Seven…"

Subaru had expected as much, but the number slammed heavily into his heart.

They'd lost five in the initial Unseen Hands ambush. It was a most cruel loss.

"…The Witch Cultists that tried to take you down?"

"All of the nine Witch Cultists here perished. Two were captured alive, but they killed themselves like all cases prior to this point… despite Ferris's strenuous efforts."

"So the enemy was completely wiped out. On our side, if we include the five scouts, our losses are twelve in total…"

"I cannot say that dividing our forces was a…poor move. Had we done otherwise, it is highly likely we would have simply increased our initial losses. Of course, it is also possible that the enemy would hesitate to attack greater numbers, but…"

Though the casualties stung deeply, neither Julius nor Wilhelm gave any hint of losing his cool. For his part, Subaru had been biting his lip enough to draw blood since the damage report began.

"That ends my report. And yours?"

"—! You don't have anything else to say to me?"

"Necessary reports come first. I had thought to ask you for your report before all other matters, but…"

In contrast to the emotional Subaru, Julius had a very calm demeanor. But as he replied, his forelocks were slightly askew, and there were traces of blood on his royal guard uniform. Of course, even he had not come through unscathed.

Gazing at the vestiges of intense combat, Subaru restrained his scattered emotions.

"…At the very least, we beat the Sloth that attacked us just now."

"'The Sloth that attacked us just now'…you say. Not a report to take solace in, it would seem."

Subaru's gloomy reply contained nominally good news, but Julius immediately homed in on the problem therein. The authority-using madwoman who had launched a surprise attack on the expeditionary force, whisking Subaru away from the battlefield, was an evil on par with the assuredly slain Archbishop of the Seven Deadly Sins—a being worthy of the title of Sloth.

"The first stage of this operation should have taken out the Archbishop of Sloth. You were more confident of that than anyone…yet, in spite of that, you call the earlier foe Sloth?"

"…Yeah, that's right. The one just now was a Sloth—a second Sloth."

The last part of that statement—"a second Sloth"—made Julius knit his brows in dismay. But given the seriousness of Subaru's gaze, combined with the events that had actually taken place, he offered no rebuttal.

"So the first Sloth defeated was a different person from this Sloth. You are absolutely sure of this?"

"I'd never forget the look on that piece-of-shit bastard's dead face. Plus, the second Sloth was a woman. There's no way you'd mistake one for the other. There's no way you would, but…"

When Subaru had first encountered the madwoman, he'd hallucinated that it was Petelgeuse. That was because he sensed things beyond their appearances that tied Petelgeuse and the woman together. It felt as if their madness had sprung from a common root—

"The authority was the same, the words and actions were the same. I've got a reaaally bad feelin' about this."

"Perhaps the first Sloth we defeated was a double, and the second Sloth was the real Archbishop of the Seven Deadly… No, there is no way to be certain of that. Besides, in this case, the real issue—"

"—Might be in a whole different league than which one was the real deal."

When Julius felt he might have speculated too far, Subaru picked up his conclusion and ran with it. The statement made sweat emerge on Subaru's brow; even Julius's face stiffened somewhat. It was a terrifying prospect. However, in light of current circumstances, it was also a logical conclusion.

Given the appearance of Petelgeuse the first time, and the madwoman the second, it was inevitable they would arrive at the same possibility.

"In other words, there are multiple Archbishops of Sloth—or perhaps the Archbishop of Sloth is actually a group with the same power, acting toward a common objective?"

"…The only Sloth I knew of was the sickly-looking bastard that came out first. But now that I've seen the next woman, I can't tell you you're wrong."

The madwoman had called herself a finger and identified with the Archbishop of Sloth.

It fit. That's what they would go with: that Sloth was multiple Archbishops of the Seven Deadly Sins working in concert.

"So without exaggeration, the fingers are parts of the Archbishop of the Seven Deadly Sins. If it is a group composed of multiple archbishops calling themselves Sloth, it would explain the breadth of the upheaval they have caused in every nation."

"So Sloth is the part of the Witch Cult carrying out the doctrine of the faith. Just the thought gives me chills."

That it was the practical arm of a larger religious group was very much a flight of fancy. Subaru wanted to laugh, but even a dry laugh failed to emerge.

If Petelgeuse Romanée-Conti was but one Sloth among many, their pleasant, orderly advance had been nothing more than a farce. That was a terrifying prospect indeed.

"In the end, this remains no more than speculation. I would like to avoid carelessly spreading unease and unrest among the others."

When the unpleasant thought closed Subaru's mouth, Julius shifted his eyes toward the expeditionary force, clumped up in one group.

"We lost twelve men, with three fingers to go… This is a rate of attrition we cannot ignore."

"—Not twelve, eleven."

When a voice corrected the number of their losses, Subaru and Julius turned toward it to find Ferris walking over to them. His white coat was sullied with blood as he wiped the sweat off his brow and pointed behind him.

"I pulled one of the heavily injured ones back from the brink. It was a really, really close call, though…"

"That is good news. To stabilize someone in that condition…as expected of you, Ferris."

"I said it meowself—I can bring back anyone who isn't dead."

When Julius said the words *good news*, Ferris gave a thin, wry smile. But his smile soon faded as he shifted his gaze in a different direction.

Subaru's eyes, drawn there as well, were greeted by the sight of someone covered with a thin cloth.

"I can't save everyone… Now I really understand the meaning of the captain's words."

"You have done well. It is not a role any of the rest of us could hope to accomplish."

"Mmm, thank you."

Ferris replied briefly to Julius's consoling words, but everyone there knew that they were a small comfort.

Head bowed, Ferris licked his lips and, after a brief pause, looked at Subaru.

"...So about what you said earlier, where's the body of the second Sloth?"

Immediately after, Subaru grimaced at the sudden change in the conversation.

"—In the forest over that way, but why do you wanna know?"

Ferris must have overheard the earlier exchange with Julius. He stared in the direction in which Subaru pointed, narrowing his yellow eyes.

"Just maybe, if I examine it, I might find some differences."

"Differences? What kind of differences?"

"Between the fingers you're worried about and the other cultists, Subawu."

When Ferris pointed that out, Subaru's breath caught. "Wait up, 'kay?" said Ferris, taking several companions with him as he went off to examine the corpse.

Perhaps examining the madwoman, the second Sloth, might give them a lead on the repugnant Archbishops of the Seven Deadly Sins, enabling them to form a plan of attack. Subaru wanted to believe that was possible.

"And besides that..."

Having watched Ferris go, Subaru went to the expeditionary force members clustered together. Subaru couldn't look straight at the row of casualties lying right beside them. The lined-up remains were covered with thin cloths, the least they could do for those who would never awaken again.

There was nothing anyone could have done for the initial five casualties who had been ripped to pieces. However, the five lives lost in the surprise attack were another story. Subaru should have realized, if no one else.

"I should've known as soon as I heard the first five were torn apart with bare hands. I'm the one who was aware what power we were dealing with. I should've noticed."

Subaru, of all people, should have recognized the cause of the deaths of those who had been slain without a single sign of resistance. But Subaru, shaken by the deaths of his allies, had let the chance slip, leading to more casualties.

On top of that, his own whisking away by the enemy had forced his allies to split their fighting strength, prolonging the combat. Had Wilhelm not pulled out, those lost during the engagement might well have lived.

"Even if it was a surprise attack, the opponent was small in numbers. Barring an exception, such as an Archbishop of the Seven Deadly Sins' authority, there was no chance of defeat. It was precisely for this reason I sent Master Wilhelm to you."

"—"

"Indeed, that authority, defying all logic, is a far greater concern. You did your duty, helping us evade it. The rest was our duty…as knights."

Listening to Subaru's murmurs, Julius set his disheveled hair in order as he offered his own view. Even Subaru was not so insensitive as to miss the consideration the words offered to him.

But it was also a fact that no words of consolation lessened the pain in Subaru's heart.

People had died in the fight against the White Whale, too.

He remembered grieving over those deaths, but not nearly as much. He'd lamented the fact that, compared to his own deaths, the deaths of others had moved his heart so little, but these deaths weighed heavily upon him.

Death was the same whatever form it took, so why did these deaths bother him so much?

That was obvious.

"…Because I was involved with these people."

Only then did Subaru Natsuki realize that he bore responsibility for those casualties.

When they'd challenged the White Whale, they had stood on the field of battle against the demon beast as a result of their own free choice. But the fight against the Witch Cult was different. These people had answered Subaru's call, sharing in Subaru's desire to save Emilia and the others; they had been cooperating with Subaru, nothing more.

"—So heavy."

Subaru had used the information gleaned from Return by Death to cooperate with Crusch and the others in subjugating the White Whale. However, put differently, it was Subaru's information that had triggered the outbreak of that battle, too. A battlefield was created, and numerous human lives met their end. Many lives were erased from the memories of others.

Subaru shared in that heavy responsibility. It was not only because he'd subconsciously averted his eyes from the burden that he had not noticed. It was more because Crusch had been so magnificent.

She led the fight against the White Whale, shouldering the responsibility for everything on that field of battle. She was aware of her own obligations, but her performance was so grand, it made you forget about all of that. And so, Subaru hadn't noticed.

Return by Death was not simply a matter of changing fate. Naturally, if Subaru took an action for the sake of some choice, some hope, some purpose, he altered the world around him.

"..."

With that all-too-late realization, he was fiercely angry with himself for being so foolish and worthless.

He'd been careless. He'd left himself wide open. The fact that everything had gone too well should have set off alarms in his mind. There had been big talk about making sure everyone got out alive, but he'd underestimated the effort required to make that happen—and this was the result.

And as a result, eleven precious lives had been lost—the lives of people who'd stood by his side.

Regret filled his head to the brim. Remorse seethed deep in his gut. The thought that there had to be something more he could have done made him pound baseless rage against his soul. Enough that he wanted to die in a fit of anger that very—

"Sir Subaru."

"—!"

Subaru was enveloped by rage sufficient to turn his vision red when that voice brought him back to his senses.

Wilhelm was standing before Subaru, staring straight at him. For an instant, Subaru's heart shuddered as he wondered if Wilhelm would scold him for his ignorance. But the Sword Devil's eyes immediately told him otherwise.

The Sword Devil's eyes were as tranquil as the surface of a lake as he gazed right through Subaru's dark eyes.

"You likely have a number of things running through your mind at the moment, none of them trivial emotions…but forgive my exceedingly great rudeness and allow me to say this."

"—"

Wilhelm's words made him unwittingly straighten his back. He didn't know what would be said to him, but whatever it might be, he needed to give it his undivided attention.

Then, with Subaru bracing himself, Wilhelm said…

"—Fight."

Spoken in a low tone, that word made the very air tremble.

But Subaru also received it as a blade—one that bit into his body, his heart, his very soul.

The ghastly aura pouring from Wilhelm filled the forest-turned-battlefield, wrenching its way into Subaru's mind and body. The hostility swept over the whole area, and naturally, the knights' eyes all fell on the two of them.

At the center of that vortex of gazes, Wilhelm continued, "Whether you feel regret, or are stricken with remorse, fight. If it is fated that you must do battle, that you must resist—fight with your entire body and soul. Do not give in for a second, a moment, a single fraction of time. Gaze at victory and crave it with every fiber of your being. If you can still stand, if you can still move a single finger, if your fangs are not yet broken, stand, stand, stand, stand, fight—fight."

"—"

The words were very similar to ones Wilhelm had spoken to Subaru before.

When he'd been smacked around with a wooden sword in the courtyard of Crusch's mansion, Wilhelm had spoken words concerning girding one's heart for battle; that was the only moment Subaru had been allowed a tiny glimpse into the Sword Devil.

At the time, after Subaru had heard those words, Wilhelm pegged him as person with no drive to become stronger. In point of fact, Subaru hadn't faced him with true earnestness. Deprived of willpower, Subaru had had no idea at the time what the Sword Devil thought or was trying to tell him.

But this time was different—and this time, he thought the message was different, too.

"You're telling me to…become strong?"

"No—I am telling you to *be* strong."

The frighteningly lofty and sharp demand thrust through his chest.

Subaru had always thought, *I wanna be like Wilhelm. I wanna be like steel.*

But now, with regret and remorse slamming against his heart, he did not think those words were the answer.

"I wanna be that way, too. But it's hard. I didn't want anyone else to die like this, but they did…because I wasn't good enough!"

Once again, he'd made the mistake of getting full of himself as soon as things were going a little bit well. As a result of his mistake, people had died. If he made more mistakes, no one knew who would die for them next.

He'd desperately tried to think of a way to avoid that, and yet nothing came. He was out of ideas.

"If I don't do it… I'm the one who started this!"

"You got them involved, you strung them along, and they died, is that it? You are incorrect."

With remorse threatening to wrench Subaru's heart out of his chest, Wilhelm spread both arms wide.

"Not a single individual here believes you involved us in this. Even if you provided the spark, we chose this battle ourselves. Everyone is here of his or her own will."

"..."

"Please stop placing responsibility for the deaths on yourself alone. They do not wish you to be burdened by this. Simply make room in your heart so that you do not forget. That is all you need do."

"Not forget what...?"

Their deaths? he wondered. But Wilhelm shook his head, putting Subaru's notion to rest.

"—That they shared this burden with you. That is all."

This time, his words made Subaru's entire body numb, as if he'd been struck by a bolt of lightning. With Subaru in shock, Wilhelm nodded to him and touched the sword on his own hip.

"Lending one's strength does not mean merely swinging one's sword. It means challenging the same foes, worrying over the same obstacles, sharing the wounds and the weight of the burdens. This we can do. This is the lesson I learned in the past."

Wilhelm spoke those words and motioned with his chin. Overwhelmed, Subaru did as indicated, noticing that the gazes of all present were focused upon him.

Each and every one of those sets of eyes burned with the same emotions as Wilhelm's.

—He felt someone had once told him not to try to fight alone.

At a disadvantage against a mysterious opponent, not a single person looked ready to cut and run. Not a single gaze said to Subaru, *This wasn't the deal*, nor did wiser voices condemn him.

"...Having at least one wiser person seems like a good thing, though..."

He let out a sigh. Simultaneously, the dark clouds dwelling inside Subaru's head rapidly brightened. This did not mean freedom from anguish. But he had left the dead end in which he'd trapped himself behind him.

Subaru had been reminded of the limits of his own head.

"Shit—!"

Subaru roughly scratched his head, gritted his teeth, impulsively stamped his foot, and turned to everyone, bowing his head.

"This is the only head I have to lower. It's low quality, so I'll lower it as many times as I need to."

Subaru entreated his comrades, whose gazes remained unchanged, saying, *We'll fight.*

Somehow, somewhere, he'd escaped barefoot from resignation and remorse.

"A lot of things…seriously, a lot of things have changed. The Witch Cult's Sloth is seriously tough. To put it bluntly, we can't even see the bottom. I get why they're treated like gods of pestilence the world over. It shook me how much damage we took just taking 'em on. It shook me, but…"

It'd shaken him because he'd mistakenly thought he ought to think, counter, and fight all by himself. Thanks to everyone there, his limbs had finally stopped shaking.

Because they thought, *Let's fight.*

"I still don't have any firm idea what we should do. But I know we've got to do this. We have to beat them. We have to beat Sloth, here and now."

However mysterious the opponent, it was Subaru's side that had started it. All they could do was defeat the enemy, whatever it took, until the battle was decided.

"—"

Turning, Subaru looked at the remains of the comrades that had fallen in the forest, remains that had instilled such remorse and such a sense of responsibility that he'd been unable to look straight at them all that time.

This was Subaru's inescapable sin. However you wanted to dress it up, Subaru was responsible for their deaths. And he would not permit himself to run from his sins any longer. Subaru wondered if he hadn't been arrogant in thinking that borrowing someone's assistance was no heavy thing.

Subaru had started this battle, and so he would shoulder it. But he didn't think of it as too heavy a burden.

And so, he was determined to carry it, even if he himself knew not how great it would become.

"We'll save Emilia and the others. We'll smash the Witch Cult flat. And to do both of those things..."

"Let us do that which is needed...not for anyone else, but because you have asked it."

And for that, our strength is yours, said Wilhelm's nod, and those of the members of the expeditionary force.

He still had a mountain of things to think about, and the number of obstacles blocking their way was yet unknown. However, these he could overcome, because he need not challenge them alone.

If Subaru had been strong enough to stand alone, he'd never have gotten out of that blind alley. Therefore, for just one moment, he thought that...

"...Good thing I'm weak and puny, then."

"—Shall we go?"

"Yeah, let's go. And lend me your strength and wit."

Death did not lighten. It remained heavy. So long as he knew this, he could struggle against it with his head held high.

Subaru Natsuki walked forward, resuming the fight.

And so their battle continued.

CHAPTER 3

THE MEANING OF HAVING RETURNED

1

The return of Subaru & Co. with the bodies of their comrades was a great shock to those who had remained at the camp.

Fortunately, nothing had happened to the camp whatsoever, but the reports of combat and casualties in the forest spread gloom among the faces of those waiting in reserve. All shared the disappointment of not having been able to partake in the battle. Like the others, they too renewed their vows of support toward Subaru.

And, having linked up with additional allies, they began to discuss their plan of action henceforth.

However, the new issues and obstacles that had floated to the surface were all difficult ones. The existence of the Archbishop of Sloth continued to stand before the expeditionary force as a high wall impeding their progress.

"First, my report after examining the corpse of the second Sloth: As you can see, the corpse is a little different from that of the other Witch Cultists. There are traces of a strange ritual."

The first to offer information was Ferris, once his examination of the madwoman's corpse was complete. The word *ritual* brought a grimace to Subaru's face.

"You mean one besides the Witch Cultists embedding magic crystals into themselves for suicide?"

"Exactly. The fusion was hard to see, but when I compared on a hunch, it became clear as day… I think the same Sloth-like cultists have the same setup."

"So this setup, it's the trigger for that authority thingy?"

"I don't know that far. But when I think of some of the cultists getting this special treatment, it makes me suspect it has something to do with the weird power the Archbishop of the Seven Deadly Sins controls."

The information suggesting there were multiple Sloths had already been shared within the expeditionary force. Given Ferris's examinations to date, the possibility loomed ever larger.

"If that's so, the problem is how many Sloths besides these two are there, huh?"

"There have been two to date, but considering what it took to bring them down, the situation is extremely dangerous. Worst case, we should presume that it is possible all the individuals known as fingers are Sloths."

"…That's jumping ahead a little much, ain't it? If they could all use that authority, they'd use it to hit back at us, right? But no one's done that."

"It would be so if the individuals known as fingers appeared as a group under the archbishop's command."

Julius's reply didn't really answer Subaru's question. But Ferris and Ricardo registered agreement on their faces.

"I see, I see. In other words, I think Julius means the fingers are like the archbishop's right hand and left hand."

"—? Aren't the right and the left hands both part of the same body?"

"Not that, more in the sense of your confidant or right-hand man. Weren't you the one to guess what the fingers were to the Witch Cult to begin with, Subawu?"

"…Ah!"

After all that, Subaru finally clued into what the three of them were saying. Subaru knew of several cases where Petelgeuse had referred to his subordinates as fingers, but he'd had to guess heavily as to the details. In point of fact, Subaru had thought that the term *fingers* was what Petelgeuse used to refer to groups under his command.

But what if, instead, *fingers* was the name borne by several special cultists, and the same authority as Petelgeuse's resided in each of them?

"So that's saying that Petelgeuse was just one Sloth counted by the number of fingers?"

"If there are a maximum of ten, and each base has a single Sloth assigned to it, that might explain why we have been lucky enough not to give them an opportunity to strike back so far. That is being optimistic, however."

"So that means three bases left, and three fingers to go…so we should assume there are three more of 'em."

One should hypothesize the worst case in any situation. Casually dismissing the threat posed by the enemy came with a stiff price. Subaru had paid the heavy tuition fee for that lesson many times over.

And given the worst-case possibility they could hypothesize at present—

"—As soon as possible, I want to begin evacuating the mansion and the people in the village."

"…To be honest, I was thinking that if you did not propose it, I would myself," Julius agreed, closing one eye.

"Now that we are uncertain of having eliminated the menace of Sloth, our greatest concern should be for their future objective—to do harm to Lady Emilia and the villagers, I imagine."

"There's less than half of 'em left now, so we should assume they're onto us bein' after 'em. That bein' the case, the biggest fear is 'em tryin' to take folks down with 'em."

With Julius and Ricardo in agreement, Subaru nodded, too, his worry evident in the creases of his brow. There was no mistaking that the Witch Cult was aware of the expeditionary force. The earlier raid had established that well enough.

"The second Sloth was waiting for us. They noticed us at some point. It's fine for *us* to be exposed at this point, but it's bad if our objective is exposed."

On a combat level, it hurt to lose any advantage, but the expeditionary force's biggest issue was accomplishing its goal of rescuing Emilia and the others. The Witch Cult ought not to have known just yet why Subaru & Co. had entered the Mathers lands.

If the Cult knew that both sides were after the mansion and village, both were certain to become battlefields.

"Right now, the Witch Cult hasn't noticed that the plain is wide open yet. If we can get Emilia and everyone on dragon carriages, they should be able to make a clean getaway."

"If Lady Emilia and the others escape, we can concentrate on subjugating the Witch Cult without any worries about the future. It's really hard to fight with a weak point like that on your shoulders, *meow*. Especially for Ferri and Subawu."

"Hurts to hear that…but that's how it is."

Having received Ferris's dry approval, Subaru asked for any objections to the plan. Fortunately, with time so precious, no objections were raised, so Subaru slapped his knee and made the call.

"Thanks, big help. We'll take the traveling merchants with us and all go to the village. No leaving me behind, okay?"

"From here, there is no telling when the remaining Sloths might attack. Your eyes will be irreplaceable, yes?"

With Julius's roundabout assent, the expeditionary force's plan was set.

"Ohh. So you're finally calling on us, then. It's a relief to get some work."

As it turned out, the traveling merchants were unexpectedly eager when they finally received the order to move out. Sitting and waiting seemed to suit them poorly.

Everything about the Witch Cult was, as usual, shrouded in mystery. But with the current setbacks, there was no option but to rely on their hauling capacity to fulfill Subaru's long-delayed goal.

"Sorry to keep you waiting, too, Patlash… Hey, don't be that angry, geez."

"—"

Patlash, left behind at camp while Subaru walked through the forest without her, was quite miffed at Subaru. The pitch-black land dragon turned her sharp, refined face aside, thoroughly sulking when Subaru called her.

"Er, I mean, it was the middle of a forest? If you tripped and broke a leg there'd be no coming back, you know?"

"This breed of land dragon, known as the Diana breed, is the highest breed of all land dragons. There are dragons specific to desert or arctic climes, but the excellent Diana breed can handle any terrain."

"Eh? Any terrain, what, you mean forests, too?"

"Forests, deserts, waterside, or glacier."

Wilhelm's lofty appraisal left Subaru gaping in wonder. He'd picked the land dragon based on his first impression, but apparently, she excelled more than he'd ever imagined. Perhaps that should have been obvious given Patlash's intelligence and ability.

"After all, it takes a pretty decent noble house to buy a girl like her, *meow*."

"Hey, stop that! Don't talk about price! That's gonna stick in my head!"

Ferris smiled as Subaru raised his voice, feeling almost afraid to mount the dragon. But Subaru thought that smile was gloomier than one from Ferris's usual self.

Subaru, largely able to fathom the reason why, stood beside his land dragon and lowered his voice.

"Sorry, making you act considerate to me like this."

"—What is it all of a sudden? Did you eat something bad? Should I heal you?"

"Don't paper over it. You said it yourself. I'm not the only one who doesn't want anyone to die."

"…"

Ferris was cowed into silence with a guilty look. Subaru had apparently hit the mark.

Subaru wasn't the only one who felt deeply responsible for the deaths of his allies. Perhaps the mental anguish was much stronger for someone with a direct means of saving others such as Ferris.

Subaru thought Ferris was strong to hold that inside him and not let it come to the surface, though.

"Maybe my saying this isn't worth much, but…having you here is a big help. Seriously."

"Oh, stop it. I know best how useless I've been. I've let eleven people die, and couldn't even stop enemies from killing themselves… I'm all talk."

"But you saved one. He didn't die, thanks to you."

As Ferris berated himself, Subaru motioned to the casualty sleeping in the back of a dragon carriage. His endurance was heavily depleted, and he had not regained consciousness. But he was in a stable condition. That was Ferris's achievement.

Subaru knew how hard it was to save even a single person.

"You're a bigger deal than you think you are. No, really, I'm totally serious."

"…Wha—? Are you trying to seduce cute little Ferri? Coming to my side of the fence?"

"I am not, and I'm not seducing you, either! I'm trying to be serious here!"

Subaru knew well enough that he wasn't suited to the role, but the counterattack, harsher than even he'd expected, left him reeling. However, Ferris's lips immediately loosened as he exhaled at length.

"If you meant it seriously, I'll take it seriously. Don't worry, I'm not questioning my purpose in life. I crossed that bridge a long, long time ago, *meow*."

"Th-that so?"

"Just, well, it might make me feel a little better? They feel like words I've heard before, so I feel relieved, just a tiny little wee bit…"

Ferris glanced sidelong at Subaru, teasingly showing with his fingers just how tiny that relief was. From that reaction, Subaru felt he'd contributed some small part to cheering Ferris up, which left him relieved as well.

“So, this is a good time, so Ferri is going to say it…Subawu, you really should make up with Julius as soon as you can.”

Ferris switched subjects so abruptly that Subaru’s eyes popped wide.

“It’s not a soon or not-soon thing… You saw, right? It’s not making up, but our clashing is water under the bridge.”

“On the surface, sure. Deep down, you’re still snapping at him subconsciously. That’s why, when something comes up, you’re dropping Julius off the list of choices first thing.”

“…”

“You can rely on Julius. Though I grant you that he’s hard to deal with and tough to understand, *meow.*”

Fluttering his palm to indicate the end of the conversation, Ferris concentrated on examining the magic crystals from the Witch Cult. In contrast to Ferris, those last words had unsettled Subaru’s mind.

Am I subconsciously snapping at him…?

When he thought about it, he couldn’t conclusively say he hadn’t been. Of course, he hadn’t judged based on such personal feelings to that point. But he had no confidence that he had his subconscious under control as well.

“…”

He’d turned his still-stern face forward when suddenly, the sweet aroma of flowers leaped into his nostrils.

A lovely little flower with blue petals was blooming on the edge of the road, swaying in the wind. Subaru recognized it and its scent, which triggered a memory of a vivid flower garden—the flower garden where he and Emilia had once spent time together.

“I really wanted to put an end to all that and have more of a triumphant return, but…”

Emotionally, Subaru wanted to hurry and hesitate in equal measure. If they continued along the highway and entered Earlham Village, he’d begin to urge the villagers to evacuate. Naturally, that meant the people from the mansion as well; in other words, a reunion with *her.*

"Would've been much cooler to see her again after taking care of it all..."

Partial. Partial. Everything was halfway. The subjugation of the Witch Cult was halfway; so, too, the duty entrusted to him at the royal capital. More than anything else, Subaru's heart was only halfway prepared to face the future, his mind-set not having changed since he'd aired his feelings several hours prior.

Subaru had yet to make up for all that he had done in the royal capital. He couldn't puff up his chest while reuniting with Emilia in a situation like that, and the knowledge caused a harsh throb in his chest.

Of course, Subaru's discomfort was not something he could weigh against her safety and that of others.

"—I committed three sins, he said?"

The words had been tossed his way just before he perished in a world dyed white. The words had convicted him as the fool who had broken his promise to her, trampled upon her feelings, and even robbed her of her life. Such was the curse left from when Puck killed him the third time around.

"Eii, cut that out! Why do I have to feel like that anyway? I'm heading to save her like a prince on a white horse. My land dragon's black and I don't make much of a prince, but I should be more up front about...er."

Fight. Had Wilhelm not told him this? That mind-set was not only for the battlefield. That mentality was precious strength, bolstering your spirit against any aspect of life threatening to crush you.

"That's how it is, huh, Wilhelm?"

"Hmm? Yes, it is so."

When he prodded Wilhelm, riding a little ahead, for agreement, the Sword Devil hesitated for a brief moment before giving his assent.

Julius, glancing sidelong at just the right time to catch the exchange, sighed as he said, "That is not something you should bother Master Wilhelm about. It is natural for you to be thinking of certain things, but would it not be better if you retained a little composure?"

"…In the first place, the stuff I'm thinking about has nothing to do with you."

"I thought you should admit you are in the wrong in this so as to clear the air, but?"

"Well logic's different from sentiment! Sheesh, that's right. Push comes to shove, that's how it is."

"—?"

When Subaru berated himself in a ragged voice, Julius inclined his head, watching uncomprehendingly.

In the middle of the exchange, Subaru became aware that he was snapping at Julius, just as Ferris had told him. Even if he accepted it logically, accepting it emotionally was a different matter.

But as Ferris had pointed out, letting it compromise his judgment was getting his priorities mixed up.

"Ah, er, yeah. There might be something I need to…say to you before we move on."

Without looking at Julius as he rode beside him, Subaru haltingly and carefully broke the ice. Subaru was at pains to choose the words that would remove the seed of discord between them as soon as possible.

Ahead, the highway sandwiched between forest to the left and right was growing narrower, but it would still be a long time before Earlham Village ought to be visible, practically tailor-made to give them time to talk.

"When we linked up on the highway, I thought we'd already made the stuff before water under the bridge…but sorry. It seems that I still haven't been able to digest it."

"…"

"It's not that I don't trust you. It's just, I guess there's still dislike of you in my mind, and that's why I've been giving out bad orders here and there… Well, that's what Ferris told me."

"…"

"No, this isn't because Ferris told me that, but we're in a situation where we all need to work together, and I agree with him that you can't have feelings of mistrust between people like this, so…"

"..."

With Julius silent, Subaru beat around the bush as he continued the conversation. He was frustrated with himself as much as with the listener's not indicating he was following along. It was beyond absurd if Subaru turned out to be the only one feeling awkward.

"Hey, have you been listening to me? It's just me talkin' like I'm the only—"

Subaru, glaring forward with a look of guilt, let spittle fly at that point as he turned to face Julius. The very fact that he made the outburst, scowling as he turned to glare at that handsome face, underlined that he'd lost sight of his original goal of a conversation to clear the air, but—

"—?!"

The instant Subaru vented, a sudden gust of wind blew, making him subconsciously cover his face with his arms. The unexpected gust, mixed with the scent of flowers, sent his forelocks aflutter, and after a moment of shock, wondering what had just happened, he realized—

—the long line of land dragons had vanished, and he was alone.

2

"What the—?!"

He immediately realized he was in an emergency situation. But he didn't know what had happened.

Wide-eyed, Subaru surveyed the area, hands still gripping the reins. The scenery around him differed little from before; he was dead center on a highway flanked by trees. The difference was that there was no sight of the allies who had been close to him mere moments before, leaving him all by himself—

"No, I'm *not* alone."

"..."

Drawing the reins close, the stiff-bodied Subaru was still riding on Patlash. The low body temperature conveyed through the saddle was intact; he figured he hadn't been split off from things he was in physical contact with.

"If that's so, some kind of spatial distortion or teleport… Then…?"

He'd been split off from his allies in the blink of an eye, so he figured the method had to be along those lines. The scenery Subaru was looking at had not changed. Maybe it was everyone *but* Subaru who'd been jumped somewhere else.

And naturally, only the Witch Cult benefited from isolating Subaru from the others.

"Shit! This ain't the time to stare into space, Patlash!"

Subaru cracked the reins and sent the land dragon galloping as he berated himself for being so slow to grasp the situation. Patlash neighed, and her strong legs propelled them in an instant—Subaru was attempting to use speed, enough to send the wind itself flying, to extricate them from their isolated situation. During that time, Subaru squinted, wary of attack from any direction.

If his guess was right, Unseen Hands might well come flying from yet another Sloth.

"…"

But in spite of Subaru's wariness, there was no sign of Unseen Hands coming. Doubts crept in, and simultaneously, uncertainty formed in Patlash's steps. The cause was the same thing that was giving Subaru pause: though they'd sprinted at full speed for tens of seconds, the scenery didn't seem to have changed at all.

Mere teleportation could not explain this situation. It made him recall a similar experience.

"This is like Beatrice's infinite corridor…? But there's no doors here!"

Only once had Subaru experienced a similar phenomenon: when Beatrice, a little girl living at Roswaal Manor, had used magic to turn a corridor into a spatial loop. At the time, Subaru's keen judgment had led him to open the correct door, immediately bringing the matter to an end.

However, it would not be so simple this time around. They were in the wild, and there were no doors to be had, correct or otherwise.

In other words, Subaru's intuition was useless for resolving the situation.

"Damn it, just after I stop worrying about things all on my own, this happens!"

He lamented that he had stood and faced one hardship with all his being, only to have this happen immediately. Subaru surveyed the area, clicking his tongue at the unchanging scenery.

"Heyyy! Anyone there?! Is it just me here?! Answer me! Someone—!!"

Subaru desperately raised his voice. Worst case, he'd be drawing the enemy to his position, but he didn't care. If he could draw even a single foe away from his allies, it was better than doing nothing at all. However, Subaru's idea was fruitless, with no sign of either friend or foe answering his call.

It was odd. It was strange. Had Subaru been sent to another dimension all by himself? He was not thoroughly versed in the rules of magic of that world; was such a thing even possible?

"Hold up, Patlash. Let's be cool… Calm down and think…"

Accepting Subaru's instruction, Patlash slackened the speed of her run and came to a standstill. That instant, when they were stopped, was the perfect moment to strike, but there was no sign of that, either.

The forest had returned to eerie silence, with nothing to hear save the wind and the voices of insects. With so many living, breathing humans erased, desolation dominated the world all the more.

The situation was truly what the world would be like if it came under the Witch Cult's dominion—

…No? No, this is different.

Once he'd thought that far, a palpable sense of wrongness made Subaru jerk his head up. He looked around the area. The scenery had not changed. However, when he focused his ears, he heard his own heartbeat mixed with Patlash's breathing, and something like the sounds of crickets—sounds that would have been extinguished if it were a world ruled by the Witch Cult.

"It's not teleportation. Then what the hell *is* it…?"

He hadn't been transferred to a place under the Cult's dominion.

Furthermore, making the same highway scenery loop over and over should have been impossible even for ultra-top mages. If that was the case, something was wrong with his premise.

He thought back to what had initially taken place. What had happened at the instant when he thought, *I'm alone*? First had been a gust of wind. That was strange all by itself.

Patlash's wind repel blessing should've been up. If I wouldn't feel shakes or wind normally, where the heck did that gust come from?

—

Something happened the moment that wind blew. No, if something was the trigger, it happened before that. If this was an attack, what stood out was…the scent of flowers?

The scent of flowers. Yes, the sweet scent of flowers. The thick aroma had mixed with the gust of wind, slipping into Subaru's nostrils, soaking into his brain. And that very moment, the aroma was thick enough to make his chest feel awful.

—?! Uh, eh, what the heck…?

The instant he thought about it, the scent of flowers, which he had ignored to that point, invaded his nostrils. He instinctively rejected the clearly abnormal aroma, instantly shielding his nose in the face of the dangerous scent.

"Have we been walking around in this flower scent all this time?"

Subaru shuddered at the indecipherable power that had slipped in without his notice. Simultaneously, he realized that if the scent was the cause of his circumstance, there had to be flowers.

Therefore, the scent was coming from—

"These flowers blooming on the side of the road."

Subaru dismounted Patlash and walked over to the flowers blooming right at the roadside. The flowers, petals gently swaying in the wind, resembled the flowers known as pansies in his world. However, now that Subaru had determined that flowers were the cause, he was suddenly at a loss.

If the flowers were the cause, should he uproot them? Stomp them underfoot, maybe? Without any firm idea of how to deal with them, Subaru decided to first snap a flower off with his hand—

"Urgh…?!"

The instant he tried to touch the flower, wriggling vines became like whips, lunging for Subaru's neck. With incredible strength, the narrow vines wrenched Subaru, the power of the unexpected attack drawing out an anguished cry.

"Ack…agh…!"

Falling on his backside, Subaru tore at the vines as they tried to strangle him.

Hard. The vines were so tough that you wouldn't think they were plants, rejecting his fingernails, trying to kill Subaru with the bloodlust of an animal. Subaru bent back, reaching out with a hand, calling for aid from Patlash.

The black land dragon stood behind Subaru, quietly staring at his battle with the flower. She merely watched, with no sign of making any move. Subaru lamented with a sense of despair. But that despair was overshadowed by the sense that something was off.

"—"

Having served Subaru so faithfully thus far, it was unnatural for Patlash to overlook this situation. Why, then, was this the case? The possibilities were twofold: Patlash had abandoned him, or she didn't see the struggle. Subaru dismissed the former out of hand, concluding it had to be the latter. Patlash didn't see it. Flower scent. Hallucination—

"…There…is…no…flower…!!"

He denied it—the flower bringing death right before his eyes. No such dangerous flower existed. Subaru was seeing a world that was not possible. Accordingly, it was a sham.

Tears clouded his vision. No, something other than tears was clouding it. Patlash's form wavered, and the fraud that he'd thought was his companion vanished. There was no one else in Subaru's virtual world.

—It was all a fraud!!

"—Ahu! Gah-ha! Geho, hnnm haa!"

The instant he shook it off, the sensation of the vine wringing his neck vanished. With a chance to breathe at last, Subaru coughed as oxygen filled his lungs, trying to see what had happened with his teary eyes.

Right in front of Subaru, the flowers that had put him through a terrifying experience were burning. Petals, vines, roots—all were enveloped in crimson flames, burning black and falling to pieces. And the one doing this was a flickering red light floating right above the burning flowers—a minor spirit.

"You again..."

It was the red minor spirit that had also saved Subaru earlier when he was the madwoman's captive. While he gasped for breath, the spirit that had rescued him from peril came right before his eyes.

Subaru immediately put his hand out, receiving the light's warmth with his palm.

"—! This means...!"

He took in that heat at the same time that the flowers finished burning away. The petals had become ash and the sweet aroma had been swapped for the stench of something burnt; immediately after, the world changed.

The highway he had thought infinite began to waver, bleeding into the sky and the forest to the left and right. The world was warping like a painting being dissolved by water. Then, in an instant, it seemed to snap right back.

The world had reconstituted itself—no, he had been freed from the illusion, and returned to the real world.

"—Subaru!"

A voice called out to him. Raising his head at the sharp voice, Subaru returned to the world as it was.

Standing right in front of him was Julius, calling to Subaru as the red spirit rested upon his shoulder.

3

"So it was you..."

"There is no mistaking that abusive tongue. I do not believe anyone could reproduce your invective toward me this faithfully."

Subaru was sour at Julius's face being the first he saw upon his return; Julius responded with mild sarcasm. However, Julius immediately pulled Subaru's arm, bringing him to his feet, and motioned with his chin toward the surrounding area.

When Subaru followed suit and looked around the area, he stood dumbfounded, gaping at the state of the expeditionary force. All the neatly lined members of the expeditionary force, man and mounted beast alike, were at a complete standstill.

"Someone has attacked us. An illusion-type incantation, but it only sent my mind astray for several seconds. At present, only you and I have returned from it. How did you come back?"

"A few seconds? On my end it was minutes. Maybe 'cause it was all in my head?"

"I never would have thought that you possess the power to resist such magic. How did you make it back?"

"Wait, everyone got trapped by this? Seconds or minutes, at this rate we'll all be stuck in place and make a real nice target. We've gotta do something!"

"That's why I'm asking you *how* you came back!"

With their mutual doubts clashing, the lack of headway aroused Julius's anger. The rare reaction shocked Subaru. Realizing it was no time to argue, he switched gears.

"It was burning the flowers inside the illusion that caused it all. Er, when I say burning, it wasn't me who burned them, but anyway, the flowers are the trigger. So by getting rid of 'em."

"Flowers…flowers, you say? I see…a suggestion incantation carried by a flower's aroma… But…"

Julius let his words trail off as he surveyed their comrades still under the spell. Then, in front of Subaru—who was wide-eyed and at a loss for what to do—he slowly raised his arms. As he did, his arms served almost like a perch as several lights emerged into view. They glowed in different colors, six in all; among them was the red light that had saved Subaru.

"You! Then that's…"

"This is the radiance given off by my little buds. I shall henceforth inform everyone of how to break the illusion—In! Nes!"

Julius, indirectly responding to Subaru, spread the fingers of his outstretched hands. The lights that seemingly glided onto his fingertips were colored white and black. The two lights intermingled, growing in intensity, and before Subaru's amazed eyes, their light enveloped the world around him.

"Wh-what's…?"

Going on? Subaru was about to say, but the change jabbed into Subaru's brain faster than he could say the words.

"Nn! Choiya! Choiya! Huh, no one's here! Where is this?!"

"Huh?"

He heard the girl's faint speech expressing incomprehension of her situation—no, strictly speaking, it was not *speech*. This was not a voice, but rather thoughts; not sound, but emotion, her will conveyed not to Subaru's eardrums, but rather directly to his brain. Nor were the thoughts hers alone.

"I've gotten lost…no, split off. This is bad, at this rate…" "Darn it, this is the worst. I keep wreckin' the forest and it don't change a thing." "This sort of trick at a time like this…! Lady Crusch…!" "Sis! Sis! Where are you?!" "TB might be crying by now!"

"Gaaaa…!"

They were flowing, flowing into him. The muddy stream of thoughts was merciless, slipping through his ears into his skull, through his skull into his brain, and pressing down upon that brain with a weight beyond what it could handle. The big helping of multiple thoughts and emotions, barbs and all, leaped around inside Subaru's skull, leaving him moaning in anguish.

He couldn't really tell if it was pain or suffering. It wasn't really pain. It wasn't really suffering. It was simply…heavy.

"—Was the sensitivity too high? I'm sorry. Please breathe deeply and bear it."

"Aarrghh, you jerk…!"

"Right now I have no time to calibrate solely for you. Getting everyone back takes precedence."

That was all Julius said before closing his eyes and ceasing to move to concentrate on his incantation.

Amid his agony, Subaru levied curses upon the handsome young man responsible for that suffering. Even when he did as told and took a deep breath, not even a smidgen of relief was forthcoming. Then, as before, his brain was filled with a multitude of thoughts. At this rate, it would soon liquefy and pour out of his ears. *I've gotta put these thoughts in order*, thought Subaru.

The muddying of thoughts and stirring of minds was Julius's doing. He'd used some kind of magic to produce that situation, allowing him to convey the means of breaking the illusion. *Think. Someone spread the flowers around inside the illusion. Several people are free of the illusion and are breaking through the vortex of thought. Still so many. So many still captured.*

Brain waves intermingled time and time again. But like thorns being removed or teeth being pulled, the number of thoughts was dropping. People were returning from the illusion's evil hand to the real world.

"At this rate, everyone shall be freed, and…"

Subaru kept scratching at his thick sweat, enduring the ragged brain waves even the ringing in his ears could not blot out. He brusquely wiped off the cold sweat dampening his brow, panting as he looked up to the sky. The next moment—

"—!"

He heard faint breathing. The source was the sky, right above Subaru's and Julius's heads. There was a break in the forest canopy in which the sun was floating in the sky, and with that sun at its back, a figure in white landed at Subaru's side.

With Julius focused on breaking the illusion and keeping his eyes closed, the figure proceeded to drag Subaru by his arm.

"Oh, wai…!"

Julius, pouring all his energy into the incantation, did not move as Subaru, caught by the white figure, nearly fell down. The figure in white, face concealed by the white robe covering it from head to toe, was set to drag Subaru off without asking. Instantly, he instinctively realized that the person before his eyes was the caster of the illusion. Of course, the Witch Cult had to be involved. If Subaru was dragged off, the expeditionary force would lose its means of resisting the Unseen Hands.

"Shit! Wait, there's no way anyone's letting you do whatever you… Uu?!"

The instant Subaru braced himself, trying to resist, his planted foot was swept away, sending Subaru flipping over, unable to even cry out. The off-the-charts martial arts skill didn't even let him get a word in.

At that rate, the figure in white would try to drag Subaru right out of that place—

"Duaaa—!"

But a cloth-rending cry and the unleashing of silver light interrupted the attempt.

Stepping forward and pounding home a sword strike was Wilhelm, the first of the others freed from the illusion. With the speed of a god, the Sword Devil unleashed his sword, seemingly to vent his rage at the one who had ensnared him in the spell. The arc traced by the slash was without mercy, set to run straight through the slender figure in white. However—

"Wbah?!"

The figure in white violently tossed Subaru into the grass and, with frightening dexterity, barely evaded the sword strike. The evasion, made with an absolute minimum of physical movement, made Wilhelm, who had been certain of a killing blow, open his eyes wide in shock.

"*—Fulla!*"

As if to blow that admiration aside, the figure thrust a cane forward with an explosion of magic. The target was the ground under Wilhelm's feet, gouging the surface out in a circle, slowing the Sword Devil down.

When Wilhelm then leaped toward his foe, slashing upward, something caught him by the chest.

"Guh…!"

Wilhelm's well-honed abdomen creaked as his body was sent flying by force unthinkable for the tiny figure's size. The cane's tip was pointed at the Sword Devil as the air twisted before it. The resulting cascade of air was about to slice deep into the Sword Devil—but a slice of steel rent it first, causing its mana to explode.

"—"

In an instant, Wilhelm went from narrowly escaping death to going on the attack, closing the distance with the white figure. Mid-range was the range at which an enemy could use magic. Wilhelm would be at a disadvantage for as long as it took to get to close range. But the Sword Devil's disadvantage was overridden by another factor—the advantage of superior numbers.

"Doraaa!!"

A great hatchet flew into the air, bearing down on the white figure's rear in a ferocious assault. Accompanied by a roar, Ricardo's blow held enough might to break through even the White Whale's bedrock-like hide. The attack, which could only blow its target away, slammed into the defenseless figure in white, sending its slender body ferociously flying away—

"What the hell?!"

But Ricardo, having delivered a blow of certain death, shouted not in victory, but in shock. The cause of that shock was the white figure sent flying—no, the enemy spinning through the air of its own volition. Frighteningly, the figure in white had turned in concert with Ricardo's strike, diminishing the power of its impact.

Subaru could only guess at the level of skill required for such a feat, which could only be called godlike.

"Your skill is splendid—but..."

"You're makin' a *big* mistake if you think you're walkin' away from this!"

Between the Sword Devil's praise and the great wolf's roar, the enemy twirled the short cane in its palms and engaged in combat.

The raging great hatchet and vertical and horizontal silver slashes leaped forth, creating a zone of certain death. The white figure seemed to dance while slipping past, weaving magic in the meantime to take both warriors on.

It was an unbelievably good fight against the two forming the main striking power of the expeditionary force. But as the battle raged between combatants beyond the ken of man, the third blade to intervene decided the matter.

"—"

"Though you are our foe, I am captivated by your skill. However, this has gone far enough."

The white figure held its breath as Julius's sword rested against its neck.

During the battle, the entire expeditionary force had been freed from the illusion. Having lost all opportunity to buy time and escape, the white figure ceased to resist. It was not just Julius, but also Wilhelm and Ricardo, from the right and left, holding the figure in check.

"The battle…has been decided."

There was nowhere to run, a fact their opponent conceded.

"…Kill me. I will not be defiled."

Surrounded by hostility, the white figure accepted its own demise with extreme apathy. The voice was high-pitched; the shoulders under the robe were slender. From the tone of voice, Subaru knew it was a girl.

Wilhelm's eyes widened at the prideful declaration; Julius's and Ricardo's eyes met. Unrest spread as the expeditionary force, now back to reality, grasped the circumstances.

"W-wait! Wait, wait! Wait a sec, please!"

It was then that Subaru, covered with grass from his tumble, raised his hand and his voice.

After being thrust into the weeds, Subaru had watched the battle, unable to help in any way, but with the match decided, the sound of the girl accepting her defeat made him come rushing to the spot.

He did it not because the opponent was a girl, but because he *knew* that voice. And when Subaru leaped forward, the opponent recognized him as well.

"—Barusu."

"Ahh, been a while since I was called that. Wait, it seriously is you?"

Deflated at the unexpected assailant's identity, Subaru let out a very long sigh. At Subaru's reaction, the person in the white robe pulled down her hood.

And so, the girl's lovely, stern face appeared, with pink hair and pale-red eyes.

"—Ram."

It was Ram, maid of Roswaal Manor.

4

"Now I suppose you will explain the meaning of all this, Barusu."

Having plunged the expeditionary force into unprecedented crisis and spectacularly giving Wilhelm and others the runaround, Ram brushed dirt off her body as her extremely displeased eyes stared daggers into Subaru.

"What's the meaning of this? Isn't that our line…?"

Squirming under the stern gaze, Subaru surveyed the sorry state of affairs along the highway. Along the highway and forest were traces of the recent battle, along with allies now freed from the illusion. Fortunately, the aftereffects from the incantation were limited to light headaches, and there were no wounded, Ram included. However, the lack of casualties did not in any way mean that the issue was settled.

How in the world did it come to this? thought Subaru, holding back a sigh as he looked at Ram.

"The gist is, you launched a preemptive strike and people fought back. Fighting your own side really sucks… Wilhelm, you're not hurt?"

"A small scratch from wind magic. I will ask Ferris about it later. More importantly, I am glad I did not get ahead of myself and slice her down. There would be no taking such a thing back."

Wilhelm lifted an arm up, showing off his sliced cuff with a strained smile. Responding to the magnanimity, Subaru put a hand to his own chest in relief.

"Wilhelm…Wilhelm van Astrea?"

Ram, arms folded while listening to Subaru and Wilhelm speak,

murmured thus when she heard the old swordsman's name. Addressed by his full name, the Sword Devil turned toward her.

"Hmm," went Ram, nodding her head. "I did not imagine the Sword Devil would be my opponent. I can accept having lost."

"Compared to my glory days, 'tis little more than a nickname. Each day, I strive to resist decay, but I cannot defeat old age. My skills are two steps behind my former peak."

"Having been laid low by such dulled skills, those words feel like irritating sarcasm."

Ram crisply cast Wilhelm's modesty aside. The Sword Devil seemed to like that attitude from Ram, but Subaru did not. He pressed Ram about the rude tone of her words.

"Hey, what's that attitude you're giving Wilhelm? Setting aside you're always like that with me, you should be politer to other people at l—ow!"

"Receive outsiders in the manner of guests, you say? I see, it is as you say. My, my, there is no excuse for my repeated rudeness, dear guests."

Flicking Subaru's nose with a finger when he drew near, Ram proceeded to elegantly bow to everyone present. As she behaved like a perfect servant, a cold smile came over her beautiful, doll-like face.

"I apologize for my repeated rudeness, but the mansion of Marquis Roswaal L. Mathers lies ahead. At present, at the command of my master, I am not receiving outsiders, so I ask that you please detour and leave."

"Slip the dagger in at the end, huh? Besides that…what the heck's that supposed to mean?"

"It means what it says. Currently, the environs of the mansion are in a state of heightened alert. I cannot allow outsiders to approach… though I suppose such words are wasted on an ingrate such as you, Barusu."

"Ingrate…?"

Subaru's expression clouded over at the appraisal he could not dismiss.

"Yes," said Ram, nodding. "Is it not so? Having received such great favor from Master Roswaal, you curry favor with another master as soon as he seems done with you. Or perhaps it was all an act to enter our good graces to begin with? If so, it would seem that you received your just deserts."

"Wait! You're getting this all wrong! You're completely misreading the circumstances!"

"So this is what a dog that bites the hand that feeds him is like."

"Listen already!"

Ram's acrimonious demeanor was a daily ritual, but the hostility included with it was the real deal. The gaze she shot Subaru's way was frigid enough to make his insides tremble, telling Subaru that something was badly wrong.

There was a reason for her to be this rigid. It was to prevent this, to not allow for any misunderstanding, that he'd—

"...Right, the letter of goodwill! That's what writing that letter was for. Didn't it reach the mansion?"

"—Letter of goodwill."

Subaru had taken pains to clear up any possible confusion about the circumstances. When he spoke the words, Ram's eyes narrowed, her reaction demonstrating that she recognized their significance.

But her reaction to the ring of those words was absolutely not a favorable one—

"...Ram, what are you angry for?"

"Certainly, a letter arrived from the royal capital. But it is useless to characterize that thing as written in goodwill."

Ram's voice had little intonation, barely holding back the fires of a burning rage. When Subaru failed to understand the meaning of her emotion, Ram snorted as she spelled it out loud and clear.

"When I think of the letter that pompous messenger arrived with... Calling a blank piece of paper a letter of goodwill is quite a farce. What did you mean by this, Barusu?"

"It was a blank piece of paper?!"

It was Subaru who was horrified at learning the incomprehensible truth. Ram continued to glare at the bewildered Subaru, anger oozing from her eyes.

"The wax was formally sealed with the Lion Rampant seal of the House of Karsten. In other words, Duchess Crusch Karsten was making a declaration of war against a rival candidate for the throne… Well, that is how we took it."

"That's crazy! Why would you decide it was that so fast…?"

Subaru was drowning in Ram's conclusion when Wilhelm intervened.

"Sending a blank letter is a method of conveying to the other party, 'We have no intent to negotiate.' It cannot be helped that they took it in that manner."

The creases of his brow knotted, a stern face on him as he shook his head toward Subaru.

"As a matter of fact, were a white letter delivered to me, I would arrive at the same judgment as she: a display of hostile intent."

"Then what happens if you seal a blank letter and send it by mistake?! If a war starts over that, what does history say—'Oops'?"

"Then one could only set the heavy burden aside and give up. That said, I did not judge hostile intent by a single piece of paper, either. But there were multiple issues, so…"

"What do you mean, multiple issues…there's even more?!"

The bad report had been more than weighty enough. Yet, there was still more on top of that?

"Two days ago, the forest around the mansion became unnaturally calm…to the point that even my eyes could catch nothing. Thereupon, an armed group appeared bearing the crest of the House of Karsten, which had declared war with the blank letter… Surely you cannot blame my little bird's heart for being on the verge of breaking?"

"Ugeh…!"

The sidelong glance Ram shot him put Subaru's flea-size heart on the verge of breaking.

Though Wilhelm had a worried look on his face, Subaru raised a hand, feeling the desire to curse Fate for the nightmarish entangling of circumstances. It was the worst diplomatic position ever.

In other words, Ram had mistaken the letter of goodwill, the Witch Cult, and the expeditionary force as signs of a hostile camp. Thus did she treat Subaru as a wicked villain who'd betrayed Emilia to Crusch.

"That's a huge misunderstanding! In the first place, do I look that cunning?!"

"Well, this is what a dog that bites the hand that feeds it looks like."

"You're still saying that?!"

"I have hardly said it enough. But it's fine. It is clear for the most part."

Though Ram's words were sharp, she'd no doubt gleaned the high points of the situation during the conversation. Perhaps that was also because she hadn't detected the intellect required for wicked scheming from Subaru's replies.

"So…you sent a blank letter by mistake and you are still Lady Emilia's dog… You're fine with that?"

"I'm not, but it's okay. Dogs are like family, so for Emilia I can be a dog, sure."

"That would be a rather base ambition, would it not?"

Wilhelm pointed out what low sights Subaru had, but Subaru, worried that the conversation wasn't progressing, shook his head. At any rate, with the misunderstanding cleared up, he had to get right to the point.

"Wilhelm included, everyone here is reinforcements—we're on your side. Anyone making you worry, we're gathered together to send 'em packing."

The worst of all misunderstandings threatened to bring the hard-won alliance crashing down. Aghast at that fact, Subaru puffed his chest out, establishing his goodwill toward Ram.

Ram furrowed her brows, so Subaru got to the point.

"I fulfilled the objective of me staying in the royal capital—an alliance between Emilia and Crusch, as equals. The people gathered here are the proof."

5

Immediately afterward, they set off toward Earlham Village with Ram in tow.

They had no time to waste. The misunderstanding-driven combat with Ram had cost them even more. Subaru endeavored to explain things to her while they headed toward the village.

That included the fact that they were allied camps. He was grateful his comrades in the expeditionary force were taking things so well. They'd accepted Subaru's earnest apology and Ram's gratitude for their help after her initial hostility, taking it all in stride. Thanks to the zero casualties, those words had ended the matter.

"You did give Wilhelm some trouble…but he even hid the wound from it."

"A fine man, just as the rumors said."

"Oh, yeah. He is, isn't he?"

"What are you so pleased for, Barusu? It is creepy."

Subaru, gripping the reins, overreacted as he agreed with the words of praise for the Sword Devil. The sight of it brought a genuine scowl to Ram's face; one of the hands on Subaru's hips jabbed him in the flank.

At present, Subaru and Ram were riding together on the jet-black land dragon's back. Subaru turned his head just enough to look at Ram, who was sitting behind him, as he thought back to the earlier battle.

"I have to ask…what was with that illusion attack earlier? I thought the only magic you could use was wind magic? No one told me about that part."

"It is a mixture of wind-type magic and a hallucinatory drug. I had truly intended only to whisk the commander away while the others were weighed down…but I never imagined *you* would be able to break free."

There Ram's words trailed off. She nodded to herself a few times and said, "You probably gained a resistance to the drug. The drug is derived from the leaves in the tea you always drank, after all."

"I was drinking that poison every time?!"

"I am kidding."

It hadn't sounded like she was joking, but Subaru did not press the issue further—not purely because he was afraid to know whether it was true or false, but also because he felt the trembling in the arms with which she touched him.

Realizing that her trying to break the tension had resulted in him blurting something out in plain sight, he said, "Sorry I made you put your guard up like that. Whatever the cause, you were pretty serious back there, huh?"

"I suppose… Serious enough to be resolved to take my foe down with me. Can I truly trust the gentlemen behind us?"

"Or what, they'll seize the chance to march on the mansion? A pretty nasty bunch is after the place, after all. Even Crusch doesn't really want that much trouble."

"…So it is outlaws lurking in the forest that are after Lady Emilia, then."

"I really did write about that in the letter, y'know…"

With Ram unexpectedly hinting at the Witch Cult's presence, Subaru could only lament the cause of the jumbled circumstances. Upon his opening the lid of his painstakingly acquired insurance, it had turned into the greatest of all traps. However, the singular fact that a blank letter of goodwill had arrived brought a different problem into sharp relief—

Namely, that someone out there had swapped his letter of goodwill, aiming to turn Emilia and Crusch against each other.

"What happened with the messenger who brought the letter to the mansion?"

"We politely granted him our hospitality. After all, I thought that he might prove useful in the event of a prisoner exchange."

"Prisoner exchange…?"

Even if a prisoner exchange with the Crusch camp truly came to pass, the only people from the Emilia camp to have returned were Subaru and Rem.

When Subaru thought back to the surprise attack, he remembered that Rem's first move had been to try to drag Subaru off without a care as to appearances. Perhaps the purpose of that aggressive operation had been to get the "imprisoned" Subaru back.

Though even if he asked Ram about it, there was probably no way in hell she'd give him a straight answer.

Either way, she already had someone from the most powerful candidate in her grasp. If the messenger proved to be a spy, she would interrogate him, simple as that.

"Anyway, you can relax about the enemies hiding in the forest. We've already smashed seventy percent of them. We have a way to draw out the last thirty percent, too."

"...The enemy is seventy percent crushed? Barusu, are you are saying that you destroyed them?"

He'd conveyed the state of the battle with the aim of changing the subject, but Ram was taken aback upon hearing the words. In modern warfare, losing 30 percent of your fighting strength was considered being routed, but even in an age without modern logistics, 70 percent was a considerable number. The Witch Cult was on the verge of being wiped out.

"But where they're concerned, they've gotta be annihilated down to the last man. Besides, the fewer they are, the more time it'll take to find 'em. Plus, it might make them desperate."

"So that is why you assembled the transportation needed to evacuate... Holing up in the mansion is a poor plan, I take it?"

"These guys would set it on fire and not even blink. We have a lot of memories of that mansion, so I don't wanna see it go up in smoke. Easy to understand why running is better, huh?"

Along with the reinforcements he'd brought were the horde of traveling merchant dragon carriages. When he explained the force's various objectives, Ram closed her eyes, sinking into thought. Many of them were the result of Subaru's own independent decision making. It was natural for her to be bewildered by it all—and yet:

"Sorry to act out of turn, but this is my decision. As for the right to decide...Roswaal's not at the mansion, is he?"

"—That's right. Right now, Master Roswaal is traveling to Garf's... to the sanctuary. Currently, I am under instructions to obey Lady Emilia's commands."

"Did Emilia order you to smack anyone approaching the village with illusions?"

"That was my independent judgment."

"Figures."

Even if she was backed into a corner, it would have been far too violent an order for Emilia to give. Subaru patted his chest, relieved at the fact.

"...You are naive to be relieved about that part, Barusu."

"Ah?"

"I said, the village has come into view."

Subaru hadn't caught her murmur the first time, so he thought Ram had repeated her words as she pointed forward. At her urging, Subaru turned his eyes to the road ahead; the entrance to Earlham Village truly was within view.

The highway, continuing to infinity within the illusion, had come to an end. To Subaru, it had been a very long road, enough to make the proper return a sight for sore eyes.

"I'm finally back..."

Not once but twice had he returned to find the village a tragic sight. When he had returned to the village before that, Subaru's mind had been whittled down to the bone. So to him, this was a first.

"But...doesn't feel like there's much of a welcome."

The expeditionary force passed through the entrance, entering the village square. Amid that imposing atmosphere, the villagers poked their heads out of the surrounding homes one after another. However, the expressions on their faces were certainly not sunny; naturally, they were ones of worry and confusion. Subaru could hardly blame them; an armed group had suddenly appeared in the village's midst.

"Ram, how much did you tell the villagers?"

"...I warned them not to wander outside the village and to stay out of the forest. I did not touch upon any of the details."

"Okay. Nice call."

If the Witch Cult was even guessed at, the village would surely be in chaos. Perhaps Ram was to be commended for keeping that part a secret, considering that she had thought the Crusch camp was her enemy.

"Hey, isn't that…Master Subaru and Miss Ram?"

"It really is. So Master Subaru has come back…"

One by one, the villagers began to realize that it was Subaru and Ram on dragon-back. With all eyes upon them, seemingly in charge of the group, Subaru got off Patlash, judging it a good time to do so. He was probably best suited to explain the situation.

"Barusu…"

"Just wait a minute. I'll talk to 'em—Wilhelm, Julius, Ricardo."

Subaru put a hand up to Ram and addressed the three heaviest hitters of the expeditionary force. He chose them because they would amplify his persuasiveness to the villagers. They weren't just reliable; they looked the part. Subaru brought the three with him as he walked straight into the center of the village square.

"Subaru, it would seem that they are concerned. Do not neglect to be considerate."

Nodding at Julius's whisper, Subaru took a deep breath before loudly clapping his hands together. Seeing the Subaru they knew so well do this made the villagers widen their eyes, wondering what was going on. Seeing from their reactions that he'd nicely gathered their attention, Subaru opened his mouth to set their concerns at ease.

"Yes, everyone's attention, please! Hi, it's been a while. It's been a few days, but is everyone doing okay?"

"…"

"I know coming back like this is really sudden, but today, I'm asking everyone to do something."

After a modest greeting, Subaru switched to the topic at hand. The way Subaru raised his voice made the villagers, surrounding him from a distance, look at one another's faces.

They all knew Subaru, and he knew all of them. Understanding their worry and confusion, Subaru spoke in the gentlest voice he could, but also laid things out very quickly. He wanted to convey the situation with haste, enough to deny them time to think about other choices—and enough to make evacuation a reality.

"Actually, the demon beasts in the forest seem to be getting bad again. These are the people brought in to wipe them out...but I want everyone away from the village until that work is done. Of course, I prepared the transportation in advance. It might not be that comfy a ride, but..."

Hiding the lie behind a layer of truth, Subaru selected words that would not startle the villagers as he continued speaking. Their memories of the demon beast–related crisis two months before were surely still fresh. He had to be convincing when he told them that the forest beyond the barrier still harbored demon beasts.

Behind him, they could see an expeditionary force formed of veterans and numerous traveling merchant dragon carriages to transport them. Even if it felt high-handed to him, Subaru pushed forward while concealing that the Witch Cult was attacking. However—

"The evacuation will be for half a day at shortest, one or two days at most. Sorry to cause trouble for everyone, but please accept this as the safest way to..."

"—Why are you lying to us like this?"

—In the end, that was a judgment formed according to Subaru's notions of common sense.

"Huh?"

Subaru's eyes widened at the sudden interjection. The one who had spoken was a youth with a crew cut. As one of the village's band of young men, he had exchanged words with Subaru numerous times.

It seemed that he'd spontaneously blurted it out, but when Subaru met his eyes, he hesitated for a moment before stepping forward.

"You bring a huge group of outsiders...to hunt demon beasts? Why tell us something like...?"

"Because, hey, it's dangerous. I mean there was the demon beast ruckus not long ago, right? We need to deal with it before it becomes that bad this time around, so..."

"Don't try to pull the wool over our eyes!"

Subaru tried to correct the precarious atmosphere, but the young man would not lend Subaru his ear. His unsophisticated face had a scowl on it, his fist shaking as he glared at Subaru.

Upon it were repressed rage and despair, and irrepressible fear.

"Master Subaru, you said you were trying to clear up our concerns, but…doing it this way is making everyone in the village afraid! We've been thinking the Witch Cult is up to something the whole time!"

"Uh…"

The young man visibly lost his temper as he shouted, instantly making Subaru's words catch in his throat.

The youngster's voice echoed around the village, spreading unrest among the villagers, and, naturally, among the traveling merchants as well. There was no unrest in the expeditionary force, but the turbulent flow of discourse made their faces grow graver as well.

"You're…not denying it, are you…?"

The young man weakly murmured, finding his answer in Subaru's silent demeanor. The sight caused an outburst of unrest among the villagers, making their pent-up worries pour out all at once.

"So the people from the mansion really were talking about the Witch Cult yesterday… Why are they in a remote place like this…?"

"That's obvious, that's obvious, isn't it? It's because the lord did something like *that*!"

"Why must he support a half-elf…a half-demon…?"

The worries spoken by one set of lips after another made it painfully clear that Subaru's efforts to smooth things over had resulted in the opposite effect. The villagers had understood long before: the unrest enveloping their village was not unrelated to Emilia, residing at the mansion of the lord of the land.

They were not conveniently ignorant. It was only natural that they would reject Subaru's plan.

"Hold on a minute! I'm sorry! I was wrong, and I apologize! But…"

"—"

Accepting that his effort to convince them had failed, Subaru voiced an apology. At the same time, he realized something.

Among the villagers, some lamented, some raged, some glared. Those negative actions were not caused by their difficult-to-resist fear of the Witch Cult. Their negative energy was trained not toward the Cult, but toward the half-elf who had yet to show herself.

"What makes you think that?! Don't you realize it's got nothing to do with half-elves or Emilia?" Subaru exclaimed.

"How can it not be related?! The Witch Cult rampages against anything related to half-demons. Even the children of the village know that much! And yet, the lord not only shelters a half-demon, he nominates her to be the nation's king! This is no joke!"

"—!"

The youth's anger shocked Subaru; the near scream cut into him like a blade. His reaction made the youth's eyes freeze over as he looked downward. But he did not amend his statement.

When Subaru looked around, he saw, to a greater or lesser extent, the same emotion in the eyes of the other villagers.

"Is that what you all think? You think it's all the fault of the half-elf in the mansion?"

There was no reply. They seemed to think silence was more eloquent than anything they could say.

These were the friendly villagers he'd spent so much time with. Though it had only been two short months, so many things had happened that Subaru felt deepened the friendship they shared with one another. That was why he had been so desperate to save them.

He'd believed that they would accept his feelings without suspicion or doubt...and yet.

"This was just me getting ahead of myself again...?"

He'd underestimated the deep-rooted fear of the Witch Cult planted in every human being of that world. Even people who believed in Subaru's innate goodness could not defy the scars of history.

That fact made Subaru weakly slump his shoulders—but the next moment, his shoulders were slapped from behind.

From very close, an individual patted Subaru's shoulders, moving parallel to him while exhaling.

"Raise your head—after all, Lady Crusch says you should never lower your sights."

"You..."

"Do you think what you're doing is wrong...? If you don't think that, you don't need to look down."

Ferris's firm declaration surprised Subaru, coming from the last person he would have expected to console him. So, too, was he surprised at the memory that Ferris's words spurred him to recall.

They were words Crusch had actually spoken to Subaru, albeit during a different time around from the present.

"Besides, wasn't recklessly picking fights at the castle a lot harder than raising your head here?"

"...Now hold on."

Ferris's taunting comment made Subaru's shoulders go slack in a way that was very out of place. Subaru wondered just how long he was going to be made fun of for that single moment. But—

"—Yeah. Compared to that, this is nothin'."

As much as his words had been rejected, he did not doubt that he was doing the right thing.

He understood that the villagers had an aversion toward half-elves. That very cruel fact caused a dark shadow to fall over Subaru's heart. But that reality was absolutely not something he could do anything about now. It was something to be changed by Emilia's future actions, with Subaru at her side.

"It's not somethin' I can do anything about just by saying 'I'm gonna change it.' Not when I haven't managed anything else yet."

As much as he thought their assessment was unfair, all he could do was show them results big enough to make them see her in a new light. And Subaru and the others were acting to create the time necessary for him to do so.

—Subaru Natsuki wanted to believe that was the reason he had come again like this.

"From what you've said, I understand how you all feel. I won't tell you, 'Drop everything and come with me.' It's natural you all have your thoughts on it. It hurts, but I get that, too."

"Master Subaru..."

"But for now, please, swallow it down. I really do understand all the feelings you're trying to put into words. So please, do as I say right now so we can speak properly about it later. The village really is in danger."

When Subaru spoke those words, training earnest eyes toward them, the villagers kept their silence, saying nothing. With silence falling over the village, Subaru thought their reaction very sad. At this rate, all he'd have done was spend time in futility.

However, it was Ram who sternly smashed the stalemate asunder.

"—The words of a servant of our house are the commands of Master Roswaal, lord of this land. You serfs never had any right of refusal to begin with. Come now, hurry and obey your instructions."

Having observed on the sidelines up to that point, Ram had stepped out of the ranks of the expeditionary force to stand alongside Subaru as she confronted the villagers. The overbearing glint in her eye and the authority of her statement surprised and unnerved the villagers.

"H-hold on! I get why you're putting it harshly, but you don't have to put it like that. Everyone has their own lives. It's only natural they'd be thrown off like..."

"It would seem you, like these villagers, are insufficiently aware of the greatness of your lord."

When Subaru objected to Ram's high-handed statement, Ram glared at Subaru with an exasperated air.

"If you incur issues or damages due to the evacuation, our landlord shall take responsibility and compensate you. If any of you object, come forth and state your names. This is Master Roswaal's decision."

The way she said it was stern; her meaning was severe as well. But though she had been uncompromising, the contents of her proposal soothed the concerns of the populace, leaving Subaru and the villagers in awe. Everyone understood: by backing up Subaru's words with the authority of the landlord, Ram gave the villagers what they needed to agree.

"Ahh, sorry for Ram's harsh way of saying it, but what I want hasn't changed. Everyone needs to evacuate the village. I realize that it's so sudden you can't properly prepare."

"..."

"That's why I'll take responsibility and talk to Roswaal about proper compensation for damages. I want everyone to at least believe me about that. Please."

Accepting Ram's viewpoint, Subaru appealed not to emotion, but to logic. Between Ram's calm and Subaru's urgings, the villagers were silent for a time. Then they nodded in apparent resignation.

They were a long way from liking it. However, they'd given their consent. The evacuation could begin.

"Sigh..."

When, with one thing settled, Subaru breathed out with relief, he was joined by the comrades standing in a row behind him. Everyone had been tense and anxious, but somehow, they'd climbed that mountain.

"I've gotta say, though."

"What?"

Subaru shared in his comrades' relief before proceeding to look at Ram, standing right beside him. Ram had a suspicious look in response to that gaze, but there was no question that it had been her words that had given the final push. He thought that was very Ram-like—hard edged, difficult to fathom, but kind.

"Having you tell people to do what I say is new. Does this mean you've accepted me?"

"Hah!"

Ram snorted. Somehow—just a little bit—he took solace in her demeanor.

6

The evacuation would last for two days at most. So it would begin as soon as the minimum supplies needed for that time were loaded.

The conditions Subaru placed on the villagers were very grudgingly accepted.

"There's fifteen dragon carriages. If we put seven people on almost each one, we should be able to get everyone aboard with room to spare."

Subaru had asked the young men of the village to take a roll call, ensuring every villager was accounted for. Now that they were evacuating, they surely didn't want to cause any extra trouble. Though they still dealt with the expeditionary force rather awkwardly, they dutifully did as they were told.

There was just one issue that couldn't be left unresolved—

"Explaining this to Lady Emilia and Lady Beatrice at the mansion, yes?" Ram said, hands on her hips as her eyes shifted to the path going from the village to the mansion.

The issues for proceeding with preparations to evacuate had been resolved. The mansion was another issue. And for Subaru, it posed the largest problem of all.

"I thought the village was pretty agitated, but what's Emilia been up to?"

The time had moved past early morning, finally entering the period one could call "morning" proper. Even if most human beings would be asleep at that hour, it was difficult for him to believe that Emilia could sleep soundly given the state of the Mathers domain over the last few days.

Ram's testimony had already made clear that Emilia had had no role in Ram's attack. But the fact that Emilia hadn't responded to the unrest in the forest tugged at his mind.

Ram responded to Subaru's suspicions by lowering her eyes with a faintly melancholic look.

"She was busy until late evening, so she should still be resting at the moment. Ever since returning from the capital in a state of despair, she has been weary, lacking any time to put her heart at ease."

"Unghh..."

"She has the look of someone who has been put through a distasteful ordeal by a man."

"Don't attach *distasteful* to it, okay?! …Not that I'm denying it…"

Her third-party opinion magnified Subaru's feelings of guilt all at once. It was natural that the events at the capital had greatly wounded Emilia. He could not disagree with Ram's scornful opinion of him.

"While Master Roswaal is absent, it is up to Lady Emilia to deal with anything amiss at the mansion and the village. But you can understand the villagers' reactions to Lady Emilia from their earlier demeanor, yes?"

"I can picture it, but I don't really want to put it into words… Rejection, huh?"

"'Rejection'? A rather simplistic impression, isn't it?"

Ram laughed loudly at Subaru's words, her face immediately turning more cheerful.

"—More like repudiation. If you have been rejected, you can always reach out again. If one's outstretched hand has been brushed aside, that means there has been contact. But what if you have been repudiated instead?"

"…"

"If it is disgusting to even touch, one must wonder how one closes the distance."

Subaru made no reply to Ram's argument, seemingly made to test him. Ram didn't seem to be looking for an answer, either. "I said something mean," she said immediately with a sigh.

"Lady Emilia realized there was something amiss in the forest and attempted to have the villagers take shelter in the mansion. Then the villagers repudiated her. She is not someone sensible enough to withdraw immediately after being repudiated, something I imagine you know for yourself, Barusu."

"But I also know that she's not a girl who'll get hit with cruel words and not be hurt."

Emilia had been trying to deal with the Witch Cult unrest in her own Emilia-like way. However, that way was not enough to soften the hard hearts the villagers bore toward half-elves.

Or perhaps the villagers' excessive reaction was the result of their speaking with her.

"So what'd Emilia do after?"

"After repeated attempts at persuasion were declined, she was unable to sit still, so she went around reweaving the barriers around the village. After all, as we had not judged the unrest to be from the Witch Cult, she feared it might be demon beasts."

"Well, that wasn't really a bad call, but..."

"After that, the blank declaration of war arrived last evening, so she was fretting about that until the morning."

"So that pops up here, too..."

While Ram spoke as if it were light banter, Subaru could only lament that the letter had done damage on another front. The report on events in the capital, evacuation preparations, Emilia and Ram's concerns, Ram's independent actions—the secondary damage was a gift that kept on giving. For such a simple trick, the effects were all too painful.

"In any case, with this much advance preparation to evacuate, Lady Emilia is unlikely to object. If we report to her at the mansion, it should make her agree immediately."

"..."

"Barusu?"

"No, I get it. Just makes my heart hurt a little."

With Ram looking suspicious, Subaru shook his head, conscious of his quickening heartbeats. Here, on the brink of a reunion with Emilia, his tension was at its zenith.

Just as Ram saw it, Emilia was *not* the kind of girl who'd reject the cooperation of so many people. Hence, Subaru's stress and worry were an issue of Subaru's own heart.

"Julius, come with me, 'kay? I'm heading to the mansion to convince Emilia and the loli."

"Me?"

As he hardened his resolve, Subaru looked around him and called for Julius. Subaru nodded at Julius, whose face showed that the nomination had come unexpectedly.

"Yeah. I'm a lot more convincing with you beside me than not. You'll be my proof that I've behaved and repented after all the stuff at the castle."

"I see, very well. If it will make the talk go more smoothly, use me to your heart's content."

His handsome face indicated consent, elegantly nodding at Subaru's suggestion. The gesture made Subaru grimace.

Ram, glancing sidelong at the exchange, sighed as she said, "A petty and very Barusu-like little trick."

"Hey, don't call it petty. Call it paying attention to the little details. Ahh, Julius, besides that."

"What is it?"

"You're the one who stuck a spirit on me, right? I want a proper explanation."

The offhanded way Subaru made the remark made even Julius look apprehensive. His reaction made Subaru avert his eyes, a guilty look on his face as he continued:

"Now look, I've been saved two times now with my life on the line, so I get that you're a spirit mage whether I like it or not."

"I would prefer you called me by the proper title, spirit knight. I employ spiritual spells, of course, but I do not recall skimping on my sword training."

Giving that reply, Julius stared at Subaru's face with utmost seriousness.

"...You are unexpectedly calm. I was thoroughly convinced you would find my being a spirit user to be distasteful."

"Even I can account for time, place, circumstances, and person once in a while. There are times when I haven't, though."

Subaru, eyes still averted, made a pained smile as he motioned toward Julius's right arm. There emerged the minor spirits that Subaru had seen during Ram's attack, seemingly orbiting the arm.

The flickering spirits numbered six in total, each one lovingly nestling close to Julius's arm.

However beautiful and fickle they looked, they were beings imbued with supernatural power.

"As you have surmised, these girls are spirits—known as common spirits—that I have formed a pact with. They are buds yet to bloom into distinct categories of spirits. I borrow their strength through my pledge to become a knight worthy of the beautiful flowers they shall become."

"So you had the red one keep an eye on me?"

One of the minor spirits resting on Julius's palm was the red one that had leaped out of Subaru's hair during the illusion. When he thought back, it was that same scarlet minor spirit that had appeared when he had been captured by the crazed woman.

All of it was Julius's doing. Twice, Subaru had been saved by him in his time of need.

"It is hurtful to hear you call it keeping an eye on you. She was protecting you from the shadows."

"...Incidentally, what was that thing you used when you were breaking the illusion?"

Julius had used some kind of magic to share the method of breaking the illusion with every member of the group. As a result, Subaru's brain had been put through the wringer from the multiple thoughts passing through it.

"That was magic cast through borrowing the power of In and Nes, combining Dark with Light...that is Nekt, an advanced magic spell. It links the Gates of all human beings within range, enabling thoughts to pass between them. Though it seems to have been rather too effective upon you."

"Yeah. I thought I wasn't gonna be me anymore."

"As a matter of fact, there is no question it is a difficult spell to employ. After all, it is a ritual to thin the boundaries between you and the minds of others. If deepened to excess, not only thoughts but also the five senses can be commingled. I'm sure you experienced the fear of being consumed by others to a fair extent?"

"That's walking one hell of a tightrope!"

Subaru was aghast at learning far too late that he had crossed a more precarious bridge than he had even imagined.

Julius turned a look of deep interest toward him and said, "But it is rare for the buds to make a mistake when tuning it. Perhaps you possess an unusually high affinity for spirits… Does anything along those lines come to mind?"

"Sorry, the only spirit I get along with is a mouse-colored cat."

On top of that, right then, he had no confidence that he could ever approach that cat in the same way as before.

"If you have an opportunity, you should try to learn the basics of spiritualism from Lady Emilia. If she is resistant to teaching you, I would be willing to aid you myself."

"I'm not sure what brought on this sudden outpouring of friendliness, but it doesn't sound like an instant process, so I'll pass for now."

He didn't deny that the suggestion held its attractions, but Subaru reflexively declined the offer. His reaction made Julius pull back, seemingly disappointed, when Subaru simultaneously remembered something.

Ferris had told him. Subaru was still subconsciously harboring enmity toward Julius—just as he had at that very moment.

"Can't I do something about that?"

The first time, Ram had interrupted, but was it not the time to properly clear up the ill feelings between them?

With such thoughts in Subaru's mind, his gaze caused Julius to incline his own head. Subaru narrowed his eyes at the handsome young man fluent with words, anguished in the attempt to somehow spit out serious words of his own. But—

"…I understand that you don't feel like putting all your cards on the table, but right now you've gotta put up with it. There'll be problems with our teamwork if we don't know what the other can do, right?"

"—Mmm, understood. If possible, I would like to put Ia on you again. Please grant your consent."

In the end, hesitation clogged up Subaru's throat, and all he could manage was to keep his statement inoffensive.

While Subaru's thoughts were elsewhere, the red minor spirit called Ia circled above his head. It proceeded to land on the crown of Subaru's head, asserting its existence with a faint emission of heat.

"Hey, this isn't gonna make me bald, is it? I'll have you know I'm trying to go through life without becoming bald or chubby..."

"She's been nestled against you until now without you even noticing, yes? It is especially so for those with a high affinity for spirits. Your Gate will acclimate quickly, and you will cease to notice her."

In accordance with this lecture, Subaru immediately stopped feeling the heat on the crown of his head. The principles were unclear to him, but she had apparently slipped inside Subaru. That faint heat was the only thing he'd felt from it.

"What should I do to call it out?"

"She responds to the name Ia. As she cannot respond to commands that are too complex or beyond her power, please do not forget to be as considerate as when approaching any lady."

Apparently, in other words, *read the mood*—not Subaru's strong suit.

"Now then, Barusu, will you finally put your cowardice aside?"

Ram, looking tired of waiting, cut into the pair's conversation. She was leaning on a fence, and her jaw was firm as she indicated the road running from the village to the mansion.

"Or do you intend to let a defenseless girl, her mana all used up, walk such a dangerous mountain road alone?"

"More like you ran out of gas doing friendly fire. To be honest, I didn't know you had that in you..."

He was genuinely surprised at her combat ability. She could even take Wilhelm on, if only for a short period. However, he could not wipe away his disappointment—including at how a crucial scene had gone up in smoke.

"Had Master Wilhelm been at full strength, I would not have lasted ten seconds. After all, my power has fallen two steps...no, four steps from its peak."

"Why'd you make it double Wilhelm's? Stubbornness?"

"Pride."

It was an exceptionally Ram-like statement, and for that matter, it was likely the literal truth. Subaru couldn't even imagine how astounding Ram had been before she had lost her horn.

"That probably accounts for why Rem dwelled on it so much…"

"Did you say something, Barusu?"

"Nothing at all, Big Sis. If I spill the beans that much, it'll make for more scary people to deal with."

"—?"

Ram was suspicious about his demeanor, but Subaru avoided saying any more at that juncture. He was hesitating about Rem—her little sister—and all the feelings Subaru bore toward her. More than any other, it was thanks to Rem that Subaru had overcome his trials at the royal capital and was standing there.

In that moment, the importance of Rem's existence rivaled that of Emilia's inside Subaru. But considering the time and place, explaining those difficult-to-describe emotions to her older sister just wasn't happening there and then.

He could face that, and all the other concerns, after everyone had overcome the current state of affairs.

"We have to explain the alliance, too, so we should grab Ferris and head to the mansion, huh?"

Someone from the Crusch camp was required for smoothly clearing up the misunderstanding from the letter of goodwill incident. They'd leave most of the expeditionary force to guard the villagers, with several heavy hitters joining him on his way up to the mansion.

"So about Ferris… What's he up to anyway?"

Subaru, searching for any sight of the kitty-eared knight in the village, finally spotted him at a corner of the village square. There rested the merchants' dragon carriages in a line; Ferris was surrounded by their owners, engaged in some kind of argument.

"It is because the circumstances with the Witch Cult have come to light. They might be venting their frustrations about it."

"Geh… Well, I suppose they would. Sorry, I'll go mediate a little."

Scowling at Julius's guess, Subaru headed toward them. Ram seemed beside herself as she watched him go. Ferris was clearly relieved when Subaru wedged himself into the center of the dispute.

"Ah, Subawu..."

"Okay, that's enough! Can someone explain to me what this argument's about?"

"They keep saying, 'This wasn't the deal'! Even though I told them again and again that Ferri doesn't represent the group..."

"That's right, pal. You're the one we wanted to talk to!"

This time, instead of Ferris, whose cheeks swelled up in a huff, the angry voices poured onto Subaru. Breathing raggedly through his nose, the merchants' representative—an individual named Kety—jabbed his finger into Subaru.

"The deal... Well, I suppose not?"

"Of course it's not! There's no mistaking what you told us: 'Help us evacuate people while we exterminate demon beasts.' And when we open the lid, what's inside?!"

Kety, his face red with anger, pressed roughly against Subaru's chest and said, "It turns out to be trouble involving the Witch Cult! This is quite a fraud, you know? What the hell are you up to, dropping that kind of huge lie at our feet?!"

Accosted in such a threatening manner, Subaru was of course taken aback by the sheer force of it.

They were right to be angry about circumstances not corresponding to the explanation they'd been given beforehand. That said, Subaru was at a loss for how to apologize to Kety, who was vehement to the point of incoherence. Then—

"If that's the case, how about we make a more tangible apology by raising the reward, *meow*?"

"—Wha...? You sure got more sensible than earlier all of a sudden."

Kety's smile toward Ferris, hiding behind Subaru's back as he made the proposal, deepened further. Inside, Subaru breathed a sigh of relief that his demand was so straightforward. If they'd gotten bent out of shape Subaru would be right back to square one. A little extra damage to Roswaal's coffers was no great concern.

"The original condition was to name our price. Can we expect double that?"

"Because you're greedy, *meow*... Where is your register? I'll review the contents with Subawu."

"Hey! Do we have to do that...? Doesn't human life come first?" Subaru's eyes widened as Ferris drove the conversation further and further afield.

Kety, having just handed the register over to Ferris, gave a mean-spirited look down at Subaru and said, "This is a huge issue related to the lives we'll be leading tomorrow. But if you don't want to, that's fine."

"...I'm just grumblin'."

Cowed by Kety's downward gaze, Subaru grudgingly climbed into the wagon of his dragon carriage. So far as he could tell, the register listed all the cargo the carriages hauled, as well as personal accessories and jewelry and the like, in an unexpectedly meticulous manner.

"Even though the owner's so violent, *meow*?"

"I had the same thought, but why are we doing this together? Go thataway or somethin'."

"This'll be done faster if two people are checking, yes? And it's not like he minds, *meow*."

Ferris snuggled against Subaru as they checked the cargo in the curtained wagon. Subaru raised his eyebrows at Ferris's pushy demeanor when Ferris narrowed his eyes and said, "More importantly...making up with Julius? Did you do it?"

"...Concerning that issue, after much consideration and study, I wish to approach the matter with positivity and discretion."

"I thought so, *meow*. I thought, *It's Subawu, so he'll mess it up for sure*. And after you said all that cool stuff in front of the villagers, too—"

Ferris put a hand on his mouth and giggled, showing no sign of ceasing his teasing look. Subaru, feeling burned at the teasing over earlier events and his lingering resentment toward Julius, continued the inspection, comparing cargo to the register.

"Well, it wasn't a bad try, *meow*? All you have to do is apologize to Julius with the same intensity..."

"Why you little...!"

"Hey now, don't start a lover's quarrel inside someone else's dragon carriage. Get the work done already."

When he talked back at Ferris for making light of his situation, Kety made his disapproval with both of them very clear. When his tall frame lumbered over, he was even more sour about Subaru and Ferris's lack of concentration.

"I can yell at you more, you know. If you'd rather I don't, get serious."

"Y-yeah, sorry. We'll do it right..."

"Uh-oh, he's angry with you, Subawu. Sheesh, you really are a handful, *meow*."

Seizing on Kety's anger, Ferris hopped away from Subaru's side. Subaru had just about had enough of his antics. But before he could raise a coarse voice—

"—So careless of you."

"Guh—?!"

When Ferris murmured, narrowing his yellow eyes, he touched Kety's exposed arm. The next moment, the tall man let out an anguished cry, his eyes rolling up as he toppled onto his side.

"Huh...?"

"Subawu, don't just stare like that. Stand watch outside so that no one notices."

All trace of levity gone, Ferris gave crisp instructions to Subaru, who was taken aback by the sudden series of events. But Subaru was rooted to the spot, unable to understand what had just taken place. Seeing this, Ferris sighed and explained.

"This person is part of the Witch Cult. I touched him to check earlier when all those people were around me; he has the same weird ritual embedded in him as the Archbishop of the Seven Deadly Sins' finger had earlier."

"—?! He's a Witch Cultist?! And a Sloth on top of that?!"

"The possibility is high. That's why I thought I'd get into the dragon carriage to lower his guard."

As Ferris replied to the wide-eyed Subaru, he checked Kety's fallen body and found something. When he lifted a hand, it was holding a cross-shaped sword furnished by the Witch Cult.

"That's one of the swords the Witch Cultists… They seriously infiltrated the traveling merchants…?"

"But we captured this one alive. The instant I touched him, I made the water in his body run wild and knocked him out. Though if I've directly affected someone even once, I can do the same thing without even touching, *meow*."

"…Meaning you can do the same thing to me. Kinda gives me the chills to hear that…"

Grudgingly, Subaru did as Ferris directed and checked on things beyond the curtain. Fortunately, no one on the outside seemed to have noticed the skirmish inside the carriage. No one else seemed to be coming aboard.

"But if one of them was a Witch Cultist, that changes everything."

"We can't be certain they don't have others among the merchants…but we can check that from here on out, I suppose?"

Subaru was chagrined at the plan backfiring, but Ferris shook his head as if it was no big deal. After that, he gave the unmoving Kety a smack on the cheek, then pressed a palm, glowing with a pale light, to his face and said, "Now, spill out everything that you're planning, would you? Ferri's hand is the gentlest in the world…but it can do such terrible things, *meow*?"

"—"

Subaru's body shuddered when he remembered the phrase *Those who know how to heal people also know how to break them.*

Ferris's request made Kety open his eyelids a crack, gazing at Ferris with unfocused eyes. His lips frailly struggled to move, but Ferris's power was supreme. He apparently couldn't move at all.

"Ferris, be careful. If he is a Sloth, even if he can't move his limbs…"

"He can still use his power, yes? That's why I have you watching, Subawu."

Just because the flesh could not move didn't mean Unseen Hands couldn't be put into motion. In accordance with Ferris's request, Subaru squared his shoulders and kept the closest eye possible on what Kety was doing.

With Subaru and Ferris both hemming him in, Kety breathed out, seemingly deflated. Then—

"—"

"What?"

When Kety seemed to murmur something, Ferris narrowed his eyes, demanding he repeat himself. Subaru hadn't been able to hear the statement, either. Kety opened his mouth once more—

"—YES."

"—! Ia! Protect him!!"

Ferris seemed to leap to his feet the instant the whisper reached his eardrums, calling to Subaru, at the entrance to the wagon—no, to the common spirit tethered to him.

Ferris's gravity, normally unthinkable for him, made Subaru stare for a second, wondering what had happened, when…

"Ah?"

With a burst of heat, the common spirit flew out, deploying a crimson wall of shimmering light around his entire body. It enveloped Subaru, completely isolating him from his surroundings—

"Now cooomes the beginning…of the end!!"

Frozen stiff, Subaru heard a shrill voice saying that right before his eyes.

The next moment, Subaru was engulfed by the flames of the exploding dragon carriage, losing all track of which way was up.

CHAPTER 4

A CRAFTY SLOTH

1

When Subaru's mind returned to reality, the first thing he took in was the powerful stench of something burnt.

It was like meat that had been barbecued to ash, stir-fried vegetables that had been fried black, completely and thoroughly burnt from too much heat inside and outside, a scent that brought one's mood to its nadir.

"—"

He opened his mouth, trying to get his voice out. He couldn't hear a thing. It was not that sound did not reach his eardrums, but rather that too great a sound had slammed into them a moment prior. A sound far too great to be termed *ringing* echoed through his skull at length, leaving Subaru to expect little from his hearing for the time being.

"—"

Subaru continued instinctively raising his voice as he relied on his other senses. His eyelids were open, but his field of vision remained pitch-black, ruling sight out. His sense of smell was dominated by the stench of something burnt, and there was a strong taste of rust inside his mouth. The fact that he lay faceup, limbs spread wide, meant he'd probably fallen onto the ground.

"—Aah."

During the time he checked to see that his limbs could move, his own voice faintly slipped past the ringing in his ears. As the ringing began to fade, he began to be able to hear himself. At the same time, he began to hear the sound of his own blood coursing through his body, and the darkness in his field of vision gradually brightened.

His five senses were functioning. Sight and vision were returning, allowing him to sense the world around him. And then—

"—!!—!—!!"

As his hearing recovered, stringent shouts flew his way. Some voices were bloodcurdling; others were those of crying children. Screams. The mansion, burnt—instantly, his thoughts came to a boil.

"—! What the—?!"

When his thinking processes recovered, bolstered by his five senses, Subaru sat up with a start and looked around the area. His entire body, covered in burns and scrapes, pleaded for mercy, but the spectacle before his eyes made him forget all that.

—Right before Subaru's eyes were the burning remains of a dragon carriage, with several land dragon corpses scattered around it.

"Ex—plosion…"

His memory from just before came back, allowing Subaru to properly grasp what had happened.

Explosion. Yes, an explosion. *Explosion* was the only word he had for the supreme might of the destruction wrought.

Such was the power of it that the dragon carriages lined alongside had been blown away and a good chunk of Earlham Village completely leveled. The homes bordering the village square had been engulfed by the spreading fires from the explosion, with flames licking at the familiar scenery.

The blackened, charred objects scattered around the area were partly the dragon carriages and the corpses of their land dragons, but that none were intact made him unable to differentiate between organic and inorganic matter. It was surely a foregone conclusion that the dense scent of burning flesh invading his nostrils was from the land dragons that had perished in the blast.

Aghast that land dragons had been blown away without a trace, Subaru bit down on his back teeth and said, "Ia! Come on out, Ia! You're here, aren't you?!"

When Subaru slapped his chest and desperately called out, the red common spirit instantly responded. The red light appeared before his eyes, making no complaint at being called on repeatedly as she silently asserted her existence with her heat.

—Subaru remembered that Ia had protected him, deploying a wall an instant before the explosion. If not for the common spirit's protection, Subaru would have died in the explosion just like the land dragons around him. However, Subaru had not been the only one in the dragon carriage. It would be meaningless if he had been the only one saved.

"Ia! The person with me… Where's Ferris?! Where's…"

"—I'm here."

Subaru was on his knees when a frail voice reached his ears. As it was truly the voice he'd yearned to hear, Subaru practically tumbled as he turned toward it. He heard the voice from the shadow of a ruined house.

"Ferris?! Are you all right, Fe—"

"All right…might be a hard sell, *meow*."

When Subaru practically crawled in that direction, Ferris, the one he sought, revealed himself out of the smoke.

Subaru had feared the worst but was relieved to the bottom of his heart when Ferris emerged. But an instant after that relief, he realized that something was very off. He was happy Ferris was all right, but he was *too* all right.

"Ia's magic wall didn't deploy in time…? Some sort of superpowerful defensive spell, then?"

"Nothing of the sort…I died once, that's all."

Ferris, with one eye closed, bore no wound worthy of the name. Unlike Subaru, he surely didn't have the protection of a common spirit, and yet his fur and flesh were in tidy shape.

But his attire was not the uniform of a Knight of the Royal Guard, but merely a tattered cloth wrapped around his naked flesh. Given the little time available, the cloth must have come from a dragon carriage curtain.

"Why are you dressed like...?"

"Well, I can't help it! Clothes can't be regenerated with magic! And more to the point..."

Ferris thrust his palm forward, interrupting Subaru's question as he turned hard eyes elsewhere. Following his gaze, Subaru clicked his tongue. The situation was even worse than he'd imagined.

—In the blink of an eye, Earlham Village had transformed into a battlefield—a clash of fire and sword taking place.

"No retreat, push them back! Cut open a path! Evacuating the villagers comes first!!"

On the other side of the village square, one of the knights shouted to that effect as he and an attacker crossed blades.

A large number of people were gathered together in the square, knights included. However, the majority were noncombatants—villagers and merchants. The expeditionary force was surrounding them in a circle while resisting the enemy.

The attackers were dressed in black robes, carrying cross-like straight swords in their hands—it was the Witch Cult.

"How did they enter the village...?"

"That's obvious: they were in the dragon carriage wagons."

"Shit!"

His "insurance" had backfired in every possible way. Subaru cursed his own stupidity and god-awful luck.

They hadn't placed any restrictions on the merchants aiding with evacuation. Realizing that the merchants had ferried the Witch Cult in made the phrase *the Witch Cult is everywhere* ring painfully true.

—Particularly if an Archbishop of Sloth was among them.

"Subawu, you don't have time to get depre—"

"I know! Scrap the evac plan! Anyway, let's get everyone up to the mansi—"

Poor strategy or not, they had no choice left but to go and hole up. The instant after he made that judgment, Subaru saw it.

Repeated spells by the Witch Cultists tore the knights' circular formation apart, causing the combat strength resisting the Cult to collapse. The black-robed figures proceeded to leap into the village square, waving their swords as they assaulted the helpless villagers.

"Those bas—!"

Their short swords reflected the flames; their glints burned into Subaru's eyes as he yelled at the top of his lungs. However, his voice could not halt the vile blades. Nor could the knights halt their wicked deeds in time.

Mother protected child. Husband shielded wife. Young stood before old. And crosses would impale them all—

"Al Clauzeria—!"

A brief moment before that tragic scene was to unfold, a chant resounded, and simultaneously, Subaru saw light in the sky.

Light spawned and swirled about in midair, swelling into a rainbow-colored aurora that poured down onto the village square.

The vivid aurora traced a beautiful arc, indiscriminately bathing the knights, villagers, and Witch Cultists with its colors. But a moment later, the effects upon them were at polar extremes.

The rainbow softly enveloped the knights and villagers, transforming into a wall for them. The Witch Cultists impaled the rainbow with their daggers, and the next instant, they were enveloped in an unimaginable shock wave that sent them flying.

The square upon which the Witch Cultists had intruded was conquered by the overpowering light of that rainbow. And this had been wrought by a handsome young man in white armor, appearing in the square as if he had flown there.

"None shall mar the beautiful radiance of the rainbow—this is the truth of the heavens."

"The Finest of Knights," master of the aurora, snobbishly spoke those words as he thrust his cavalry saber toward the sky. The cavalry saber that had swept the Witch Cultists clean was surrounded by the lights of five common spirits—all except Ia, who had been assigned to Subaru. The way Julius had turned the battle around at its darkest moment was truly worthy of his other name.

Seeing the result for himself, Subaru clapped his hands as he rushed over to Julius.

"Incredible! Good job, well done! You really let loose! I'm glad you're here for once!"

"Somewhat vexing praise, but I shall accept. I am glad you and Ferris are safe."

Julius, thanks to whom the front line had recovered, was relieved to see Subaru and Ferris rushing toward him. But unfortunately, there was no time to celebrate their safety.

"Sorry, I messed up. There was a Sloth with the traveling merchants, but I couldn't deal with him."

"It is the result of the enemy outthinking us. I have no intention of criticizing you. Right after the dragon carriage you and Subaru entered exploded, the Witch Cultists in the village went on a rampage. The damage from the explosion and the surprise attack is not shallow, but I had TB and Ram evacuate the wounded to the mansion."

"There's a lot of enemies, though. The evacuation didn't go well, I take it?"

Julius had avoided spelling it out, but the authority of Sloth was without doubt the cause of their disadvantage. That power could change the course of battle all by itself, and Subaru's eyes were the only counter.

And if he could not fulfill that duty, all they could do was await their fated destruction.

"Anyway, we've got to smash all the Sloths! I'll do the looking! Julius, lend me your strength!"

"Of course. Ferris, link up with the evacuees and treat them. You are our lifeline."

Subaru clenched a fist, Julius nodded, and Ferris winked. Acknowledging their mutual roles, the three instantly separated. Subaru and Julius were to wipe out the Sloths; Ferris was to bolster the knights and villagers and form a defensive line at the mansion.

"Now then, stand up! We'll head to the mansion and hold out there. Run, run!"

With Ferris's gallant voice at his back, Subaru turned his attention to the clashes of blades he heard all over the place. The combat, far fiercer than what had come before, showed that the Witch Cult had gotten serious.

"How many Witch Cultists are in the village, roughly?"

"The precise number is unclear. However, there were many participating in the height of the battle. The entire force of the remaining fingers has likely entered the village. Clearly, this is a difficult foe."

If there were three fingers left, and each had ten people with them, the number of enemies had to be creeping toward forty. Beyond tangling with a force of that size, the expeditionary force had people to protect, a disadvantage that put it in a difficult situation. However, there was hope—if the enemy's entire force was assembled in the village, at least.

"If we can take down the last three Sloths, we can win this in one… Ah?!"

Subaru saw a chance to turn things around, but that instant, he saw the sky ahead blotted out by blackness. Directly above the flames in the village, countless black hands were covering the sky. The numbers were straight out of a nightmare.

"—Unseen Hands!!"

When Subaru looked up and shouted that, Julius's expression grew graver still. But his eyes were glazed; he could not see the same nightmare. In a sense, that was fortunate. After all, it would not be strange if seeing lethal violence on such a scale caused the heart to falter.

"Probably under there…!"

Subaru had to take Sloth on, but someone was taking Sloth on without him.

His intuition soon became firm belief.

The black hands cascaded from the sky, destroying trees, houses, and the ground itself with their overwhelming power. It was without cessation, over and over again, *destroy, destroy, destroy*—fueled by the anger of being unable to finish off one's foe.

"We have to hurry! Wilhelm's fighting right near there!"

There was only one human being who could take Sloth on without Subaru.

2

Wilhelm broke through the downpour of invisible attacks by moving beyond the limits of his own vision.

He swayed from left to right, suddenly accelerated and decelerated, did as many flips as he could, toying with his enemy and drawing ever, ever closer through each repeated skirmish.

The authority known as Unseen Hands would be a dangerous attack even if it weren't invisible. It could freely alter its range and direction, both able to overwhelm the enemy with numbers and destroy him utterly with a single blow. These constituted countless advantages in every kind of battle, making it the ultimate technique for bringing death to one's foe.

Only because he was the more experienced fighter was Wilhelm able to manage.

"Accordingly, I shall nail you to the wall here and now, Witch Cultist—!"

"It cannot, cannot, cannot, cannot be! To think you would resist to this extent!!"

To the fore, farther down the road, a tall man stood opposite Wilhelm. His posture, with his head bent at an unnatural angle, resembled that of a doll that oozed creepiness as some human hand toyed with it.

In point of fact, the madman had lost free use of his flesh; instead, it was the authority that held his body in its grip and controlled it, but such considerations were worthless to the Sword Devil.

What he required was the fact that the man standing there was an enemy, and one of the three Sloths remaining—the man, dressed in traveling merchant attire, did not appear to be making the slightest effort to conceal his identity.

He'd slipped into Subaru's painstakingly arranged "insurance," craftily manipulating it for his own wicked intentions. Simultaneously, Wilhelm wondered about the safety of Subaru and Ferris, who should have been right by the dragon carriage that had exploded. But in the heat of battle he instantly thrust such melancholy thoughts aside, and the Sword Devil immersed himself in his own fight.

It wasn't that he lacked concern. He would never be able to face his master, Crusch, unless Ferris returned safe and sound. However, his heart pleaded that he did not really need to worry too much.

They would break through that crisis, Subaru and Ferris both. Such was the great faith he had in them.

"Rrrrraaa!!"

He swung his sword, splitting the earth, kicking up a shower of dirt that allowed him to read the arcs of the invisible attacks. With superhuman evasiveness, Wilhelm broke through the wall of bloodlust burying the path between him and his foe and charged.

He didn't need to concern himself with Subaru or Ferris. This had been the only thing he'd wanted to begin with. What he could accomplish was settled from the first moment he'd held a sword in his hand.

"Such favor, to increase the numbers so! Such tenacity in the face of them! Such conviction! As a diligent disciple, I cannot praise it enough! Ahh, ahh! Oh, love! My brain is shaaaaking!"

Different eyes, different face, different voice—even so, they shared the same madness-filled look. Though a different being with a different appearance, this Sloth was obsessed with Wilhelm just the same. As he received the repulsive praise, Wilhelm moved farther from the battlefield, pursuing the Archbishop of the Seven Deadly Sins on his own.

Given the current balance of forces, he was the only one who could take the madman on. He was the only one who could keep the damage to a minimum and strike the man down.

Wilhelm glared at the insane man before him, increasing the speed of his steps. The invisible attacks slammed down, trying to pursue him, but the Sword Devil sprinted like an arrow, leaving them behind.

"—"

Heedless of the shower of dirt, Sloth recklessly repeated the invisible attacks. It was as if not only was he insane, but his tactics were stupid, as well. Of course, the duel would be settled just as stupidly.

"—!—!!—!!"

The madman made some kind of lament, but Wilhelm, running

straight forward, did not hear. He stripped away all that was unnecessary, charging forward as he became a single blade, the steel that would rend wickedness asunder.

Naturally, as he drew closer the obstacles increased. The number of grazes grew greater, and the inside of Wilhelm's body was bathed in sharp heat as he poised his sword, lashing out.

The earth split apart, and the madman's posture tilted. Wilhelm turned his sword tip toward the center of the body's mass, driving it home.

"—I have you!"

There was not even slight resistance to the tip of his blade. The feeling of rending a life was one the Sword Devil had oft tasted.

His treasured sword impaled the madman through the left of his chest, completely destroying the beating heart within. Not even Ferris could have pulled him back from the brink of death. The merciless strike had brought his life to a conclusion.

"...Yes, if it was you, then..."

Failing to die instantly with the blade running through his back, the madman spewed blood as he tried to say something. Wilhelm drew his sword back to cut his last words and testament short.

It was then that the madman said into Wilhelm's ear, "When you focus on fighting invisible arms, you lose sight of what you *can* see... Lazy, is it not?"

"—"

His thoughts contorted for a second.

An unnecessary crack in the Sword Devil's belligerence was pried open, as if he was trying to think of what the words could mean.

An instant later, the madman lunged at Wilhelm, his shaking arm raising a dagger. Then, without hesitation, he employed the dagger to stab his own left eye.

Through the eye socket, the tip of the blade invaded his skull, piercing his brain and cutting short his own life.

"Wha—?"

The instant the blade robbed him of his eye, and his life, light surged out—

3

The instant he rushed around a demolished house and onto the broken road, the earth shook.

"—"

The shock wave coursed underfoot; the shudder in the air made it hard to breathe. Then, as Subaru sprinted forward, the delayed flames and wind from the blast followed suit, mowing down everything in front of him.

"Whoaaa—!"

"Don't move! Aro! Iku!"

With Subaru frozen in place, Julius raised an arm before him, calling out to the spirits glowing green and yellow. A green blade came to be, and a bulwark of earth and stone rose before them. The wave of heat rushing from ahead was sliced apart before bouncing off the stout wall, protecting the pair from its wrath.

"What happened?!"

"I do not know. Just before the explosion, I felt like I saw a human silhouette pass through, but..."

As the reverberations of the blast relented, the two rushed past the broken ground toward the center of the blast zone. The surrounding area looked as if it had sustained a ferocious shock wave from the blast, enough to send the rooftops flying off brick homes. Naturally, there was a crater in the ground at the center of the blast, adding poignancy to the sad tale.

And when Subaru saw who lay at the center of the blast zone, his voice went cold.

"Wilhelm...?!"

Raising his shaking voice, Subaru rushed over to the white-haired, aged swordsman who was lying curled on the ground. He had sustained grave wounds from blast winds and flames over his entire body; it was almost strange to find his body in one piece.

His face was a grimy black; Subaru couldn't tell if it was from blood, dirt, or burns. But he was faintly breathing. Knowing at least that was true, he let out a long, long breath.

"But he's in big trouble at this rate! We've got to get him to Ferris, or—"

When Subaru went down on one knee, intending to carry Wilhelm, Julius stepped beside him and said, "It does not seem things will be quite that simple."

Sensing the urgent warning embedded in those words, Subaru lifted his head.

Julius swept the tip of his drawn cavalry saber around the area. His reason for doing so was simple: the enemies he was holding in check hailed from several directions, not just one.

Carrying cross-shaped swords, Witch Cultists blocked them on each of four sides. But that was not the largest problem. A final person arrived with the four, removing her hood as she appeared.

It was a small-statured woman, with short hair the color of black tea.

The cultist's hands were empty; she stood before them seemingly defenseless and wide open. However, her bloodshot eyes and the way she hurt herself, biting her shorn-nailed fingers, were all the proof they needed that she was the most dangerous of all.

After Petelgeuse, the madwoman, and Kety, this was the fourth Archbishop of Sloth.

The woman bit the nail of her right thumb, twisting her hand as she tore the nail off. The sight and liquid sound of blood droplets and exposed flesh made Subaru grimace in pain and disgust.

"Comin' out one after another with timing like this… How many of you are there, damn it?!"

"Why, why, why, why…why is it youuu yet live? All of those measures, and yet…why is it you do not fall before my diligence?!"

"Well, that's my line! Cut it out already! Doing continues over and over like this! You have some kind of grudge against us?!"

Probably words of complete and mutual hatred, enmity, and vilification were the only ones Subaru and the woman could share. Then Wilhelm stirred in his arms.

Perhaps it was due to external stimulus, but the Sword Devil was still unconscious when his lips faintly moved. The way his anguished breaths held increasing anger toward their foe felt ghastly to Subaru.

It was almost as if he was subconsciously trying to tell them something—

"Wilhelm?"

"Same…ne—per…"

He couldn't completely make out what the trickling voice tried to say. And the Witch Cultists were not merciful or polite enough to wait for him to hear it once in coherent form.

Subaru was clutching Wilhelm on one knee when the woman turned a nail-less finger toward him and shouted.

"You! If the lazy you and the diligent you backed away, all would be firm! All would be decided! Everything arriving at its proper conclusion! Thus, scatter here! Scaaatter to the winds!!"

Spewing spittle, the woman put her hand into her own robe. However, she did not find what she was looking for. Pulling her hand out, she gnashed her teeth hard enough to break them. Subaru had a hunch as to why she was in such a mortified rage. That flash of insight let Subaru understand what role was his to play.

Witch Cultists were on all sides, whereas Wilhelm was gravely injured and Julius was exhausted. The only one left to take on the fourth Sloth was Subaru Natsuki, useless at anything but decoy duty.

But even if his Witch Cult attraction was of no use, there yet remained something he could do.

"Julius, can you fight off the four besides Sloth while covering Wilhelm?"

"Subaru?"

Shifting his gaze alone, Julius gave Subaru a slight, questioning rise of his brows. However, there was no time to explain the fine details. Subaru glared at his amber eyes and repeated himself.

"Can you do it? If you can do that…I'll do what I can do."

"—"

"Right now, you're the only one I can count on. If you're willing to put yours in my hands…I'll put mine in yours."

"Put what?"

It was obvious. Subaru responded to Julius's words by pointing at Sloth and saying, "I'll smack that idiot. I'll fight and take your life in my hands. In return, I'm putting my life in yours—so can you do it?"

Subaru declared his determination to take on the Archbishop of Sloth single-handedly to Julius, his one and only ally. At his words, Julius drew back his sword.

His hesitation and silence lasted a second. Julius closed his eyes, opened them, and poised his sword.

"If I did not say I could do it, 'twould be my shame as a knight."

"Fair enough—!!"

They were still at a disadvantage. Subaru knew it was reckless. But his battles had always been reckless. So once again, his disadvantage was like a tightrope. He'd simply cover his eyes—and run across.

Subaru, gently laying Wilhelm down on the spot, put a hand into his own pocket. The Witch Cultists were gradually tightening the encirclement, but he detected no sign of Sloth moving a step. Subaru did not underestimate her. Distance and range were meaningless words to Sloth.

But that only applied to every opponent who wasn't Subaru Natsuki.

"Now, let us finally end this! Great love abooove all! Exalted love above all! Before my diligence, to repay Her favor! You were born worthy of being the first offered up to..."

"Hey, chick Petelgeuse— Look at this."

Subaru called out to the madly raving Sloth with a snort. Then, he stuck his hand in his pocket.

—When he withdrew his hand, he was holding a book bound in black. It was the Gospel that Subaru had recovered from the corpse of Petelgeuse Romanée-Conti—

"You're looking for this, right? The thing sent by Miss Witch you love so, so much."

"Thief!! So IT truly was you who had it?!" Sloth screamed, eyes bulging.

The way she'd rummaged in her pocket had made Subaru realize something was off.

The other two Sloths had done the same thing. They'd searched for something that ought to have been in a certain pocket with their hands, been irritated not to find it, and raged at he who had stolen it. The object of their desire had been the same: that single book.

"Guess you even tried digging up Petelgeuse's corpse to get the Gospel back. I've heard of book junkies, but come on, robbing graves to get a book back?"

"Silence! Cease your prattle! Give that book back, right—"

"Hey, don't shout. If you get too angry, you know—your brain'll shake."

"—! You mussst die!!"

No one present could outdo Subaru when it came to taunts and provocations.

As Sloth exploded in a rage, the shadow at her feet swelled up. The shadow split into an innumerable horde above her head, seemingly covering the sky in pitch-black hands whose fingertips bore down on Subaru all at once.

But if the intent was to kill Subaru, that was the wrong call.

"My favor! The manifestation of my love! Crumble BEFORE them, sinner—!"

Sloth shouted, and the black arms pressed toward Subaru like an avalanche. The veritable manifestation of destruction loomed before him like a tsunami as it advanced.

To Subaru alone, it was all too visible. And even to him, the attack was far too obvious.

"Ra-aa—!"

The evil hands were countless, but slow. Now that he had witnessed, however imperfectly, combat between superhumans, they looked like stopped flies to Subaru. No, that was going too far. They were like flies in flight. But they were by no means impossible to evade.

Subaru took a large detour, evading the savagely onrushing horde of Unseen Hands. The Sword Devil would have leaped between them, but such inhuman feats were beyond Subaru. He used his endurance to make up for it.

The bombardment of power had missed its mark, the invincible authority wasted by its user.

"My authority...?! Then, you shall die at the hands of my disciples—"

"Unfortunately, I have been tasked with denying you that option."

By the time the woman, realizing her failure, regained her composure and commanded her underlings, it was too late.

Sword in hand, Julius assaulted the Witch Cultists, vividly hindering them from pursuing Subaru. On top of that, the cultist in the direction in which Subaru had fled had been tragically caught in the wave of evil hands and dismembered.

"Huh, huh, huh?! You took out your own guy?! What kind of a sorry villain are you?!"

"G...gah...! How dare you, dare you, dare youuuu! My disciple of love!!"

"Don't gimme that, you're the one who mixed us up! Tunnel vision! What, are you *lazy*?!"

Subaru raised his middle finger as he rearranged the trademark phrase of Sloth.

Just as intended, the woman was incandescent with voiceless rage, savagely running after Subaru as he fled.

"—Julius! Manage your end somehow! I'll handle mine!"

"A most vague command. But understood."

To Subaru, thrusting a fist and raising his voice, Julius raised his cavalry saber aloft. Now that they had divided the battlefield between them, Subaru's and Julius's battle lines were wholly separate.

On Julius's side were the wounded Wilhelm and three Witch Cultists. For his part, Subaru had one Sloth, mad with rage—the right person for the right fight.

After all, Subaru had no chance against the Witch Cultists, and had the best chances of anyone against the Archbishop of Sloth.

"See ya later!!"

"Fight valiantly!"

Vowing to meet again, Subaru left Julius behind and darted across the battlefield. Evil hands rolled across the ground like a surging sea, but Subaru could see them. He leaped over them and took off, unharmed.

"Wait, wait, waitwaitwaitwait, I say! You despiiicable, foolish knave!"

As Julius began his clash of swords with multiple opponents, Subaru drew the madwoman off to another location. To draw Sloth to a place where her attacks would ensnare no one else, unwittingly doing just as Wilhelm had. Subaru pressed a hand over his heart, seemingly ready to burst, and ran at full strength.

He had a destination. He would not go as far as to say that reaching it was linked to victory. However, if he arrived there, he could buy time for victory to come calling. For that reason, he ran and ran toward it.

"—! You can't—hit me! You're one—heck of a klutz!"

Behind Subaru, the madwoman chased after him on her own two feet. However, her speed was slow. In addition, for some reason, her deployment of countless Unseen Hands was sporadic, allowing him to narrowly evade them even while on the run. He was completely shaking off her ability.

The number of arms chasing him was some sixty or seventy, clearly the most of any Sloth to date. In spite of that, her skill in using them was the worst so far. The balance was all off.

That being the case, it must have been the first and foremost Sloth, Petelgeuse, who'd used his authority with the greatest skill.

"I guess Petelgeuse really was the main Sloth…not that it matters!"

He could think about that later. It didn't change the fact that all the Sloths had to be wiped out. He didn't have time to reach for anything else. If Subaru's foe wasn't in tip-top shape, all the better for him.

He curved around corners, darted down the straightaway, curved around another corner, and leaped.

"Made it—! But…"

Arriving at his destination, Subaru surveyed the area. There were signs of combat all over the place, and the fallen did not stop at one or two people. He saw not just Witch Cultists but knights and beast people among them. Subaru felt blame for his own powerlessness pressing upon him.

He closed his eyes and forced it back. The next moment, he leaped sideways and rolled, evading the evil hands striking where he had stood. The ground split open, causing a cloud of dust to rise. Behind it stood the hate-filled Sloth, huffing and puffing.

The number of arms stretching from her back was greatly diminished, limited to some twenty or so at present.

"Guess you learned you were wearing yourself out."

"And ooonly for making me realize that do you have my thanks! However, your escape ends here! Or do you still possess some way to resist?!"

"Way to resist..."

When those words trailed off, Subaru blinked for just a moment. Along the line of his gaze was the madwoman, and behind her—

However, he immediately hid behind an impetuous smile.

"...love and courage, I suppose."

Subaru licked his lips and made a big fuss as the madwoman stood with her arms spread wide, her eyes full of bloodlust. His statement sent the eyes of Sloth bulging wide, causing her creepy voice to begin to laugh.

"Very good! Then challenge my faaavor with this love of yours!"

"I said love *and* courage!"

Taking a breath, he went into a sprinter's crouch and practically leaped as he rose, shooting his body forward. After having fled so thoroughly, he now charged straight forward, leaping into the woman's flank. Sloth blinked in surprise and, perhaps thinking charging in was the height of idiocy, instantly flew into a rage.

"This is your love?! Your love has this little resolve?! No crafty schemes, simply running like a fool, ahh, your love is so reckless! So powerless! So thoughtless! In other words, *lazy*!"

"Ooooh—!"

Subaru let out a shout from the pit of his belly, as if to overwrite the despair the woman's shout drove his way. Shout and shout he did, enough to make himself hoarse, calling out *love*, and calling for *courage*.

"Then you shall die, and pay for your laziness with your lo—"

"Now, Patlash—!!"

"—! What are—?!"

The impact cut off the latter half of the cry of surprise.

Sloth was triumphant one moment; the next, her diminutive frame was caught by the land dragon charging into her side. Its huge frame, several hundred kilograms in mass, slammed right into the defenseless woman's body, blowing it away as if it were a leaf.

"—"

The woman proceeded to bounce along the surface of the village square, flipping over as she sailed into a half-destroyed house. The glass window made a sound as it shattered; the house, unable to take the blow, was smashed, and dust slowly rose from it after.

The blow, even greater than he had imagined, sent Subaru leaping to glom the land dragon's head and rub her nose.

"You did great, awesome teamwork! Above and beyond the call, Patlash!"

"—"

With Subaru trying to kill her with compliments, Patlash raised her head and gave a high-pitched neigh.

Subaru returned to the village square he'd started from, luring the woman to Patlash, the dragon's valuable legwork part of his escape plan. But having failed to locate her just after arriving, he'd started to worry that he'd been wrong, and she, too, had been burned to a crisp—

"When I saw you'd doubled back behind her—that was a seriously devilish move."

The instant his shifting gaze located the land dragon behind Sloth, he seriously shouted like a girl on the inside. The next instant, with zero prep work, he and the land dragon did a combo attack, pulling it off perfectly. This was the result of trusting everything to love and courage—albeit *love* really meant "bluff" and *courage* meant "reinforcements" in this case.

"Now, it'd be great if that settled things, but…"

Climbing onto Patlash's back, Subaru glared at the wreckage of the house Sloth had sailed into. If she'd died from the crushing weight of the mountain of debris, it would be a big help.

But—life just wasn't that easy.

"…IT seems I was being prideful."

The mountain of rubble collapsed, and from under the remains of the roof, countless shadows welled up all at once. The wriggling, pitch-black arms writhed like tentacles. A tiny figure rose up from the middle of that black mass.

It was the madwoman—bloodied and reduced to a state half-living, half-dead.

Her head was bleeding from lacerations it had suffered, and her left eye was completely taken out, impaled by a shard of glass. The right half of her body, caught up in the collapse of the house, was dyed crimson, and Subaru doubted her slender arms or legs were now of much use. From the looks of her, there was no doubting that she was wounded all over.

And yet, having said all that, the vigor and madness displayed by her right eye was greater than ever.

"You...yes, you certainly are a diligent human being. Yes, diligent! Compared to you, having come so far, using everything at your disposal to challenge your foe, I was so very careless! Architect of my own ruin! Neglectful! Insufficient! I was too prideful! Ahh, I was so *lazy*!"

"—"

Her demeanor and the statements themselves did not differ from those of the other mad people in any way. Even if she did have a new thought, he could deal with her the same way provided there was no extreme change in her tactics or repeated attacks. Now that he was riding Patlash, able to dish out speeds far greater than Subaru himself, it was even easier.

Having played for time, Subaru would deliver as decisive a blow as possible to defeat this Sloth—with neither having a decisive way to win, the fight would come down to whichever found a way to finish the other off first.

But the woman cruelly laughed in the face of Subaru's resolve.

"I will show you my favor. That is the first thing you should accept. If you do not acknowledge it, adhering to the only love you know, and as a result sinking into laziness, that, to me, would be the greatest and vilest of acts...and furthermore, one I shall correct."

"...Shit."

As the madwoman continued her murmurs, the countless evil

hands moved toward the sky. Watching the spectacle, Subaru cursed, suppressing the shudder in his creaking heart.

Before his eyes, each of the many arms took hold of the wreckage of the collapsed house.

"That's her best option, damn it."

An instant after his rueful declaration, the rampage began.

She hurled the wreckage of the house at them, the building becoming shrapnel that poured onto Subaru and Patlash all at once.

4

The means Sloth had chosen was her best option against Subaru because it did not use Unseen Hands.

In other words, put briefly, all she had to do was stop Unseen Hands from attacking directly, using the evil hands to attack indirectly instead. The attack speed of Unseen Hands itself was less than that of a punch from a normal arm; if you didn't panic, they could be dodged, even in great numbers.

But if the evil hands grasped things and threw them, the speed was incomparable. The pure physical might they possessed went far beyond human norms. The missiles they threw traveled with a speed rivaling that of a major-league fastball.

On top of that, what she launched at them was, at minimum, the size of a human head—a single solid hit would be fatal.

"Patlash! Out of the village, into the forest! Without cover we're dead!"

"—!"

Subaru clung as tightly to Patlash's head as he could; she accelerated at the same time he gave the order. She had probably come to the same conclusion before hearing his command, but either way, charging into the forest was the right call.

In the hands of those pitch-black limbs, broken pieces of the brick house served as fine weapons of murder. Fortunately, thanks to the thrower's lack of technique, the control was awful. In spite of that, the flying rubble unleashed showered down like rain. As with a poorly aimed firearm, a few hits and you were just as dead.

"—"

A ferocious sound arose as flying rubble mowed down trees right beside them, exploding into the ground just behind them as they galloped forward. Bounding over the earth, they wove about as the entrance to the forest into which they had leaped turned to charred plains in the blink of an eye. Impact, destruction, impact, destruction—they alternated over and over.

"Guooo!"

Subaru lowered his head to narrow his profile even a little. All he could do at the moment was cling to Patlash. A piece of flying rubble grazed the land dragon's black hide, gouging the hard scales and causing blood to spurt out. But Patlash's speed did not lessen, nor did she raise any outcry.

Though they sprinted over poor footing, she galloped with the ease he'd been told about. Patlash's contributions, which were beyond Subaru's expectations, had saved him. But letting her literally shoulder all the burden wasn't a solution.

When he looked behind him, the actions of the madwoman pursuing them were burned into his eyes. Even if he regrouped and found a way to fight, it meant nothing if he couldn't predict her actions. At the very least, if she couldn't keep up with Patlash, that'd make things go a lot smoother—

"—So much for Patlash's speed!"

"Yesyesyesyesyeeeeeeeeeeeeeeees—!!"

As Subaru made a disparaging shout, it was overridden by the hateful voice repeating itself. The mad voice was launched from a height surpassing that of the trees of the forest, literally right above him.

The woman was now far overhead.

Her diminutive, beat-up body was curled up with her hands around her knees—put crudely, a somersault pose. She remained in that pose as she used Unseen Hands to grab her own body, hurling herself through the sky—as in a game of catch, she tossed herself from one hand to another as she chased after Subaru and Patlash.

Whatever it looked like, it was disturbingly fast. Sprinting through the forest, Patlash was breaking sixty kilometers an hour.

However, if you disregarded her moving only in straight lines at low accuracy, the speed of Sloth, flying like a human cannonball, was butting against a hundred.

It wasn't much of a difference, but Subaru couldn't shake her off at that range. At that rate, with her looking down at them, they'd be wonderful targets for her sniping. Furthermore, Subaru lacked the means to reach the madwoman as she moved far overhead.

"Can't go back to the village. With her like that, no way we can draw her back now."

Besides, Subaru would be at an even greater disadvantage if she linked up with the Witch Cultists. Subaru was the only one who was still a good matchup against Sloth after being backed this far into a corner.

"But at this rate, I'll be hit sooner or—"

"—!"

As soon as he said it, "sooner" came calling.

A flying clump of brick hurled at them squarely connected with Patlash's head, sending the leather helmet covering the top of the land dragon's head flying. Her posture heavily tilted as blood poured from her head. Subaru bit back an anguished cry, earnestly pulling on the reins to keep them from bowling over.

"Patlash!!"

There was no way shouting to her would give her strength. It could not be so, but the way Patlash dramatically slammed the ground with her foot, refusing to tumble, he thought it just might be true. He'd have to praise the land dragon ten times as much for guts alone. But the flying rubble continued, and blood kept flowing. At that rate, victory was out of reach—

"After lasting this long, even if we get deep in the forest, at this rate..."

Continuing the war of attrition had poor prospects, but he couldn't find any leads for a counterattack if they didn't buy some time. However, the damage just now had already stamped a time limit on Patlash. He couldn't expect the same performance from her as before. If he was going to have a flash of inspiration, it needed to be that moment, because if not—

But such a convenient turn of events had never happened to Subaru before, and it likely never w—

"—Just now…"

Subaru bit his lip in anger at the absurdity of it all. That instant, he saw something out of place in the background of the forest they were passing through. The question of what it was tugged at his mind; the instant suitable information floated up, he pulled back on the reins.

If things were as Subaru remembered, it was worth a shot. When a plan to achieve victory offered itself, you bit.

"Patlash, left!"

"—"

Patlash was bleeding when Subaru gave the order. For a single moment, she shifted her eyes in that direction, as if to ask, *Are you sane?* and *Are you sure about this?*

It was natural to wonder if he was sane. However, if sanity kept victory out of reach, madness was indispensable.

Subaru answered his favorite dragon's silent question as he stood straight, giving the reins a heavy flick.

"That's right! Patlash, head for the light in the woods!!"

He shouted, repeating and emphasizing the command. Patlash glared forward, and hesitation vanished from her eyes and gait. Apparently, she greatly esteemed Subaru's judgment. She had put her life in his hands.

The land dragon's feet seemed to scrape the earth as they drove into the forest floor, braking hard as they changed course. The wind repel blessing cut out, and Subaru gritted his teeth to endure the momentum threatening to throw him off. Right after he held on, on, on for dear life, they accelerated, running down to the left at a steep angle.

"No matter where you run, there is nowhere to hide!"

The madwoman did not miss Subaru and Patlash's sharp turn and roaring descent. The angle of the hurled rubble shifted, and the trail of sylvan destruction followed suit. Verdant trees burst apart; the split, fallen trees were immediately recycled, grasped and hurled to spread the destruction further. Death followed close behind them.

"—"

Even as that cascade of destruction pursued them, Subaru ordered Patlash to follow the flickering light he'd seen from the corner of his vision—one that might prove a literal beacon of hope.

The land dragon zigzagged left and right as she ran, making herself a difficult target even without pulling farther ahead. Subaru wondered how arduous it must have been for his steed to go at high speed down a steep incline with a wounded body, but no matter how much his head might ponder, an answer would not be forthcoming.

"Do you not know when to give in? What is ALL this running, running, running? And where does it all lead?! Your actions only prolong the inevitable… No! No, I will not!"

Sloth looked straight down at Subaru and Patlash as they continued fleeing at full tilt. However, the woman's words were cut off at that point as she jabbed a finger into her crushed left eye in apparent self-rebuke.

She proceeded to gouge out the flesh, causing blood to flow once more, her voice shrill with bitter resentment and delight.

"I must be neither careless nor prideful. My task unfulfilled, brought to death for the first time, I must part ways with my doubts, my fate, my distracted thoughts!"

Killing carelessness with self-mutilation, Sloth continued her attacks, hurling relentlessly.

The ground exploded, and flying rubble ripped through the air; a fragment clipped Subaru's shoulder, making his bones creak. He threw his head back, bit down a cry of pain, and groaned as he endured. He would not cry out before Patlash.

But their chase scene was finally coming to an end—

"Gah—!"

A blow conveyed through the earth made the ground beneath Patlash's feet disappear. A moment later, the land dragon's huge frame floated skyward. By the time Subaru noticed, he didn't even have time to scream as he rotated hard in midair, holding on to the reins as he thrashed about, and fell hard toward the ground, his entire body slamming fiercely into it.

"Aghh…!"

They vigorously rolled downhill. When they stopped, Subaru had lost track of which way was up.

He was hurting all over, but miraculously, he couldn't see any sign of mortal injury. No matter how much his limbs were torn up, his head was still attached to his body.

But that good fortune seemed only to have managed to push his death a tiny bit into the future.

"IT seems that finally…the time to end this has arrived."

"—"

Subaru lay faceup, watching Sloth descending from the sky.

When she landed, the woman dismissed the evil hand that had carried her, standing beside Subaru, still unable to move. Then she gave a bloody smile full of satisfaction and tendered a hand down to him.

"Now, return my Gospel. It is not for the likes of you to possess."

"Gos-pel…"

Murmuring in a broken voice, Subaru obeyed the woman's demand, putting his hand into his pocket. His fingers found the cover they sought. Fortuitously, it had not fallen from his pocket during all the time they'd been chased.

"If you want it…take it…!"

Grasping the book, Subaru pulled it out and mischievously tossed it into a thicket. The woman's hand reached out, grasping nothing but air; she opened and shut her fist as she let out a sigh.

"It would seem your attitude regarding my favor, and the things of others, has NOT improved."

The woman shook her head; her apparent lament had an echo of disappointment. Subaru coughed. He'd never imagined that the madwoman would make an appeal to reason and common sense.

The woman went over to pick up the book Subaru had thrown. Meanwhile Subaru moved his head in an attempt to locate the fallen Patlash. He found her; her breaths were labored, but she was all right.

And ideally positioned.

"Ahh, guide for my love, proof of my favor…! Finally within my hands… I am deeply MOVED!"

The woman clutched the recovered Gospel to her chest as she shed tears. Holding the written word, her crazed love in tangible form, the woman shifted her head, turning a mad smile toward the barely alive Subaru.

"You fought bravely. You fought well, worthy of such praise! You and your land dragon resisted so well, so diligently! In praise of your actions, I shall grant thee mercy!"

"…Mercy?"

"YES! Mercy! If you have any last words, I shall burn your words into my very soul, never to forget them for eternity! Now, say what you will!"

He was surprised that the madwoman would show her opponent compassion after a hard-fought battle. She only made room for it because she'd recovered the book and had victory right before her eyes, but it was an unexpected side of her even so.

Then Subaru, taking the madwoman up on her offer, lifted up a hand.

It was his left hand, opposite of that which had thrown the Gospel. He was holding something in it.

"Do you know what this is?"

The question made a suspicious look come over Sloth. The words were different from those she had sought, but the woman peered into Subaru's hand. It held a magic crystal, small enough to rest in a palm.

Giving off a white light, it was—*not* a one-shot-one-kill trump card. By itself, it held no power to turn the battle around. In the first place, there were things like this all over the forest.

And properly speaking, it belonged among the others, not in his palm.

"This is…"

"A barrier magic crystal. They're stuck on trees all over the forest. You didn't notice?"

"..."

Subaru wondered if her silence meant that she hadn't noticed, or that she didn't understand what he was saying.

He didn't really care which. The plan was already in motion.

"What are you sayi—?"

The woman, her disquiet at Subaru's last words evident, suspiciously reached out with a hand.

Just before her hand arrived, the plan went operational.

"—!!"

Sensing something leaping toward her shoulder, the woman instantly tried to turn around.

She never made it.

From behind, the fangs of the demon beast breaking through the forest sank deep into her neck.

5

He'd had his suspicions. The possibility had grazed his head several times while they'd been on the march.

The kicker was when Julius and Ferris looked as if they doubted their ears when he told them the area around the mansion and village was a giant demon beast habitat.

Demon beasts harbored nothing but hatred for all living things. The battle with the White Whale had soaked that terrifying aspect of their nature into his bones. But at the same time, he wondered…

The demonic, canine Urugarums in the forest, as well as the White Whale, hated Subaru's physical makeup and saw him as an enemy. If so, didn't the same go for the Witch Cultists, who saw Subaru as an ally?

—And now, firm proof of that hypothesis rested right before his eyes.

"Gaaaaaaa!"

Impaled by sharp pain and the sudden impact, the madwoman looked unaware of what had happened as she screamed.

With the leaping demon beast's fangs in her neck, the small-statured woman could do nothing to throw him off. The black-furred demon dog was large enough that it made the tiny woman look like a child standing beside an adult.

The woman was swung up and down by the demon beast maw clamping down on her, slamming her into the ground several times. The woman went limp, drained of strength. Without hesitation the demonic canine held her down, withdrew its fangs, and went for the final blow.

With a growl, it opened its maw, this time aiming for the woman's windpipe. Perhaps it meant to snuff her life out; perhaps its action was pointless, the fruit of its murderous instincts. Subaru could not tell which.

He could not, but the madwoman was not one to go down without a fight.

"Filthy beast…! Unseen Hands!"

Pressed against the ground, the woman shouted, and instantly, her wriggling shadow became evil hands that mowed the demon dog down.

Bathed in the invisible attack, the demon dog cried out very much like a puppy as it tumbled heavily. But it instantly got back on its paws, howling as it moved anew to rend its prey apart—

"Wait! That's enough!"

But Subaru intervened, barrier crystal in hand, putting a halt to its aggression.

The demon beast was in a leaping stance as it growled, glaring hatefully at the white magic crystal in Subaru's hand. The beast slowly backed away, perhaps compelled to do so by the power residing in the crystal.

Subaru and the madwoman might have been the pair the demon beast could least overlook. Even so, the demon beast did not leap at them. Its fangs quivered; it growled and drooled as it leaped backward. The demon beast proceeded to mingle with the thickets, its footsteps growing more distant.

There was no way it had let them go. It probably meant to watch and wait until he let go of the barrier crystal.

Watching the demon beast's retreat, Subaru let out a long sigh before turning his head, looking down at the madwoman. Stopping the Urugarum demon beast from finishing her off had certainly not been an act of mercy.

There had been no need. From the way her guts were already spilling out from her belly, the woman must have already known this for herself.

"How can this be? To think, at a demon beast's…"

"You didn't do your homework. This whole area's a demon beast habitat. They just isolate it with the barrier."

The back of her neck bitten off, the woman was unable to move, covered in mortal wounds. Perhaps she was already blind; her one remaining eye, lacking any spark, did not turn Subaru's way.

The results weren't sufficient to call the operation a *success*. He'd been saved by happenstance and a flash of inspiration, clutching victory by a hairbreadth. After all their history, to think an Urugarum would appear in a place like that…

"Roswaal, you bastard…you said you'd wiped 'em all out."

Cursing his all-too-secretive supporter, Subaru knelt on one knee at the woman's side. He picked up the Gospel that lay right beside the woman, bloody and on death's door.

Even if Subaru couldn't play decoy himself, the book could still be used as bait in scenes to come. The battle with the woman had proven its worth well enough.

"I don't know what happened to Kety, but at most, there's two fingers left…we'll smash 'em."

"Mm-mm-mmm…"

Subaru looked down at her. "Oh, it's reckless? Undoable? How many of you have I taken down? Learn already, geez. Though no point saying that to you now, I suppose."

"—"

On the brink, the woman twisted her lips at Subaru's words. The bleeding from them wouldn't stop. Blood trickled from the corners of her lips as the woman smiled, boldly greeting her impending death.

When Subaru saw her like that, it sent the greatest possible chill up his spine.

"Go ahead…hold it, for now. But…soon…"

"…"

"Soon, I will taaake my love back."

At the end, that part came out loud and clear before the woman's smile faltered, her life signs coming to an end. It was death, plain and simple—an end from which there was no coming back.

It was the fourth, or perhaps the third, death of Sloth he had witnessed.

"Shit…what was she trying to tell me anyway?"

Subaru scratched his head as he looked down at the dead woman's face. The inside of his mouth was dry, and he felt that his arteries had oddly quickened for reasons unrelated to stress and nervousness.

For the first time, without relying on anyone else, Subaru had brought another person to death in the midst of combat. That fact made his knees faintly shake. He clamped his teeth down and sighed at length.

The woman had set a curse upon Subaru just before her death. It was a curse he could not dispel right that moment.

"...Can't stay standing around. Even if one's down, there's still Sloths left."

Brushing hesitancy aside, Subaru turned his eyes away from the corpse and rushed over to Patlash. The land dragon looked pretty beat-up from the furious tumble, bearing countless wounds over the entirety of her body.

And yet, when the land dragon sensed Subaru's approach, she stoutly rose to her feet.

"Sorry, Patlash. I really want to give you a break, but I still need you."

"..."

When Subaru declared he would push her further, Patlash silently turned her back to him in response. He mounted, unable to count how many debts he now owed the land dragon after the last half day, the last several hours in particular.

Drawing the reins, he ordered the helmetless land dragon to return to the village. The barrier crystal in his hand was warm, steadily continuing to warn of the presence of demon beasts.

Perhaps the demon dog was lurking in the thicket, watching them that very moment. He paid no heed as they took off running.

"The Sloths left over, the Archbishop of the Seven Deadly Sins' fingers...probably one left!"

At the height of the battle in the village, Subaru and Julius had headed toward the source of the Unseen Hands. There, they found an explosion, and at the center of that explosion, Wilhelm. Subaru had no doubt Wilhelm had been fighting that Sloth until the instant just prior to that. He was sure the Sword Devil had struck down his foe.

He deduced that, just as with the dragon carriage explosion, something in Kety's possession had caused it. If Kety had been defeated by the Sword Devil, he might have blown himself up to try to bring Wilhelm down with him.

If that was true, there was one finger remaining—and that ought to be the last Sloth left.

"If we can deal with that one, we just need to mop up the regular Witch Cultists and we win!"

He finally saw a beacon of certain victory. But that glimmer was far back in Subaru's mind.

To escape the madwoman's attacks, he'd had to flee deep into the forest. He was far from the village, where the battle was surely still raging. Every second spent running uphill felt like a lifetime.

"—?! Shit! He really did come out!!"

Clenching his teeth, Subaru glared up at the sky, shouting with anger and nervousness. The sight was even worse than he'd expected.

Once more, black hands stretched from the other side of the forest up to the sky before his eyes, pointed toward the village. Subaru was still far away. His shout could not reach the people those arms were aimed at.

If they swung downward, more would die. Knights. Beast people. Villagers.

Lives would be snuffed out. Lives that belonged to people Subaru knew.

Raising a voiceless scream, Subaru prayed for the black, evil hands to disappear.

As if responding to Subaru's lament, Patlash, battered all over, increased her speed. They practically flew over the lip, charged down into the forest, and raced to the village on the verge of being violated once more.

"Sloth!!"

As they galloped, he yelled hard enough to rend his throat.

The village bore vast traces of destruction: human corpses were strewn all over the place; flames were raging, mingling with someone's crying voice in the air. Even in a world filled with the sound of swords clashing, he instantly knew who the madman must be.

The fifth Sloth was a very thin, balding, middle-aged man, tearing at his bloody face as he laughed maniacally.

"—"

Subaru instinctively knew that this was the last one. The madman turned, seemingly drawn by Subaru's certainty.

They exchanged gazes, acknowledging each other as enemies. However, the man played the most horrific of opening moves first.

"Ahh—my brain is shaaaaaking!"

Already, countless arms swung up, blocking the heavens before they came crashing down alongside an angry, unhinged shout. The attack became a cascade of death, no doubt intended to violate the village to its roots, crushing anyone and everyone to death by sheer force of numbers.

"Gotta stop him!" Subaru cried with determination, but it was a cry of despair, for he had no power with which to do so.

And a moment before the madman's act of brutality proceeded to repaint the world in black—

"That is far enough, villain."

—he heard a voice.

And that voice took everyone aback.

Standing in a daze, they looked up at the sky, unable to move.

"Enough—I will tolerate no more violence from you."

For above the myriad wriggling black hands, the sky was covered in the pale glow of absolute zero.

CHAPTER 5

A PACT FULFILLED

1

The pale light danced violently, covering Earlham Village, crimson from blood and flame, with its twinkle.

The frigid air spawned fine fragments of ice, reflecting the light to create a fantastic sight—a phenomenon known as diamond dust, robbed of its beauty by the reality of the tragedy beneath it.

"Enough—I will tolerate no more violence from you."

The beautiful voice cut through that surreal scene like light through a clear piece of glass.

The battlefield was dominated by that voice, clear as a bell, and everyone's eyes were stolen by the girl who appeared upon it.

Her long, silver hair flapped in a warm wind. Her violet eyes were imbued with a powerful will. Her beauty was so great that none who witnessed it could ever forget. Her outward appearance was enough to draw the eyes of others several times over.

However, in that instant, her appearance was not why she had stolen the gazes of all present.

Everyone's eyes had been stolen for no reason beyond the overwhelming awe of her presence.

"..."

The sound of steel against steel, the cries of anger and sadness, and even the flames burning homes fell into silence, seemingly holding their breath.

In such a world, the silver-haired girl—Emilia—quietly gazed at her foe.

"Emilia..."

When Subaru put her name on his lips, all of his complicated feelings enveloped him.

Of course it had come to this.

There was a battle raging on the mansion's doorstep. Villagers were evacuating to the mansion one after another. Someone was fighting to protect her. There was no way she would stay quietly shut in.

Emilia's eyes contained sorrow—and enmity toward the Witch Cult that had created the field of battle.

"Step back, villain. I won't...let you do such terrible things."

"Ahh, how can this be...?"

Identifying the madman standing in the square as her enemy, Emilia pricked him with a stern tone of voice. However, the madman was hardly thrown off by that voice; his blood-smeared face registered surprise before beaming with delight.

Sloth twisted his body, stretched both hands toward Emilia, and continued to smile as he shouted.

"Ahh, ahhh! What a fortuitous, wonderful day! Such marvelous fate! To think such a wondrous opportunity would come to fruition! Truly, the living image! Never, amid these repeated trials, did I believe I would have the chance to come across a vessel of such magnitude...!"

"...What are you saying?"

So deeply moved was the fifth Sloth that he wept, a flood of tears pouring out of him. Seeing the madman's out-of-place tears, Emilia raised her eyebrows, bewilderment plain on her face.

"Ohh, ohh, O Witch...the beacon of love that guides me...!"

The madman stumbled forward, narrowing the range between himself and Emilia. Perhaps her reaction was part of what stirred him so deeply. With the distance counting down to ruin, Emilia turned a palm toward him.

"Don't move! I won't warn you again."

Emilia kept her palm thrust out, making the statement as the madman stepped closer. However, her call for him to halt never reached the madman's ears. He took one step, then another, narrowing the distance—

"This time! Or the next! Someday, someday, I shall…!"

"I told you, don't move."

As she had said, this time was not another warning. She coldly switched from an ultimatum to an implementation of force.

The light wildly dancing in the sky cracked open, and a surge of mana froze water droplets in the atmosphere. This created a total of four sharp, icy spears—and these, she launched in an instant.

"—"

The chill of overwhelming death was merciless. A single blow would sever the thread of life without fail; a being impaled with a solid blow would have his flesh dyed white, frozen down to the soul to become an icy statue. However—

"No hesitation, no pity, no mercy… Truly, truly, truly a diligent decision!"

"…Aren't they your allies?"

The madman energetically laughed beside the Witch Cultists now frozen beside him, having shielded him with their bodies. The sight made Emilia uncomprehendingly furrow her brow.

Responding to her doubts, the madman tilted his head at a ninety-degree angle, stretching an evil hand to a frozen subordinate, shattering him.

"They are disciples! Furthermore, my fingers! However, before you, before the vessel, these things bear no meaning! It is the same even for ME! Right now, now, nownownownownownownownow! My will, my reason for existence! All of it, unto you!"

"—"

"Unto you, unto you, unto you… However, that is not where it must end."

To Emilia, aghast at his madness, the madman opened his eyes wide and raised a bloody finger. He trained the crushed fingertip on Emilia—or, more precisely, Emilia's left shoulder.

Atop her slender shoulder, a little cat spirit was nestled against her silver hair. It was to this being that Sloth turned his hated.

"Spirit, spirit, spiriiit! Diminutive in stature, knowing neither love nor righteousness! Unaware of just how grave a crime it is to cuddle up to the vessel! Ignorant, in other words, sinful! What blasphemy!!"

Sloth vented excessive rage and hatred toward Puck. However, when the madman addressed him with a torrent of enmity, Puck trained cruel eyes upon him.

It was an expression unimaginable on the spirit that had been so gentle and carefree daily—no, Subaru knew that look, what Puck looked like with bloodlust honed to a tip.

Subaru knew the mighty power resting inside that tiny body, for he had experienced it for himself.

"Unfortunately, being with her is the reason for my existence. I do not need anyone's permission, nor do I intend to seek it—besides, you're the unpleasant one here."

Both were set in their ways, making the hatred they turned toward each other all the clearer. The madman had rebuked Puck with fierce emotion; Puck responded to the madman's disgust with scorn.

At that rate, the slightest touch would set them off, and the clash between two beings of immense power would truly begin.

"Wait, that's..."

"You're the one who needs to wait, Subawu. Settle down, now..."

When Subaru tried to intervene on the brink of hostilities, someone suddenly tugged him back by his sleeve. The force took Subaru by surprise; Ferris, who'd appeared at some point, was the one pulling his sleeve. Ferris, still wearing the tattered mantle from earlier, stroked a heavily wounded Patlash as he sighed at Subaru.

"Subawu, she's terribly wounded, and so are you. You need absolute rest. That's an order, *meow*."

"Like this is the time! I can't just make Emilia fight that..."

"It was Ram and I who decided to call Lady Emilia—trust her a little, okay?"

With a stop put to his nervous feet, Subaru grimaced at Ferris's words.

In response to the perplexed Subaru, Ferris closed one eye and said, "Trust that the person you want to protect isn't only fit to stand back and watch."

2

Considering the harsh exchange just before, the battle began in eerie silence.

"—"

The walls of icy mist Emilia had scattered around her were smashed as she leaped heavily backward. Just then, the ground where she had stood until a moment before exploded; she blinked at the clumps of excavated dirt.

"So you really can't see them at all."

"This needs extra attention."

Puck whispered from atop Emilia's shoulder. She straightened herself out as she lightly touched down on the tips of her toes.

The invisible blow wielded by the madman—as Ferris had informed her beforehand, Emilia's eyes could not catch sight of the fists. But she had ways to defend herself even without seeing them.

She surrounded herself with a body of icy mist, dodging when she sensed outside intrusion. Puck had suggested the method, and with his capabilities, it was far from impossible to pull off.

"I'll get close and hit him right away."

As Emilia murmured, the ground tapped by her tiptoes was being dyed white. Centered on Emilia, the frost covering the ground spread farther, turning it into frozen earth for a twenty-yard radius around her in the blink of an eye.

It was a familiar sensation under her soles. Influenced as she was by the forest she had been born and raised in, gliding on ice was second nature to her.

"Before my love, such petty moves! Tricks! SCHEMES! Merely futile resistance!"

The man shouted at the gliding Emilia, reaching top velocity from the first step toward her. The next moment, he pressed on with an oppressive cry, ripping away the icy mist floating around her. But by the time the invisible arms broke through the mist, Emilia's body was nowhere to be found.

Gliding over the ice, Emilia was running circles around the man to throw off his aim. He tried chasing and getting in front of her, but nothing he tried resulted in a hit. Freely dispersing ice over the ground, she could escape anywhere.

And before the invisible arms could hit her, Emilia's reliable protector completed his encircling snare.

"I understand you falling for my beloved daughter. I'm very proud of her. But no pests allowed."

"Nn—?!"

The instant Puck made this laid-back statement, thick walls of ice rose up, surrounding the man on four sides. His path of escape blocked, the man's eyes went wide with wonder, leaving him completely defenseless.

Immediately, the icy walls let out a creak as they shot spikes from the surfaces within.

There was nowhere to run; a lethal attack without any forewarning.

Prey struck squarely would be impaled inside the walls, frozen to the last drop of its flowing blood, and shattered.

It was an attack that embodied the innocent cruelty under Puck's adorable surface. But—

"—Naive!! Naivenaivenaiveveveeeeee, yessss!!"

A bellow rose from inside the icy encirclement. The next instant, the icy walls broke into smithereens with a high-pitched sound. The ice-turned-shards twinkled as the man leaped out of them, unharmed.

The instant he was showered in spikes, he'd created a wall of invisible force against the interior of the walls of ice. Unable to withstand the pressure from within, the icy walls had been smashed to pieces.

"That mere tricks could defeat me is absurd! A trial is not so easily—"

"Eiiya!"

"—Kwaa?!"

However, when the man, proud of his victory, trod across the ice, Emilia launched from her powerful glide into a flip. Emilia's kick, slipped in without a sound, drove into the man's defenseless solar plexus. The speed and force of the unexpected kick were of sufficient power to lightly blow the man off his feet.

"This time…eh?!"

Emilia proceeded to beat the man to where he was due to fall and deploy her magical energy, making icy flowers bloom—but the spectacle she witnessed made her doubt her own eyes.

Tracing an arc, the man she had knocked away halted in midair, flying up in another direction. The movement was unnatural, as if something had caught him out of thin air before hurling him in another direction—

"Using it like that…"

"Ahh, the repudiation of thought is the essence of Sloth! Apply! Redirect! Reappropriate further!"

When the man, dancing in the sky, reached an arm toward her, Emilia instantly formed a pillar of ice, driving it toward her opponent. But as the icy pillar flew toward the man, it struck something and shattered, failing to reach him.

In contrast, with the oppressive force coming from the man undiminished, Emilia glided across the ground, moving forward—and proceeded to use the momentum from her glide to sail into the air.

"—"

With both rising into midair, Emilia and the man exchanged glances.

Madness met righteous indignation, and once again, it was Emilia who first went on the attack. The next things she created were multiple icy disks that she pounded toward the man, sending them through the air in erratic curves.

Stranded in midair, the man could not dodge the icy disks surrounding him above, below, left, and right.

"Yesyesyesyes, YES—!!"

However, the man did evade the flying, icy disks, moving unnaturally via the most absurd of methods. He bounced erratically in the sky, and though he was uncontrollably spun round and round, the man escaped the disks, shouting in delight.

"What was...what?"

"THIS is love!"

When the creepy movements made even Emilia exclaim, the man gave a reply that was not an answer. His ferocious desire to return the favor transmuted into stabbing bloodlust that made goose bumps stand on Emilia's pale flesh.

The man's combativeness was more than a match for her wariness. He poured his hostility into the hands he powerfully brought together—

"Be baptized by Her favor, the symbol of my love! Prepare to undergo the trial!!"

"—!"

When Emilia felt the icy mist being destroyed, her face stiffened for the first time in the battle. That was the result of detecting the invisible menace unleashed upon her from all sides, denying her any avenue of escape.

She was in the sky, unable to move freely. The difficult-to-evade blow was truly retribution for the earlier attack.

"—"

And then the center of Emilia's chest was impaled, brutally run through.

The destructive power gouged out her breasts, punching right through her chest. The man's eyes bulged at the results, the wound so deep that he could see through to the other side.

"This is the result of Her favor! The fruit of my love! The proof that the Witch responds to my love! But there is no cause for despair! Even if what is within is lost, the vessel is ours to—"

"Eiiya!"

"—Kuwaa?!"

The man's declaration of victory was interrupted by a kick. The blow from behind sent his body flying.

Beyond the sheer force of the kick to the man's blind spot, completely unexpected from his point of view, he had no idea what had happened. Before him was Emilia, with Puck riding on her shoulder, clapping his paws with no hint of sarcasm.

That instant, the ice statue of Emilia pierced through the chest shattered into dust. Even the light had been fine-tuned to create a false Emilia that looked just like the real thing.

"That's no good, looking away in the middle of a fight—you'll get sucker punched, you know?"

The man she had kicked into the sky, spinning round and round, had no time to get his bearings. He'd fallen for Puck's fake Emilia hook, line, and sinker, exposing his defenseless back.

And with that setting the stage, Emilia couldn't miss.

"You won't get away this time."

"—!"

The man was hurtling downward from the kick when his arms and legs were buried in manacles of ice. He was no longer able to move, no longer able to resist, and Emilia's blow was already prepared in full.

The man slammed into the ground; his frozen limbs pinned his body there. From midair, Emilia proceeded to fall straight down, aimed right at the man's torso.

The man's eyes widened as the distance narrowed. Then he laughed at the fast-approaching Emilia.

"Ahh. This—is truly diligent!"

"Thank you—now die properly!"

Descending straight down, Emilia thrust the heel of her palm into the laughing man's torso.

The force made his bones creak. The man let out a painful cry, stunned by the blow. But the cry lasted for only an instant.

The next instant, the place touched by her palm began to freeze over. Not only his limbs but the man's entire body was dyed white, freezing to its core.

"—"

Unable to even raise a death cry, the man became part of an ice flower in full bloom and perished.

That was how the battle between Emilia and the man was decided.

3

Watching the outcome of the battle, Subaru was rooted to the spot, unable to make a sound.

"—"

Overwhelming was insufficient to express it. From start to finish, Emilia had soundly engaged the enemy, splendidly succeeding in striking down the final Sloth.

"You see? It's just like I said, *meow*?"

In place of the dumbstruck Subaru, Ferris, standing beside him, expressed admiration for Emilia's battle. His basic healing magic had closed up the land dragon's wounds; now he reached a hand out to heal Subaru's.

The touch of his slender fingers made Subaru aware of the pain of his own wounds once more. He had countless bumps and scrapes all over his body; in particular, the right side of his body *really* hurt. He'd taken a hard hit when he and Patlash had been bowled over in the forest.

"Ah, Subawu…doesn't this really hurt? Your ankle, your shoulder…"

"Where's your bedside manner?! Put my mind on the parts that don't hurt or something!!"

"Ahh, this might be pretty bad. You might die from it, *meow*..."

When Subaru made a grandiose show of pain, Ferris teasingly poked his ribs. When his teasing hand withdrew, Subaru sighed as he looked toward Emilia once more.

It was unclear what Emilia felt concerning the madman's death. But there was a trickle on her pale cheek; Subaru saw a shining tear rolling down it.

It must have pained her spirit to take another person's life. If so, that was Subaru Natsuki's sin—it was his powerlessness that had drawn Emilia and the Cult together.

"..."

However, Emilia looked surprised at the rolling tear on her face, quickly wiping it off. Perhaps the spirit on her shoulder had said something to her, for Emilia knit her brows with a conflicted look.

She didn't even know why she'd shed a tear. That was how it looked to Subaru.

"...?"

As Subaru watched Emilia, he suddenly noticed deep emotions strangely stirring in his chest. The multiple thoughts toward her somehow seemed like separate, foreign emotions.

For some mysterious reason, he had a deep urge to scratch his brain. It was almost as if—

"My, my, they're all so hasty."

Ferris, hearing battle cries in the distance from all over the village, gave a slightly pained smile as he spoke. Now that Emilia had struck down the final Sloth, the battle was nearing its conclusion. The Witch Cultists being fought in every corner of the village had largely been slain, and cries of victory filled the sky.

The Iron Fangs were particularly boisterous, but it was not only in the beast people that victory bubbled to the surface. The knights who had fought and survived raised their swords, letting up shouts of their own.

To Ferris, a healer, the real battle had now begun, for the number of casualties, and the number of casualties who could be returned to health, rested upon his skill.

Of course, pouring cold water on his comrades when they boiled with victory was the one thing he could not do, but—

"Ferris."

"Yes, *yes*, Ferri at your servi—er, Old Man Wil?!"

When addressed, Ferris turned around with a lighthearted greeting, but was taken aback at who the speaker was. Behind him was Wilhelm, breathing raggedly as he dragged his half-bloodied body around. The heavy burns and countless lacerations on him truly justified the word *half-alive*.

"Wait a—! You can't walk around with those wounds! If I don't lay you down and heal you right now—"

"I can wait. More importantly, there is something crucial I must say."

"You might die, you know?! Don't tell me it's more important than your l—"

"Even so, I must speak it now. Where is Sir Subaru?"

In contrast to his level of injury, Wilhelm's voice was filled with vigor and drive. He would have fallen on the spot, save for sheer will.

Both surprised and exasperated at the fact, Ferris immediately looked back and said, "Subawu? He's right h—"

He ought to have been rooted to the spot, hemming and hawing over what to say to Emilia.

And yet—

"—Subawu?"

When Ferris looked back, Subaru Natsuki was nowhere his eyes could see.

4

Clutching his head, he barreled through the thickets, running deeper and deeper into the forest.

He had to get as far as he could, as far as he could manage, as far as was humanly possible; far from the village, far from the square, far from his friends—and far from Emilia.

"Haa, hu…haa!"

Short of breath, he earnestly, desperately ran across the poor footing of the forest. Sweat was in his eyes, and his heart hurt as if it would leap out of his mouth, but he couldn't be bothered to care.

The image of a silver-haired girl turned away from him was burned into the back of his eyelids. She would turn, their eyes would meet, and they would speak words of reunion—but that was a moment he could accept no longer.

It was not that he was ashamed to meet her face, nor was it timidity of any kind. He had a different reason.

A terrible, abominable reason.

"—"

"Subaru, where are you going?!"

"—?!"

Subaru had headed toward the uninhabited depths of the forest, and yet someone had called out to him even so. He stopped; his eyes turned back, watching the slender figure with wonder.

He was a handsome young man, with short, light-purple hair and a look of elegance and refinement—Julius Juukulius.

Julius, wiping his bloodstained uniform with a sleeve, put a hand against a large tree beside him as he gazed at Subaru.

"I am glad that you are safe…but what happened? I hear cries of victory from the village. If you are here like this, that Sloth must have been slain. And yet, why are you here?"

"…"

"If something troubles you, please, speak of it. After all that, we are comrades through thick and thin."

Hand-combing his disheveled hair, Julius spoke patiently to the stiff-faced Subaru. Just as he'd said, Subaru could still hear their comrades' voices from the direction of the village.

They were still close enough that he could hear them, even though he needed to be farther, much farther away…

After all, if he didn't get farther away—

"Subaru?"

Julius knit his brows at Subaru's persisting silence, saying nothing. Sensing that something was off, the knight took a step forward, approaching with concern in his eyes. It was the look of concern one gave the ill or wounded.

However, it was not his body that was the problem. Ferris's no-frills healing let him move without any difficulty.

—That was why he was using that flesh to the fullest.

"Suba—"

"Julius, get away fro—but it is TOO late!!"

"—?!"

Desperately, Subaru resisted with all his body and soul, managing to partially hold it back. But even the fragmented, cut-off words made the knight instantly put distance between them to avoid the risk.

"Subaru" raised an arm, swinging it in the air, and tilted his head in dissatisfaction—at a ninety-degree angle, straight to the side.

"A fine reaction, yes! Though this flesh resists, you evaded WELL. You truly, truly, truly are a diligent person! All the greater the pity…"

"—I had a bad feeling when I was suddenly expelled from Subaru's body."

On one knee, cavalry saber drawn, Julius murmured with frustration. Complex emotions swirled in his yellow eyes: anger, regret, and inexhaustible hostility and hesitation.

Seeing the wavering of his eyes, "Subaru" squared his shoulders in approval.

"All the more promising! The way you are, you think, you waver, is all proof of your diligence! The only thing that sullied that was your base, filthy soul…"

"Truly, it is he who has been sullied by something base and filthy. Namely, you—"

Mad hatred and hatred mixed with righteous anger clashed as Julius and "Subaru" glared at each other, their fierce emotions at polar opposites. And then—

"Julius! Subawu!"

With a great sound of running feet, a high-pitched voice intervened, riding through the trees. A jet-black land dragon appeared, kicking up a cloud of dirt, and riding on its back were Ferris and Wilhelm.

Atop the dragon, Ferris's eyes widened as he saw Julius and "Subaru" facing off. Wilhelm leaped down from the dragon, standing at Julius's side. Then he turned to "Subaru" with a grave look in his eyes.

"Sir Julius, Sir Subaru..."

"Master Wilhelm—that is not Subaru."

Hearing Julius's hushed reply, Wilhelm radiated hostility, clenching his teeth enough to make them creak.

The atmosphere tightened. Their faces contorted—Ferris's with worry, Julius's with righteous anger, Wilhelm's with fierce emotion. "Subaru" was the only one having a good time, clapping his hands as a crazed smile came over him.

And then—

"Now that you are assembled, allow me to reintroduce myself—I am the Archbishop of the Seven Deadly Sins entrusted with Sloth..."

His head tilted at ninety degrees, "Subaru" opened the front of his jersey—and the madman laughed grandly.

"Petelgeuse Romanée-Conti!!"

Thus did he give his name.

5

He'd been wrong. He'd been mistaken. Subaru had failed to grasp the most important thing about his enemy.

He had been mistaken about the evilest, most important part of Petelgeuse Romanée-Conti.

The Witch Cult's Archbishop of Sloth was not multiple beings bearing the titles of ten fingers.

It was a single spiritual entity named Petelgeuse, attaching itself to the flesh of others.

* * *

"Truly fine! Truly a splendid body! It has been decades since flesh has felt so comfortable, the perfect resource for supplementing my lost fingers!"

"How dare you…?! Get out of Sir Subaru's body right now, heretic!"

"For what purpose, and with what right do you say such a thing? It is because you robbed me of my precious fingers that I must inhabit this body as a last resort!"

Wilhelm grasped Petelgeuse's face, bending his head back while yelling into it. But the madman responded with Subaru's face and Subaru's voice and, for the pure enjoyment of it, scratched at his throat.

The painful sight of gouged flesh and blood scattering mortified Julius and the others.

"Your qualifications are by no means poor. Unfortunately, you have engraved too many excess rituals into your fleeesh. This makes you fundamentally unsuitable to be my finger."

"—"

"Diligent old bones! Your flesh, too, is unsuited to be my finger! Even if I must praise the spirit, your flesh is an unsuitable vessel for love…ahh, how tragic!"

To Ferris, and then Wilhelm, Petelgeuse pointed his finger and shook his head. They did not understand the finer details of what his declarations meant. But putting aside that he could mean nothing good, they understood that they were unsuitable in his eyes. And then—

"—And above all else, a spirit user. You are the MOST incompatible of all. The hindrance of your impurity aside, you would become a fine finger of mine. Is THIS answer enough?"

"Unfortunately, I shall not cast the flowers aside, even if they were to abandon me. Perhaps a madman like you cannot understand such feelings."

Julius responded to that extraordinary malice with a reply of utmost enmity. The contents thereof made Petelgeuse's eyes go wide; the next moment, he slapped his knees, seized by laughter.

"Madman! Truly, that IS the proper term! Yes, I am crazy for love! Love, undaunted love, mementos of love, affectionate love, kind love, warm love, benevolent love, thirst for love, reverent love, love of family, climactic love, private love, pure love, cherished love, gushing love, filial love, trusting love, deep love, virtuous love, sensual love, bitter love, profound love, charitable love, spiteful love, faithful love, gracious love, humble love, biased love, delusional love, fraternal love, romantic love, love, love, love, loveloveloveloveloooooooooovvvvve!!"

"Damned fool..."

As Petelgeuse made his insanity clear, Julius focused his hostility at him while pleading to Subaru's soul.

"Subaru! Open your eyes! You are too good to be taken over by a madman like...!"

"It is futile! This flesh is already under the control of my mind! Though it attempts to RESIST, it is fruitless, meaningless! This body is already my finger!"

"No one is speaking to you! Subaru, think! What did you come back for? Why do you fight? Did you not shout those very words to me?!"

While disparaging Petelgeuse, Julius wrapped his six colored spirits around his cavalry saber, raising it high. The powerful, rainbow-like light repelled the darkness in the forest, its radiance dazzling the eyes for a brief moment.

This created a faint gap in Petelgeuse's thoughts, which had completely smothered Subaru's to that point. And then—

"Wh-what is this?! What are...? As if you need it spelled out, you stupid jerk...!"

"—!"

The madman opened his eyes in shock, rocked back by the torrent of emotions surging up from within. Halting as they were, the words that trickled out of his mouth were a glimpse of the mind of the owner of that flesh.

In short order, Petelgeuse's look of shock was forced back, replaced from beneath by the look of Subaru breathing painfully.

The transformation made Julius and the others raise their voices, seeing a glimmer of hope.

"Subaru!" "Subawu!" "Sir Subaru!"

"I am…Petelgeuse Romanée-Conti… Shut the hell up, I'm Subaru Natsuki…!"

Push back, push back. Bury everything in the dark dregs of the mind.

"You are merely…mumbling in my ears…you will soon falter… Do you really think…you can defeat the likes of me, by strength of will…?"

With bluff, a show of pretense, he tried to take back, seize back his own mind.

If he didn't, he was on the brink of surrendering to the urge to destroy himself that very moment. Or perhaps of wanting the destructive arms to stretch from his shadow and lay waste to everything around him.

"—"

Was that urge a darkness that enveloped Petelgeuse around the clock?

If so, he could, on one level, understand and sympathize with the madman's aberrant actions to date.

Immersed in such madness, he injured himself to maintain his sanity.

If he was constantly coated in such powerful madness, small wonder he'd become mentally unbalanced.

Was this the world as Petelgeuse saw it?

"I do not seek your understanding!"

Those were the first words Petelgeuse spoke when he broke past Subaru's resistance.

The voice that had spoken such madness, such crazed delight, such fury, now spoke with a mind that was indifferent, unmoved.

It was a darkness that chilled Subaru to the bone more than any of his madness ever had.

And then he understood—he couldn't let this darkness come to the surface.

"…Do it, Julius."

With Petelgeuse's resistance slackening, he'd settle it while he was still in control.

For that purpose, Subaru chose the method most likely to succeed. That sword held the greatest possibility for beating Petelgeuse.

When addressed, Julius was aghast; his eyes widened, and his lips quivered.

"What are…you saying?"

"Sorry, but…it's only a matter of time. If you…don't stop me now, we can't win…so before that happens…"

"No! Subaru, you must reconsider! I am both a knight and a spirit mage, a spirit knight who swore to aid you in your objective. I cannot break that oath now!"

"You swore with me to…protect Emilia… Pretty sick of me, I know."

The reply Subaru wrung out of himself made Julius grimace in anguish.

He'd always maintained his elegance and composure. With that demeanor to go on, Subaru was a little surprised at the expression he was making. Subaru had never dreamed that he'd hesitate after coming this far.

"And you had something to speak to me about later."

"…Sorry. But no can do."

He remembered the words spoken the instant they'd prayed for each other's good fortune in battle at the height of the fight with Sloth. He should have cleared the air before that, but in the end, after dragging his feet, he hadn't said it in time.

"Wilhelm, don't do anything rash…"

"I pushed myself to reach this point. I absolutely will not accept an end like—"

Wilhelm was heavily wounded, having delayed treatment for his injuries to rush over with all haste. Subaru could only praise the Sword Devil, forcing a body that should not to move through willpower alone, but this darkness could not be swept away by skill with the sword.

Subaru gave a momentary, limp smile before leaving things in the hands of the last person.

"Ferris, please."

"You can hate me for this, Subaru—I hate me, too."

At Subaru's words, Ferris—the person there who most hated the cruelty of life and death—nodded. He seemed to somehow have known he would be called upon. With tears in his eyes, he pointed a finger at Subaru.

The gesture triggered an abnormality in Subaru's core—namely, a scorching pain, as if his blood were being boiled, burning his entire body with unendurable heat.

"Ga—aaaa—!!"

Hot. Hot. Hothothothothothothothothothot—

His throat was hot. His eyes were hot. His body was hot. His tongue was hot. His nose was hot. His hands were hot. His ears were hot. His feet were hot. His blood was hot. His brain was hot. His bones were hot. His soul was hot. His life was hot. Hot, hot, hot.

His blood was literally boiling, his internal organs were simmering, and the high-temperature steam his brain gave off clouded his vision.

"Aaaaaaa—?!"

From somewhere other than his melting ears, he heard the echo of a death cry that was not his own.

One body was inhabited by two minds. Naturally, burning the body meant burning the mind of the madman with it.

There was no escape. At this rate, that soul, trapped in its vessel, would be sent straight to the afterlife.

"—"

He suffered, he writhed, he convulsed, and finally, his body could move no more.

Petelgeuse could try his sore loser act again, but it wouldn't work this time. Inside Subaru, his days were done.

"Ferris! Why…?"

"No one else could do it, right? This is what Subawu wanted."

"Even so, to inflict such pain on Sir Subaru like this—"

"—! Do you think *I* wanted to?! To use this power, power I have for Lady Crusch's sake, that I promised to use to put her on the throne, like this…!"

The voices of lament, regret, anger, sadness…they sounded so distant.

Lacking the strength to even shift his head, Subaru silently apologized for forcing Ferris to stain his hands like this. With Julius hesitating, and Wilhelm beyond reach, Ferris was the only one he could count on.

It was the same method he'd used to make Kety faint inside the dragon carriage that later exploded. Subaru's body had been directly healed by Ferris, so Ferris could interfere with Subaru's mana without touching him.

The result was plain. The power, and suffering, were beyond Subaru's expectations, almost enough to make him regret his choice.

But those feelings were overshadowed by his guilt of forcing such a deed on Ferris.

Ferris's power was the power to heal others. That was the source of Ferris's pride, his mission in life, and the part of himself he treasured above all else. Subaru had made him use that power in a terrible way.

He just wished he could utter the word *sorry.*

"—"

Lying on the ground, unable to move, Subaru felt something touching his face. His eyes felt like a haze, displaying nothing. But Subaru recognized the hard, grainy sensation from somewhere.

It was not from Julius, nor from Ferris, nor from Wilhelm, but from someone else related to—

"—"

With Subaru's life flickering like a candle in the wind, he felt Patlash, the jet-black land dragon, nestle close to mourn his passing.

Probably, these were the top four on the list of people he'd caused trouble for—no, Emilia and Ram were missing from that list. And he was truly grateful neither of the two was there.

"Subaru."

He sensed someone standing opposite Patlash, speaking with a forthright voice. He didn't even have to think about who it was. Full of determination, the voice could be none other than that of "The Finest of Knights."

After all, there was no knightly knight in that place save he.

"It was my inadequacy that forced you and Ferris into an unpalatable decision. I shall surely pay for this sin someday."

Don't dwell on stupid stuff like that, was exactly what he didn't feel like saying.

Dwell on it more and more, damn it. Don't you ever forget it.

I won't ever forget. This pain, this powerlessness—

"—"

For a moment, there was silence. However, that did not break the knight's resolve.

Sensing the feeling of cold steel on his neck, Subaru let out his breath at the apparent fact that he would soon be sent on his way.

"Sir Subaru, I am very sorry."

"Lady Emilia will probably cry."

The voices sounded distant and broken to him. Everything was vague, incomprehensible.

There were promises. To never forget. To take something back. To definitely come again.

It ends here? Absurd! I cannot…not like this! Right when I have found a suitable vessel! On the eve of the trial's completion! A finger! If I have a new vessel, I cannot be destr…

—Shut up and go to hell.

6

He fell, fell to an unknown place far, far away—

Somehow, he'd died again. He'd probably lost it all once more.

He surrendered everything to the abyss. This was the familiar embrace of failure after he pathetically lost his life.

* * *

Look back at the world.
Look back at your failures.

Don't forget. Don't forget. Do not forget.

Ferris's tear-filled voice. Wilhelm's lament, shaking with regrets. Julius's resolve and remorse, so great he probably gnashes his teeth over it—*Don't forget, ever. No matter how low you are, don't ever let go.*

Thus, another life came to an end.

However, nonetheless, even so—Subaru Natsuki continued.

Whatever happened, no matter where he came back, no matter how much suffering he carried with him, his struggle would not cease. He would repeat and do over, for that was what he swore.

With a strike, and a sound, everything plunged into darkness.

And so it was interrupted. It was severed. And then—

"I love you."

Together with that soft, gentle, fleeting, and cruel breath—

Subaru Natsuki lost his life, and the world was born again once more.

<END>

Afterword

Hi, how are you? Tappei Nagatsuki here, known in some quarters as the Mouse-Colored Cat.

Once again, I thank you very much for your patronage of Re:ZERO. The series now exceeds ten books in total, with this the eleventh! The tale has become deeper still.

Also, thanks to all of you, this eighth volume goes on sale just prior to the airing of the Re:ZERO TV anime. These are exceptionally fun days for me, both as an author and as a viewer.

Now then, since we're on that topic, I'd like to touch on anime issues ever so slightly.

The anime production companies and all their related staffs have already been announced on the Re:ZERO public homepage, so you can see for yourselves that it's quite an impressive member list.

As a matter of fact, when I heard all kinds of things about that from Mr. the editor, I was like, "Huh?" and doubted my eyes and my ears several times.

After that, the day progressed as we talked about this and that, and I raised the idea of actually meeting everyone involved sometime, somewhat expecting that this was nothing more than a pipe dream, and if it wasn't, wow, if it really happened, it'd be a pretty big deal.

Ever since the announcement that a TV anime was set to be

produced, I have received words of congratulation from many people. This includes people who began reading the work from published books, people who knew of it from when it was just serialized on the Web, fellow authors and old friends—lots and lots of people.

I am very sorry that in contrast to all the warm words of encouragement, I was unable to answer all your questions. No, it's not just from being secretive and guarding against careless leaks of information; the biggest reason is that as the author, I haven't really heard very much.

It's not that they wouldn't tell me; it's that I was afraid to ask—so I didn't.

I think you understand, but human beings tend to doubt anything that sounds too good to be true. My book becoming an anime is on the top of my list. I worried that the instant I carelessly said something I shouldn't, these dreamlike days would vanish like little bubbles…so I retreated into my author's shell.

Of course, there were screenplay conferences, and when I was there after recording sessions I popped my face in as much as I could, doing everything I could to cooperate as the original creator. But all the people at the anime studio were anime pros—and professionals at work are quite a sight to behold.

I think the Re:ZERO anime will turn out very well. Go ahead and get your hopes up.

It's starting in April, so let's have fun with it together!

Though the current discussion is winding its way toward a conclusion, allow me to indulge in a bit of author selfishness and extend these afterword pages a little further. Why? Because I have a lot I want to say!

Actually, in the same month I am writing this afterword, February 2016, your author went to a signing event in Taiwan at something called the Comics and Animation Festival.

For your author, it was the first time overseas! The first time in Taiwan! The first signing event! Sorry, I lied about the signing event part. It was my third, but anyway, it was an event full of firsts for me.

* * *

It may come as a surprise to you, but Re:ZERO is actually published overseas as well. Re:ZERO isn't just popular in Japan; the anime/manga/novels have become popular abroad.

This time, the Comics and Animation Festival I'd had such high hopes for had a large collection of anime popular in Taiwan. During the festival, there was Japanese anime plastered at every turn. I suppose what surprised me even more was the incredibly fervent welcome I received from all the fans in Taiwan.

Truth be told, your author was a jumble of worries his first time overseas. I was crossing an ocean, crossing a language barrier, wondering just how many people would actually be there—

The event was wonderful. I'm not kidding when I say I wanted to hug every last person there. Thank you, Taiwan!

Speaking of the language barrier, the Japanese of the fans participating was very, very good. Seriously, I was completely blown away when everyone got "E M D" instantly.

Of course, overseas publication means publishing a translated edition. This Re:ZERO translation was done by a publisher called the Chingwin Publishing Group, and I thought I should earnestly bow my head to them for how faithfully they conveyed the work to the readers of Taiwan.

Also, staffers from this same Chingwin were always guiding your author around Taiwan when he was trembling like a fawn his first time overseas. They welcomed me as if I were some kind of celebrity, fed me good food and tasty mango shaved ice, and really went out of their way to make it a wonderful trip for me.

Truly, going from a narrowly read Web novel to print, and before I knew it, to its being read by all kinds of people overseas and even turned into an anime—it really does feel like a dream.

Though I still lack the courage to pinch my cheek, all this gives me the strength to work hard so that these dreamlike days never end.

Thank you, Taiwan! And best regards going forward, Taiwan! Of course, Japan, too!!

* * *

Now then, the additional pages are at an end, so I shall move on to the customary words of thanks.

First, Mr. I the editor, thank you very much for always greeting your author's reckless demands with a smiling face. It was very reassuring to have you come to Taiwan with me. But sticking with your author when he had the bright idea of signing two hundred extra books was indulging me a bit too far.

From there to Otsuka-sensei the illustrator: I know I say this every time, but thank you very much for your beautiful illustration pages. As usual, you did a wonderful job with them. Also, thank you for responding to my sudden request for a limited illustration for the Taiwan event. You indulge me.

Kusano-sensei the cover designer: The series now exceeds ten books, with each and every one a spectacle, this one included. Please go big, captivating, and fun forevermore. Thank you very much.

Matsuse-sensei and Fugetsu-sensei handling the comic versions: I am truly grateful for your drawing such moving images monthly. Seeing your drawings is an urgent reminder that I need to keep these girls really cute. Thank you very much.

To others, everyone at the MF Bunko J editorial department, sales managers, copyeditors, bookstore salespeople: Truly, thank you very much.

And to those at the Chingwin Publishing Group, in particular Mr. Ryuu, you were a very large help to me. Let me borrow this space to thank you very much.

Finally, my greatest of thanks goes to all of you who have read this book, and to all of you readers who have given me such warm support. Please give Re:ZERO, anime included, your best regards going forward!

Now then, let's meet again next volume!

February 2016
Tappei Nagatsuki
(still unable to stop shaking with the anime about to start)

AFTERWORD

Since Mr. Petel had a lot of illustrations this time, here's Rem and Beako to get that bad taste out of your mouth!

オツカシンイチロウ

Shinichirou Otsuka

"Lady Felt, it is all right, you need not be so embarrassed. The dress suits you very well."

"Exactly who's worried about it?! Now even Old Man Rom is putting me up to this stuff. Is anyone on my side like at all?!"

"It could not be otherwise. I am your ally, Lady Felt, your one and only knight."

"You really are a knight in name only! Fine, let's get to the point so I can finish quick and get out of this dress!"

"Yes, as you wish. First, it is hereby announced that *Re:ZERO -Starting Life in Another World-* will be broadcast as an anime beginning in April."

"Huh, anime… Wait, you're serious?! Where in the world did you read that?!"

"In this book, as well as information announced on the Re:ZERO public homepage. It is written that Subaru's exploits, as well as his fateful encounters with you and me, are recorded therein, Lady Felt."

"Stop saying *fateful encounters*! That makes it sound special or something! It was total coincidence. Er, beyond that…the second volume of Monthly Comic Alive's Arc 3 serialization is on sale right now along with *Re:ZERO* Vol. 8!"

"Lady Felt, Arc 3, Volume 2, that would be when you appointed me as your knight…"

"Don't talk like we're some kind of pair! Are you *trying* to tick me off?! Ahh, anyway, the comic's out, too! Also, ne next novel's coming out in June, while the anime's still airing!"

"One can reread the novels, watch the anime, and enjoy the comic…an excellent opportunity to immerse oneelf in the world of Re:ZERO. Lady Felt, why not take this opportunity to face the books and tales rather than flee rom your desk?"

"Ha, as if. We don't have time to stop. It's because we're doing so much that this 'tale' thingy is coming together o begin with!"

"Lady Felt…"

"Okay, talk's over. I'm headin' off to change clothes and give Old Man Rom a piece of my mind!"

"Understood. Next time, I shall arrange a dress that is easier to move in."

"Listen when people talk! I told you, I *hate* dresses!!"